HEAVEN IS HIGH

ALSO BY KATE WILHELM

The Barbara Holloway novels:

Death Qualified

The Best Defense

Malice Prepense

Defense for the Devil

No Defense

Desperate Measures

The Clear amd Convincing Proof

The Unbidden Truth

Sleight of Hand

A Wrongful Death

Cold Case

The Constance and Charlie novels:

The Hamlet Trap

The Dark Door

Smart House

Sweet, Sweet Poison

Seven Kinds of Death

A Flush of Shadows

Justice for Some

The Good Children

The Deepest Water

Skeletons

The Price of Silence

HEAVEN IS HIGH

KATE WILHELM

MINOTAUR BOOKS ✹ NEW YORK

This is a work of fiction. All of the characters, organizations, and events portrayed in this novel are either products of the author's imagination or are used fictitiously.

HEAVEN IS HIGH. Copyright © 2011 by Kate Wilhelm. All rights reserved. Printed in the United States of America. For information, address St. Martin's Press, 175 Fifth Avenue, New York, N.Y. 10010.

www.minotaurbooks.com

Design by Kelly S. Too

Library of Congress Cataloging-in-Publication Data

Wilhelm, Kate.
    Heaven is high : a Barbara Holloway novel / by Kate Wilhelm.—1st ed.
        p. cm.
    ISBN 978-0-312-65860-1
    1. Holloway, Barbara (Fictitious character)—Fiction.   2. Women lawyers—Fiction.
3. Emigration and immigration—Fiction.   4. Oregon—Fiction.   I. Title.
    PS3573.I434H43 2011
    813'.54—dc22   2010039076

First Edition: February 2011

10 9 8 7 6 5 4 3 2 1

HEAVEN IS HIGH

1

Barbara had looked over the two letters she had written on behalf of her clients. One of them had paid her in homemade tamales, and the other had promised to pay something as soon as possible. She folded the letters, put them in envelopes, stamped, ready to go. She glanced at her mail and decided nothing there needed immediate attention and turned to the newspaper. Reagan was going somewhere or other; the city council members had wrangled about something or other. Either nothing else was going on or her attention span was such that nothing was registering long enough to form a memory. Now what? she asked herself. All that expensive education, she thought derisively, all that time wasted in studying law, in preparation for a couple of letters about petty problems or reading escape fiction. A book a night was her current routine, and she had a stack of books to return to the library later that day. Before or after a long walk was the only pressing issue to be decided when she got around to it. A relentless rain was stalling even that decision.

After she quit pretending to read the newspaper, she continued to sit at her desk and gaze at her office. Room enough for her desk, a comfortable enough chair, one other straight chair, and many boxes of things, stuff. It was sufficient even if there was little room to move.

The house was tiny, but it was a real house, not an apartment with people just a wall away, coming and going at all hours, laughing, yelling at each other, opening and closing doors. Living. She wanted no one close enough to hear, and this cramped, miserable house provided that solitude. Furthermore, she thought angrily, she didn't give a damn what her father thought about it. Not that he had said anything, but his expression the previous night, even that stony silence, that one sweeping glance around followed by a refusal to look anywhere but at her had been eloquent. At dinner, he had made his outlandish proposal.

"What I'm doing these days is coming in on Tuesday morning," Frank had said. "I work on the book with Patsy, on through Wednesday and Thursday, and go back out to the McKenzie place on Thursday evening to deconstruct the cross-examinations. And that means an apartment or a hotel or something for a couple of nights each week. I hate hotels, and you can't rent an apartment for just two days a week. I want to rent a nice big house or apartment and you can live in it and let me have one bedroom for those two nights when I'm in town. Good idea?"

Conniving, cunning, conspiring, and ever so innocent. She had shaken her head. "Dad, why don't you just spend those two nights at my place?"

"And sleep on the floor?" Frank's astonishment at the idea was quite real, his rejection as swift as a reflex.

"It's called a futon, Dad. It makes a bed, and it's on a platform, not on the floor."

He wouldn't give up, she knew. He wanted her back in the law office where he was one of the two founding fathers, and he wanted her back in his house. Although he claimed he was retiring, he was keeping his spacious office, which she suspected he intended to hand over to her when and if he ever really retired. He had told her to make use of it, use the law library, the interns, whatever she needed. She could almost envy him, she thought, not for anything material, but for the new enjoyment he was finding in his second career as a writer. He was writing a book on cross-examinations and loved doing it.

She should just tell him it was over, she decided. She was looking for her own second career. She would never return to his law offices. Never. The real question for her was what second career. And that was a pisser, she added, nodding. She wasn't fit to do anything else, hadn't trained for anything other than to practice law. She should have had a double major, one that would allow her to move right into social services of some sort, or the financial system as a counselor or something, or even medicine. Meanwhile, this tiny office was sufficient for the tiny problems neighborhood people brought to her doorstep. Rent problems, landlord problems, fences or lack of fences . . .

The ringing of her doorbell roused her from her thoughts, and almost regretfully she left the little office to see what impoverished neighbor needed a bit of legal advice.

At her door was the biggest, blackest man she had ever seen along with a diminutive lighter woman. He was at least six foot six, possibly even taller, and appeared to be as wide as the door itself. The woman at his side was almost doll-like in comparison.

"Ms. Holloway? Could we have a few minutes of your time?" he asked. "We need advice from an attorney." He was holding a dripping umbrella. He closed it and added it to the one in a bucket on the stoop. The steady rain that had been falling all morning was still pounding down.

"Of course," she said, and moved aside for them to enter. He ducked when he passed through the doorway, and the room became crowded instantly. Barbara looked around, then motioned toward the only chair that would accommodate him, one she had chosen for comfort, her own reading chair. "I'll take your coats to dry out in the kitchen," she said. And she would bring in a straight chair for the woman. The only other place possible was the futon. The office was out of the question. He might break the single visitor's chair she had.

When she returned a minute later with a kitchen chair, he said, "My name is Owens, Martin Owens, and this is my wife, Binnie. She was born mute, so she won't do any of the talking, but it's her story that's brought us here."

Barbara held out her hand to Binnie and for the first time really examined her face. She had been too conscious of Martin Owens's size to study his wife before. She was a beautiful young woman, no taller than five feet, with a shapely body that her T-shirt and jeans did nothing to detract from, fine cheekbones, short dark brown hair with a little curl, and expressive, large, milk-chocolate-colored eyes. It was unmistakable that she was terrified. Her hand was very cold and trembled in Barbara's.

Martin Owens's hand enveloped hers as they shook, but his grip was surprisingly gentle.

"What can I do for you, Mr. Owens?" Barbara asked after they were all seated.

Binnie had moved her chair as close to him as possible, put her handbag on the floor, and reached for his hand as soon as she sat down. Barbara suspected his grasp of it was as gentle as his handshake had been.

"We want to know if there's an appeal process for a violation of the immigration law. If they will take circumstances under consideration. How to go about starting such a process right away. I mean, if they order someone to provide proof of citizenship, or demand a birth certificate, or something of that sort, if there's a way to make them understand why it can't be done. At least not soon."

Barbara held up her hand. "Mr. Owens, I'm afraid I'm not the person you need. Please understand that there are specialties in law, exactly as there are in medicine. You wouldn't go to a brain surgeon for an appendectomy. I'm a defense attorney, not an immigration attorney. It's outside my field and I can't answer your questions. What I could do is find you an attorney with the training to do so."

He shook his head and leaned forward. "Just hear me out, please. Just hear me out. I think you are the one we want. A few months ago a couple came to the restaurant, friends of ours, and they talked about you and that case you'd just won, the woman accused of shooting her husband up on the McKenzie. She's their landlady and they knew about that case. They said you'd take on the devil himself and beat him."

Barbara felt her stomach lurch and her heart threaten to implode. She caught her breath and quelled her impulse to jump up and order them out of her house. Her self-imposed isolation fortress had just collapsed.

"Tawna and James Gresham," Owens continued, "said you were the best lawyer there is and if we ever ran into trouble to tell you about it first. I know what you've been doing for folks around this neighborhood. We all know. You listen to them, really listen and help them. That's what I asking for, Ms. Holloway. Let me tell you about it. Ask for your help."

She nodded silently.

"It's a long story," he said. "First, my part. I was one of six guys from the Giants NFL team. We rented a yacht and went cruising in the Caribbean, stopped here and there, did a little fishing, some snorkeling, drinking, smoking, and were having a blast. The skipper put in at Haiti. We'd heard a lot about it, that it was a hellhole, and some of the guys wanted to see for themselves. We only stayed two days and planned to leave before dawn and some of us went to town, got back late, and turned in. I found her hiding in my stateroom." He motioned toward Binnie, who nodded.

"She was wet and crying. And trying to tell me she couldn't

talk, but I couldn't make heads or tails of it and started to get the skipper. She caught me and pulled me back and held my sleeve while she looked for a piece of paper. She wrote that she was mute and a man was going to sell her to be a slave. She swam out to the yacht, pulled herself up and on it, and went inside the first door she came to, mine. I hauled out a dry shirt, told her to get herself dried out in the bathroom, and tell me about it. She was a sight in that shirt, I can tell you."

He paused, looked at Binnie for a long moment with a big smile, then sobered and said, "I didn't turn her in. I hid her, brought her food, and didn't say a word. Then, when we got near Miami to dock, the Coast Guard hailed the skipper and ordered everyone on deck. They said they were coming aboard, searching for a kidnapped minor female. I told her to hide in the closet and went on deck with the others, and the Coast Guard guys boarded and searched the whole boat. There wasn't a trace of her. We were about half a mile offshore and she was gone. I thought she had jumped overboard and drowned."

Binnie had ducked her head, her hand remaining in his, and he continued to lean forward as if ready to leap up from his chair. Barbara thought that she couldn't have stopped him from telling the story if she had tried.

"Okay," he said. "We docked, and the group broke up. We were due to report in another week to start training, and I'd planned to rent a car and drive up to Atlanta to spend a few days with my mother and sister. I got the car, but I didn't leave Miami Beach. I rented a cabana and spent the next three days driving up and down the coast, reading every local paper there was, watching television news, listening to the radio news. I expected her body to wash up and planned to give her a decent burial at the very least.

"She found me instead," he said. "She spotted me driving and got the license number and then began checking motel parking lots, hotel lots, whatever she could think of, and she found me.

She was starving and dirty. She had swum ashore and had kept out of sight, looking for me. What if I'd left the way I planned? I felt as if it was meant to be, fate, something like that. We were meant to be together. I hid her, and we went to my mother's place. They fell in love with her, Mama and Adele, my sister. That's where we were when she showed me a thing she'd worn on a ribbon around her waist from the time she was thirteen or fourteen. Her mother made it for her. A little tube glued shut, watertight. I had to use a hacksaw to open it. There was a tiny scroll inside."

He released Binnie's hand, patted it, then said, "Show her the message."

Binnie looked at Barbara, her big eyes questioning. When Barbara nodded, she reached into the bag at her feet and removed an envelope, extracted a folded paper, and handed it to Barbara.

"It was rolled up so small for years," he said, "Mama flattened it with an iron. I had it Xeroxed on a regular-size paper and put the original away in a safe. That's the copy."

The message was centered on the 8½ × 11–inch paper where it took less than half a page. The writing was very small and neat, almost schoolgirl neat, like a penmanship sample for a test. Barbara read it slowly.

My name is Shala Santos and Lavinia Santos is my daughter. My sister is Anaia. She married an American named Lawrence. I do not know his surname. We are citizens of Belize. I was a passenger on a freighter on my way to my fiancé's parents in Jamaica and we were attacked by pirates. Every man aboard was murdered, including my betrothed Juan Hernandez. He was Lavinia's father. Domonic Guteriez took me to Haiti where he held me captive. When he learned that my father was a businessman, he tried to ransom me back to my family. An emissary arrived, but when he discovered that I was pregnant, he declared that I was not the daughter of Augustus Santos, and that Shala Santos had perished at sea. I became a slave to Domonic. When Lavinia was born mute, he grew fearful and believed she was cursed, that a birthmark over her heart was a sign of the curse. I told him that if he harmed her, the curse would punish him severely and he never touched her, and ordered me to keep her hidden away. He never let my daughter leave the house with me for fear I would escape with her. Now I am ill and know I shall die. I write this in order for my daughter to have knowledge of her heritage. I have told her that she must escape alone.

Barbara reread the message even more slowly, then put the paper down on the futon. Both Martin Owens and Binnie were watching her intently. Binnie's hand was again in his.

"Your mother passed away? Then you swam out to the yacht?"

Binnie nodded, but Martin said in a mean tone he had not used before, "There's one other little bit to add to that. Domonic was negotiating the sale of my wife to a pimp. He had prostituted her mother and planned to turn Binnie over to a guy who would do the same thing to her. A day or two after her mother died, she heard them bickering over the price. That's when she ran away." He kept his voice low, but it was more frightening than it would have been if he had shouted the words.

Binnie pulled her hand loose and touched his arm. When he turned his gaze to her, her hands moved rapidly in what Barbara thought must be American Sign Language. After a moment, he shook his head hard, and she made the same gestures even faster. Barbara had the impression that if her words had been spoken, she would have been shouting.

When he shook his head again, she reached for her bag, and this time pulled out a notebook and pen.

With an agonized expression he put his mammoth hand over hers and said to Barbara, "She wants me to tell you she'll kill herself before she'll go back to Haiti."

2

———

Exactly what did you hear from the immigration people?" Barbara asked.

"We have until next Friday to produce a certified birth certificate," Martin said. "And we can't do it. As for an expert in immigration, a special lawyer, we tried that. After we left my mother's house, we went to Chicago to consult such a lawyer and he said our only choice was to go to INS, that sooner or later they'd catch up with us, and the longer we dodged them the harder they'd be on her. They'd deport her, Ms. Holloway, send her back to Haiti. He said that letter from her mother didn't mean a thing, it isn't a legal document, and that if that man, Domonic, claiming to be her father, accused the team of kidnapping a minor for immoral purposes, I could probably buy him off, but that would be a tacit admission of his claim. Catch-22."

"Please excuse me for a minute," Barbara said, rising from the futon. "I'll put on coffee and copy the names on that message from your mother, if I may."

"Let me make the coffee while you get the names," Martin Owens said, almost leaping to his feet, drawing Binnie up with him.

"One more thing, Ms. Holloway. That lawyer said that by resigning, leaving the NFL like I did, I probably made them suspect that I was the one who kidnapped her."

Well, of course, Barbara thought, but she said nothing, and walked into the kitchen with both of them at her heels. She pointed to the coffeemaker and the cabinet. "Help yourself. I won't be long."

In her office she sat for a minute before glancing at the words. Pirates! Slaves, curses, kidnapping charge, transporting a minor for sex not only across a state line but from one country to another! Belize! She didn't even know where Belize was. It was hopeless, too implausible to accept without a lot of proof. And they had none at all. Obviously Martin Owens was intelligent, and apparently Binnie was, too, and she was courageous, if their story was anywhere near the truth. They both understood the situation. But Barbara knew how unlikely it was for INS to show any leniency whatsoever. Young single women looking for a way out of their own country, looking for an American husband, were anathema to immigration officials. The fact that she had landed one would only confirm their suspicions. Marrying an American citizen conferred citizenship automatically for legal immigrants, but not for Binnie. Without a Social Security card, birth certificate, visa, or driver's license, without a scrap of paper to attest to her identity, she was an undocumented illegal immigrant, and she was subject to deportation. Impatiently Barbara stepped off the carousel that, no matter how fast it whirled about, always returned to that bleak starting point.

She knew there was nothing she could do for them beyond finding someone qualified to give good advice, possibly intercede on their behalf, on the chance that the attorney they had consulted had not been a real expert. She suspected that what he had told them would be repeated, however. She also knew she could not simply send them away, not after reading that letter. She shook her head. Not just that, but rather after seeing how Binnie had reached for his hand, how he had looked at her. His expression had been so soft, so loving it had been wrenching. She felt she had to give them some hope, a glimmer of hope, while she searched for the right attorney.

She copied the names, and when she left her office she took her legal pad with her along with the letter.

Martin Owens had put cups on the table and he said the coffee was nearly ready. He had brought back the chair she had taken out for Binnie. "If there's another chair I could bring in, maybe it would be better here."

"In the office," she said, pointing. "I'm afraid it won't be very comfortable."

"I'll try not to break it," he said, then grinned as if he knew exactly what she had meant.

For the next hour she asked questions and they answered without hesitation. They had stayed in Chicago for several months, but too many people recognized him, and he had become alarmed, afraid someone would pass the word to someone who would notify immigration. They went to Las Vegas, where they were married.

Barbara interrupted to ask how Binnie had learned ASL, if she had gone to school. Binnie shook her head and her hands spoke to him.

"No school," he said. "Her mother got hold of a book and they learned it together. Binnie taught me. I'm not good at it the way she is, but she thinks there's hope for me."

Binnie's smile at that was radiant, beautiful. Her hands moved rapidly, and he shook his head. She looked at Barbara and first pointed to him, then held up a thumbs-up sign of approval.

"Okay," Barbara said, smiling. "After Las Vegas, what next?"

"New Orleans," he said. "I got a job in a restaurant, cooking."

She imagined that he meant flipping hamburgers, but he went on to say, "See, I got this scholarship to Georgia Tech, you know, for football. No one expects the players to do much in the way of classes, just patty-cake stuff, but I got into culinary arts. I always liked to cook and I had a knack for it. I didn't care if they thought it was just another easy way to get classtime credits. And a little restaurant management, courses like that. So in New Orleans, I got a job in a pretty good restaurant and learned a lot more and we stayed there for a year and a half, then headed up here to open a restaurant. I thought enough time had passed that we'd be off the hook, on the back burner, a buried file, something like that. I was wrong. Another mistake on my part."

"When did you leave Haiti?" Barbara asked Binnie then.

She held up three fingers, and he said, "Three years ago, in April."

When Barbara asked how old she was, Martin answered, "Twenty-one. She was eighteen when she swam out to the yacht."

"It's important," Barbara said. "It will give us a clue about when the piracy occurred, a possible starting place."

He looked at Binnie, who looked down at her hands, then nodded slightly. "She isn't sure," he said. "Her mother told her at one time it was her tenth birthday, but she never said exactly when her birth date was. She thinks her mother lost track of the time, the date. She had no way to keep up with it. Ms. Holloway, she was really a slave, no clock, no current newspapers. She picked one up now and then, and she taught Binnie to read using newspapers, but they usually were out-of-date. She lost track."

Then surprisingly he spoke to his wife with his hands. To Barbara's eyes he appeared to be as adept as Binnie was. They held a silent conversation while she waited.

"I asked her if she would be willing to show you the things she wrote down for me before I could understand ASL," he said. "She wants to let you read her notes."

Not me, Barbara thought. Someone should read them but not me. She nodded however. Soon after that she said, "Let's leave it for now. I need a little time to make some inquiries. As I said, I'm not an expert in this field. Tell me how to get in touch with you. I'll try to make it by tomorrow afternoon. Saturday at the latest."

He gave her two telephone numbers and mentioned the restaurant. "We'll be open tonight and tomorrow night, then I'm closing until this is over. We'll be there tomorrow from about ten in the morning until about ten thirty or a little later. We don't take new customers after nine."

When she went to the door with them, he took her hand in both of his and said, "Ms. Holloway, thank you. More than I can say, thank you."

She watched them walk out into the rain, with him holding the umbrella over Binnie. She wanted to shout after them, "Don't thank me! I don't have answers for you!"

In her kitchen again she refilled her coffee cup and took it to her office to make a few notes. First call someone. First, she amended, find out who would know about immigration law. She leaned back, thinking, sipping the coffee. It was very good, the best she'd had in her own house, she realized. How had he done that? Her coffee, her coffeemaker, and excellent coffee, proving something that she didn't like to admit. A lousy cook, she couldn't even make a decent cup of coffee.

Herman Krugman, she thought suddenly. Of course. He had lectured her class on immigration law a couple of times. It was twelve thirty, three thirty in New York, not a bad time to call, if he was still at Columbia, if he was still teaching, if he had the faintest memory of her and would take her call.

After going through two different offices, she got his number and an answering machine. She left a message. She would call again at five thirty.

Looking at the names she had copied, another thought surged. If Martin Owens really was suspected of kidnapping a minor, why hadn't the FBI come for him long before now? Why hadn't there been a big splash in the newspapers about it? A player in the

National Football League suspected of kidnapping a minor, even she would have heard something about it. If Domonic Guteriez claimed her as his daughter, was that the name he had given for her, Lavinia Guteriez? Certainly she would not have used that name anywhere, at any time. She would have used her mother's name, Santos. Had she called herself Binnie Santos on the marriage license? If yes, then why had the Chicago attorney leaped to the kidnapping charge? Martin Owens must have brought it up, and she had not thought to tell him not to talk about it, not to talk about any of this again with anyone. Next time, she ordered herself. Tell him next time.

If she had decided to take them on as clients, she would have kept them much longer, asked many more questions, demanded answers, but she had kept it superficial, knowing she had to turn them over to someone else. She knew too damn little even to do that much, she thought in irritation.

She needed more information, she decided. How much of that story was pure fantasy, how much real? Her decision about the library had been made for her, she realized, leaving her office to put on a poncho and pick up the books to be returned. She needed the library and the archives of *The New York Times*.

She hurried now. In two hours she wanted to be back at her house to try Krugman again.

It was twenty-five minutes after two when she entered her house later. She left the library books on the end table in the living room, that night's reading material, two books on Belize. She also had a dozen or so articles she had photocopied that she took to her desk. Her shoes were wet, and her poncho was dripping. No umbrella was quite big enough to keep the rain all the way off. In her office a minute later, wearing warm house slippers, and after leaving her poncho on the shower curtain rod, where as many drips hit the floor as hit the tub, she placed another call to Krugman's office at Columbia. This time he picked up the phone.

"Ms. Holloway, it's always a pleasure to hear from former students," he assured her when she apologized for disturbing him with the long-distance call. "How can I be of assistance?"

She explained the situation briefly without mentioning names. "I've become a defense attorney," she said, "and my lack of knowledge about your area of expertise is woeful, I'm afraid. I don't even know anyone on the West Coast who is an expert."

"Ms. Holloway, it is doubtful that anyone can be of much help in such a case. Without papers, a passport, visa permit, a Green Card, Social Security number, and so on, there's little recourse but to return her to her country of origin. If, as you say, there is some question concerning what country that is, it becomes a little more complicated, but I would assume there's a photograph of the girl the father claims was kidnapped, and if she resembles the person in such a photograph, probably the case will be concluded expeditiously by returning her to her father with the understanding that in her home country she will have access to the legal system to appeal such a decision. If the young woman has done nothing to draw attention to herself, applied for a passport or a Social Security card, something of that sort, or has broken the law and has been arrested, since she has married, with a name change, there seldom is a reason for the immigration service to take notice of her, unless they received a tip. But even if that is a given, that someone has tipped them off, the pertinent facts are unchanged. She is in the country illegally and almost certainly will be sent back home. I can give you the name of someone in your area to represent her, but I'm afraid such information does not immediately come to mind. In a day or two perhaps."

"I would appreciate that very much," Barbara said. "May I call you again early next week?"

"Yes. Monday or Tuesday. I'll make a note, my dear."

Tuesday, she thought with dismay after hanging up. With the deadline on Friday, that was cutting it too close. Her father might know someone, although it was not his field any more than it was hers, but he knew a lot of people. He might know an expert. She called his office and had to settle for Patsy, his secretary.

"Oh, you just missed him," Patsy said. "He left five minutes ago. He said he has some shopping to do, and he wants to get home before dark. You know how awful that drive is in the best of weather, and a day like this one. . . . You have his number out there, don't you?"

"Of course," Barbara said, and thanked her. Okay, she told herself, stymied. Coffee, and get to those articles. She nuked leftover coffee, never good but better than any she might make, she admitted to herself. Then she returned to her desk and began to read.

"My God!" she muttered after the first two articles. Piracy was alive and thriving in the Caribbean, off the African coast, in Indonesian waters, other places. She'd had no idea. So that part of the message Shala had left her daughter very likely had been true.

She was immersed in another article concerning contemporary slavery, again all around the world, when her doorbell rang. Not at all regretful about leaving the disquieting article, she went to see who was calling this time.

One of the reasons Frank objected so strenuously to her housing arrangement was the fact that she admitted strangers inside. "You're inviting danger," he had snapped when she defended the practice that she knew was somewhat less than prudent. The man on her stoop that late afternoon would be chalked up in her father's column, she thought. He was at best nondescript, middle-aged, tired-looking, wearing a dripping wet, shapeless raincoat and an equally wet slouch hat down low on his forehead. He had one hand in his coat pocket.

"Yes?" she said cautiously, keeping the chain on her door.

"Ms. Holloway, Jeffrey Nicholson." He pulled his hand out of his pocket and, shielding it with his body, showed her an official ID. "DEA," he said. "Drug Enforcement Agency. May I come in?"

She opened the door. Inside, he looked at the rug at his feet and said diffidently, "Maybe there's someplace where the water won't hurt anything?"

It wouldn't hurt the cheap rug, but she nodded, motioned for him to come along, and went to the kitchen. "Drape it over a chair, I'll bring a towel to put down."

After spreading a towel under his coat, she said, "We might as well sit in here, Mr. Nicholson. What can I do for you?"

He placed his hat on the towel and pulled out a chair. "This is fine. Thanks. Ms. Holloway, I've come to ask you to assist the agency in an ongoing investigation. I don't want to take a lot of your time, so I'll try to explain quickly."

Barbara sat opposite him at the table and waited. Don't judge a book by its cover, she thought, and don't judge a man by the sound of his voice. But Nicholson's voice was high-pitched and rasping, the kind of voice that, if he were a hostile witness in court, she would encourage to talk on and on, knowing the jury would find it as irritating as she did.

"It concerns a big drug-smuggling enterprise," Nicholson said, "one that involves people here in Eugene. We have reason to believe that your city is one of the major redistribution centers for drugs smuggled into the country and sent on to other cities up and down the coast. And the focus of our investigation is this neighborhood."

If Eugene had a slum, Barbara knew, it was this area, with some of the poorest of the poor, unemployed, unemployable, immigrants with minimum education if any, many with no English. And some, most of those she had met so far, very good people who simply were impoverished. She knew there were drugs, but probably no more than in the university neighborhood, just more likely to get the possessors into trouble.

"Exactly what are you after?" she asked. "Assist you in what way?"

He looked very earnest as he said, "We've been unable to get a reliable informant in the area, and we really need one. There are a couple of snitches who tell us things now and then, but they are as likely to lie as not, and that's not good enough. We think you might help with that effort."

She shook her head. "Mr. Nicholson, as an attorney I sometimes give advice to local residents, but my oath as an attorney would prohibit disclosing to anyone whatever matters I discuss with such clients. I can't help you."

"No, no," he said. "We understand that relationship, Ms. Holloway, and we respect it entirely. We wouldn't think of asking you to break your confidentiality oath to your clients. Never. It's an urban legend that where federal agencies are concerned the right hand doesn't know what the left hand is doing. But there are times, Ms. Holloway, when that isn't true. For instance, we know that the immigration service is homing in on Mrs. Binnie Owens as an undocumented resident, an unregistered alien here illegally. And we also know that Martin Owens, a football star, is a hero to many of the young people here. They look up to him, respect him, and they confide in him. We are asking you to tell him that if he will simply relate to us any information he hears concerning a shipment, a delivery, anything about who the headman is of the ring operating here, anything of substance that he hears, we will come to his assistance in negotiating an appeal with immigration. We can be of great help to him and his wife, Ms. Holloway, if he will cooperate with us. Will you deliver that message to him? That's all we are asking of you, to deliver the message."

"Why don't you tell him yourself?" Barbara asked coolly.

"When you're in trouble with one government agency, would you even listen to a second one?" he said, spreading his hands in a discouraged manner. "We wanted to approach him before, but without any leverage, it appeared pointless. He's clean, young, suspicious of the government and somewhat fearful of it. With cause at present, I must admit, with cause. Now, with a little leverage, an offer of help in his real trouble, he might be willing to assume such a role. And, Ms. Holloway, it would benefit those young people he already befriends. Whenever we can take drugs off the streets, it can only help society as a whole. Surely you would agree with that."

She rose from her chair and said, "I'll deliver your message, but I won't advise him in any way concerning it. Was that all, Mr. Nicholson?"

"That's it," he said, reaching for his hat. "Thanks for giving me this time." He put on his coat and hat and followed her from the kitchen after a swift glance about. In the living room his glance lingered a moment on the library books as he adjusted his hat down low again and buttoned his coat. "I'll be in touch for his answer," he said at the door. He opened it and left with that.

She locked the door, then returned to the kitchen, deeply troubled. She was very much afraid that she had found out who had tipped off the immigration officials about Binnie's status. And to do that and now demand that Martin Owens become a stool pigeon for them was so reprehensible that she thought that if she knew of an anarchist group she could join, she'd become a card-carrying member immediately. It had not been a simple request; it was a demand. It was blatant criminal extortion.

3

It was eleven when Barbara closed her book about Belize and wandered into her office to make a few more notes and reread the ones she had made earlier.

Something was wonky, she kept thinking. Something was nagging at her without defining what that something was. Jeffrey Nicholson, she jotted his name with a question mark. Domonic Guteriez, another question mark. After Nicholson's name she wrote the question: Why did he come to me? How did he know to come to me?

One of his stoolies could have informed him, she thought. But she didn't believe it. In that kind of rain? An unreliable stoolie tagging along after Martin Owens and his wife? One who knew that she was an attorney living in this wreck of a house? It seemed unlikely. Yet Nicholson had known that. If he already had a stoolie who knew it also, why did he say he needed Martin? Why bother with her?

As for Domonic, why hadn't he continued to press the kidnapping charge? To all appearances the matter had been dropped, or the FBI would have become involved. There would have been publicity. Had Martin Owens paid him off?

Back up just a little, she decided. Martin and Binnie got the letter from INS the day before yesterday. It had been in their mailbox when they got home at ten thirty or a little later, and they stewed about it for one day, then came to her door. Nicholson had shown up hours later, and he had come knowing she was an attorney. It didn't add up, she thought irritably. It was all too damn fast.

One of the articles she had read was about Haiti, which the World Health Organization had described as having a high incidence of the new scourge, AIDS. Superstitious, with a strong belief in witches, curses, even zombies, one of the poorest nations on earth, practically denuded of its trees, with attendant soil erosion, chronic food shortages. Corrupt government. If INS deported Binnie, escorted her from a plane to return her to Domonic, she would vanish to a bordello somewhere and never be found again. Even if Martin got a visa to follow her, he would fail.

Barbara shook her head. Not her goddamn case, she reminded herself. She was as helpless as Martin Owens in this matter. But she wanted to talk to them again, a long talk. And she wanted answers to the questions she had written.

Before she left her office an hour later, she wrote one more note on her pad: Call Bailey.

She placed the call at eight thirty the next morning. When she asked if he was free, Bailey said, "Depends. What's up?"

"Can you come around at ten? I'll explain when I see you."

"The old man's office?"

"No. My place." She gave her address.

"I've got another job going, so I might not have a lot of time," he said in an aggrieved-sounding voice, his skepticism over the address no doubt on his mind.

"Let's talk about it when you get here," she said. "See you later." She hung up.

From one of the articles she had read, a brief profile of the NFL linebacker Martin Owens, she had learned that he had made a lot of money in the six years he had been on the Giants, but also that he had spent a lot of money, buying his mother an expensive house, another slightly less expensive one for his sister's wedding present, new cars for both, and that he had established a substantial trust fund for his mother. She had cleaned houses in Atlanta to support him and his sister. And he and his buddies had rented a yacht for three weeks and probably had indulged in other extravagant holidays, as well as expensive toys. Barbara hoped he had kept some money. Bailey Novell, the best private detective west of the Mississippi, according to her father, did not come cheap.

Bailey usually was prompt, and he was that morning. Barbara, watching for his old Dodge, already had her jacket on, purse in hand, when he pulled to a stop at the curb behind her own car.

She met him on the sidewalk.

From his appearance Bailey was exactly the kind of danger her father had warned her about. He looked like a bum dressed in thrift store clothes that didn't quite fit. He looked perfectly at home in this poor neighborhood.

"Let's talk a minute in your heap," she said.

He was looking past her at the house, badly in need of paint, with an unkempt yard that had a mixture of wild grass and weeds growing luxuriantly that wet spring. "You've got a nerve, talking about a heap," he said with a shrug.

He got in behind the wheel and she settled into the passenger seat. The rain had yielded to a fine mist and their breath fogged the windows almost instantly.

"So what's up?" he asked.

"You know who Martin Owens is?"

"Never heard of him."

"The football player."

He gave her an appraising look. "You kidding? That Martin Owens? Sure, who doesn't?"

"He has a restaurant here," she said, and described the broad outlines of the situation. "Anyway, I wonder if his restaurant is bugged. And I wonder if my house is. For openers."

"You flying solo?"

She nodded. "I assume Owens has kept some of the money he earned playing football. I'll find out. But keep the cost down. Just in case I have to pony up."

"Barbara, come on," he said, sounding offended. He could do that well. "So what do you want me to do?"

"I want you to go to the restaurant. I'll take my car and follow you, and I'll invite them out for a little spin while you see if there's a bug. How long will it take?"

"Hour, maybe less, depends. You want it out?"

"Nope. Don't touch it if it's there. Then back here, and do the same. If I'm clean, then we can talk about the next step. Okay?"

"Okeydokey," he said. "Where's the restaurant?"

She gave him the address and the key to her house, and left his car to get into her own. A few minutes later they were both stopping at the curb outside a neat house with a small sign swinging in the yard, MARTIN'S RESTAURANT. It was only six blocks from her own house.

This house was very well maintained, freshly painted white, windows shining clean with brilliant white café curtains, flower boxes sporting blooms on a narrow porch, and a walk bordered by gold daffodils.

Barbara left Bailey by his car as she went to the door and rang the bell. When Martin opened the door, surprised to see her there, she put her finger to her lips and motioned him to come out. Beyond him Barbara saw Binnie standing by an open door, probably to the kitchen, Barbara assumed after a swift appraising glance about. The restaurant was tiny, with a few booths, half a dozen tables, and little else. It wouldn't take Bailey very long. Binnie, at the door, looked as surprised as Martin had been. He turned to her and spoke with his hands. At her nod he followed Barbara out and to Bailey. She introduced them.

"I suspect that there's a listening device in there," she said to Martin. "If there is he'll find it. Can you and Binnie leave for half an hour or so, take a little ride with me so we can talk while he goes about his business?"

Martin's face had frozen in alarm at her words, and his hands clenched.

Barbara put her hand on his arm and said, "Relax. Take it easy. I may be altogether wrong. Overly cautious."

"I'll get Binnie," he said tightly. "I want to talk to you."

This time Bailey followed him into the restaurant and a minute later Martin and Binnie came out.

"I'm afraid you'll have to ride in front," Barbara said when Martin opened the back door. "No legroom back there for you." She tried to ignore the look of terror on Binnie's face and went around to get in behind the wheel. Martin barely had legroom in the front seat, but it couldn't be helped, and she didn't intend to go far. Just to the parking area at the base of Skinner's Butte. She told them it would take only a few minutes and they drove in silence until she pulled into a parking space. Ahead was a swatch of grass, then the bike path, and beyond that the flashing Willamette River, her favorite walking place. That day she remained in the car, twisted around to see them both and started. The windows soon fogged so heavily that no one passing by could have seen inside, which suited her just fine.

"A couple of questions first," she said. "You got the letter Tuesday night. Did you talk a lot about it that night? All day Wednesday, and after you saw me yesterday?"

"Sure, we did. That's all we could think of."

"Right. What all did you talk about? What options did you voice out loud? When did you first mention my name?"

He rubbed his eyes, glanced at Binnie, then said, "Ms. Holloway—"

Barbara held up her hand. She didn't know when it happened, but in her mind they had become Martin and Binnie, not Mr. and Mrs. Owens. "Let's get less formal. I'm Barbara." She pointed to him, then to Binnie. "Martin and Binnie. All right with you?"

He smiled a big, expansive smile that made him look like a kid, but it didn't last more than a second and he was sober-faced again. "Barbara, we're scared to death, to tell the truth. Yeah, we talked. You know, out loud, ASL, a mix of both. I talked about running, just getting in the car and taking off, down to Tucson maybe, get across the border and keep going. Maybe if I could speak Spanish, I'd still be talking about that. I don't know when we thought of you. Late the next day?" He looked at Binnie and she nodded. "Yeah, late the day before we showed up at your door."

"And after you left my place? Still talking about it?"

"Sure, all day, this morning. Why are you asking about that?"

She told them about Nicholson's visit, his message. Martin looked as if it left a bad taste in his mouth, but Binnie seemed willing to consider the proposal. She made rapid hand gestures and Martin shook his head. "Be an informer? Spy on folks who trust me? Not my style," he said flatly.

"Have you applied for a driver's license, a Social Security card, any official identification?" she asked Binnie. She shook her head hard. "I think someone tipped off the immigration people. There was no reason for them to get you in their sights otherwise. And for Nicholson to show up the way he did makes me wonder if his people haven't been spying on you, Martin. The timing is too close, too coincidental, and I have little faith in coincidences."

"Why? Why would they?" he asked in bewilderment.

"That's the real question, isn't it?" Barbara said. She glanced at her watch. "We should be getting back soon. I'd rather not raise any questions right now about your silence in the restaurant for too long a period. But first, is there someplace you can go to keep a low profile, out of sight for the next few days, maybe most of the week? Someplace where we can talk freely?"

They had a silent conversation with their hands for the next minute or two. Then Martin said, "I told you we heard about you from Tawna and James Gresham. They've invited us out to their place a couple of times. We never made it yet, but we could go there. You know where they are, up the McKenzie? I think it's called Turner's Point, something like that."

Barbara felt as if every cell in her body shrank at the thought of going back there. Martin was still speaking, but now he sounded a long way away.

"We'd be okay there. I don't think a soul would dream of looking for us there."

Barbara nodded. She opened her window and turned on the fan to clear the fog. When she spoke again, her own voice sounded strange, hollow. "Did you mention their names at all? Out loud, I mean."

Martin glanced at Binnie and after a moment he said, "I don't think so, not until we turned up at your place anyway."

"Good. I want Bailey to drive you out there, if you agree. He would make sure you weren't followed. I don't want you to drive because if there's a bug in the restaurant, there's no way to know about your car, how secure it might be. For the rest of today, tonight, don't say a thing out loud that bears on anything we've said, anything about the whole situation, and especially don't breathe a word about the listening device if there is one. Okay? I'll come in with you and tell you again about Nicholson's proposal, and you say something like you'll have to think about it, talk it over. Will you do that? Put on an act?" She suspected that they would have a lot of conversations about it in the days to come. "It would be absolutely normal if you keep talking about that, in fact, let them know you're considering it."

"Sure," Martin said. "Barbara, are you all right?"

"Yes. It's getting a little stuffy in here. I'm fine. I'll ask Bailey to pick you up tomorrow, whenever you say. If you call Tawna or James, use a pay phone somewhere, not your own."

"We can be ready by ten in the morning," Martin said after another silent conversation with Binnie. He reached in his pocket and brought out a card and wrote on it. "Our home address."

"Thanks," Barbara said, and turned on the engine, engaged the gears, but paused before backing out of the parking space. "I'll come out to the house on Sunday, after you get settled in. We'll have a long talk then. You should have my phone number, in case you want to get in touch with me." She wrote it in a notebook, ripped out the page, and handed it to him.

"We haven't talked yet about paying you, Barbara. I'm good for it," he said as she drove back to the restaurant.

Bailey would be pleased to hear that, she thought with relief. Again, she had failed to bring it up herself. Because this is not my case, she told herself sharply.

When they reached the restaurant, Bailey met them in the dining room. He held up his finger, one bug, and indicated the kitchen with a jerk of his thumb, then without a word he saluted and left. Barbara repeated Nicholson's proposal and Martin responded exactly right. "I'll be in touch," she said at the door. "Take it easy, you two."

Done, she thought, returning to her car. She would give Bailey some time at her house, buy some sandwich makings to feed him, and go on from there.

4

When she opened her door later, Bailey stepped out from the bedroom, saluted, and stepped back in. She took her groceries to the kitchen, left the bag on the table, shrugged out of her jacket, and went into her office.

Twenty minutes later, Bailey came to the door. "You're clean."

She glanced at the several boxes on the floor. "Those, too?"

"Just the one on top. Barbara, you plant a bug, you want to make it quick and easy, not start unpacking boxes to hide it. In, out, done, that's the way. A day later same thing, in, out, done. You need padlocks on your doors. I can do them. There's dry rot in your bathroom. What's in the bag?"

"Lunch. Let's make some sandwiches."

A few minutes later, at the table with ham and cheese sandwiches, beer for him, she told him what she had. "Nicholson's a creep. Forget him for now. According to the letter Binnie's mother wrote, her sister, Anaia Santos, married an American, Lawrence somebody. I want his name. And the father was a businessman, name Augustus Santos. Sometimes a grandfather has more regard for a grandchild than for the child who strayed off base. Company, business, how influential is he, the usual background. I want to get in touch with him, but I don't want to go in cold. And finally, what happened to the kidnapping charge? Why didn't Domonic Guteriez pursue it? You'd think with a rich American sports figure, he'd be hot after big money. Why wasn't he?"

As she listed her Christmas order, Bailey grew more and more disgruntled. "What's Belize? Besides a name. Never heard of it. You want me to go traipsing off to a foreign country God only knows where it is, and what language, or if they shoot Americans on sight. Come on, Barbara."

"It's a tiny country in the Caribbean, nestled in the armpit of the Yucatán. English language. Gained independence a few years ago. Before that governed by British Honduras, British law system, no doubt. Two traffic lights in the whole country, which is sixty-eight miles wide and under two hundred miles from north to south. Exporter of sugar, mahogany until they cut down all the trees. One of the major marijuana growers until Reagan sent in planes to spray the fields last year. They're still doing it. With marijuana on the decline, down to less than two hundred tons apparently—" She stopped when Bailey snorted, then continued, "They could be looking for another way to bring in the big bucks. Could be the reason the DEA got interested in Binnie, if they know there's a connection. What more do you want? If Santos is a prominent businessman, in a country that size he shouldn't be hard to find."

Bailey's gloom did not lighten. "And the sister married an American. Whoopie! When?"

"Binnie thinks she's twenty-one, but she may be younger, and the sister was already married when Shala sailed out with her lover. Start there, around twenty to twenty-two years ago—1960 on. There should be a record of the piracy and murder of the crew and others."

She gave him the address Martin had provided. "They'll be

ready at ten in the morning, straight out to Tawna and James Gresham's house at Turner's Point. You know where it is?"

He nodded. "I'll get word to them to meet me at long-term parking at the airport and go from there. In case a neighbor spots me at the house."

And that was why she wanted Bailey, she thought. He took account of things like that and she had not. "Right. You said you had other work going on. Can you get to this right away, like yesterday, in fact?"

"Yeah. You realize you're just like your old man? He always wants things yesterday," he said morosely, then grinned. "This is more fun. Watching you tangle it up with INS and the Drug Enforcement Agency is a hoot. If the IRS and or the FBI get involved, I'll give you some pointers on skipping out of the country, up to Canada, and on to Finland or someplace like that."

"Thanks," she said. "I'll keep it in mind. I'll go out to Turner's Point on Sunday and talk to them, but Binnie doesn't know any more than what her mother told her." She hesitated a moment, then added, "Bailey, Martin can pay. And Dad isn't to get involved in this. No way, not even a hint."

"Gotcha," he said. "He'll have to be on the outside to post bail bond or something." He stood and pulled on a raincoat that looked to be fifty years old. "I'll be in touch." Everything about him screamed slouch, even his amble to the door, but he delivered. That was what mattered, Bailey delivered.

She wanted a long walk more than anything, she decided. There was nothing else she could do until she saw Martin and Binnie on Sunday, and called Krugman back on Monday or Tuesday. She thought uneasily about Bailey's words, tangling it up with the INS and the DEA. But she had given Martin Nicholson's message and if they were listening, they'd know that she had done her duty, as a good citizen should. She put away the remains of lunch, pulled on a jacket, and left to take her walk.

That day the river was a restless palette of gray, black, and silver, with white lacy foam where rocks created ripples. High with spring runoff, the river seemed in a terrible hurry to reach the sea, a futile, never completed task, a goal as unreachable as the horizon.

She walked briskly, and every time her mind switched to the ordeal of facing the McKenzie River, she forced herself to veer off to a different direction. Days after announcing that she and Mike Denisen were going to marry, she had lost him; the river had claimed him. She had not been back since the night that she waited for word.

Binnie and Martin, she veered back to them, deserved something other than a Chicago attorney who so easily discounted the message left to Binnie by her dying mother. He was like a surgeon doing a tonsillectomy without noticing a knife in the patient's back.

Finding the right attorney might take some time, and they didn't have time. That was the problem. Maybe the grandfather would come through for Binnie, she thought then, but without real hope. His emissary had judged Shala an imposter when she turned out to be pregnant. After he returned to Belize and made his report, no doubt Augustus Santos had believed his daughter was dead. But it was possible the emissary had told him the truth, that Shala was alive and pregnant. It was possible, she repeated more firmly. It was possible that he would embrace a grandchild.

Two dazzling white egrets skimmed the surface of the racing water, a beautiful rare moment never captured in art. She stopped walking to watch them, and in her mind she heard Mike's joyous laughter that last day.

She began to walk again, more briskly than before. Another disquieting thought came to mind. Was she letting herself become involved with Binnie and Martin despite her lack of qualifications because they obviously were very deeply in love? Letting it become personal was always a mistake she knew. An attorney could not allow personal feelings to enter a case. But they always did, she added, and with this one more than usual.

All right, she told herself sharply. Consult a specialist, but oversee it, manage it yourself. She damn well knew there was a knife in the patient's back. Something was rotten about the whole affair that made it more than a simple illegal alien, immigration matter.

When she returned home, she found a message from her father on the answering machine. Of course, he would have checked in with Patsy, and she would have told him Barbara had called. She thought for a moment before returning his call. She couldn't go out there without seeing him. He would be furious and hurt, when he found out, and he would find out. And she had no intention of getting him involved with Martin and Binnie. She knew that he would tell her to turn them over to someone knowledgeable about immigration and butt out, that immigration played by its own rules and she knew diddly about what they were. Good advice that she would not heed. She dialed his number.

"Hi, Dad. Phone tag, my turn. I thought I might drop in for a visit Sunday, if you're home and free."

"I'll be both home and free," he said. "And I'll make you some dinner."

"Yum," she said. "Sounds good. Can I bring anything, good bread, wine?"

He said she could pick up a loaf of French bread, nothing else, and that was that, she thought when they hung up.

In his house overlooking the McKenzie River, Frank regarded the phone thoughtfully. Was she trying to face down demons? Deal with her pain by confronting it? An act of healing? Something else? Barbara had many facets, he knew, and many of them remained hidden, buried, not to be pried out of her. He would never attempt to unravel her mind, but it left him feeling helpless to offer anything that might ease her pain. It was too deep, too well hidden. What he could do, and did as often as she allowed, was to see to it that she got a decent meal at least once a week, and hope to go on from there. And try to avoid anything that might send her packing ever again. His biggest fear was that she would leave again, stay away for months or years. The fact that she was coming out to Turner's Point, to his house, an event he had not invited or expected, was hopeful, he told himself. He would air out the upstairs room she had used before, but he suspected that was a meaningless gesture. He certainly would not push for that extended a visit, just hope it might happen.

He began to consider what would be an especially fine meal in honor of her visit and, humming to himself, he went to take a duckling from the freezer. Barbara was very fond of duck with that special garlic and lime sauce he had found.

Barbara continued to sit at her desk, thinking of next steps. A letter of agreement with Binnie and Martin, making it official that she was representing them. More, she decided. A letter to the immigration service, on office stationery with the Bixby-Holloway imprint. Petty thievery seemed quite minor compared to tangling it up with two big government agencies, she thought mockingly. She would go to Frank's office on Saturday when she was unlikely to meet anyone and lift some letterheads and envelopes.

5

Everything was exactly as she remembered it, Barbara thought that Sunday, leaving the highway for the gravel road that led to Frank's house and a short distance beyond. The rise of the high Cascades as backdrop. The same tall, dark fir trees, a tangle of brambles on one side, a madrone visible now and then, gleaming red where sunshine shafted in to touch it, ferns, and multicolored lichen. The smell of the river. Changeless, eternal woods here, eternal mountains, river. She shook her head, acknowledging that that was her human arrogance at work. Actually, it was all in flux, connected in a dance taking place in a time frame not visible to her limited vision. Her passage through it was like that of a meteor streaking through space.

She pulled into Frank's driveway and parked, picked up her purse but left her briefcase in the car. He would wonder why she was bringing a briefcase out for a family visit.

Frank greeted her with his arms spread. "Good weather for a drive in the country," he said, embracing her. "Good to see sunshine, have spring arrive, maybe."

"Maybe is always the right word about weather," she said, smiling.

She tossed a light jacket on a chair and went to the living room with him. He had moved a small table and two chairs close to the fireplace where a low fire was burning, sparing her the kitchen windows with a broad view of the McKenzie. She recognized and appreciated the gesture.

"Coffee in the carafe," Frank said. "Have you had lunch?"

"Yep. And breakfast. Dad, I'm not going hungry. Honestly, I don't go hungry. But coffee would be good. How's the book coming? I thought I might read a bit of it, if you're willing to show it."

"Willing? Try delighted. I've been coming across some pretty incredible cross-examinations, and decided to give a whole chapter to some so rotten you have to question motivation of the defense, or in some cases the prosecution. Although generally you know damn well what's driving that side. The scoreboard."

She laughed with him, and for the next hour read his manuscript and made comments. Then, laughing harder, she put a page down and said, "Dad, he'll sue you! You can't get away with saying things like that."

"Verbatim quotes from the court transcript," Frank said complacently. "I hardly even mention what an ass he is, what he missed. A passing reference is all. I consulted an expert on libel."

"Who?"

"Me."

She stood. "With that I need some air. I'll take a walk, inspect Nell's walnut trees, maybe drop in on Tawna to admire her newest jewelry creations. Do you mind?" Tawna taught French at the university, and she made fantastic jewelry, her true love.

"Take a walk, Bobby. I have things to do in the kitchen. Have a good walk. Tell Tawna and James hello for me. I hardly ever see them."

She picked up her jacket and left, then stopped at her car to get her briefcase. It was a short walk through the woods to Nell Kendrick's property with a grove of black walnut trees that would be ready to harvest in a year or two. The valuable wood would make Nell a rather wealthy young woman. Adjacent to the maturing trees younger trees were growing sturdily, another harvest in twenty years coming along. Seedling trees would not be ready, Nell had told Barbara, for about seventy years. A long time between edible nut in the ground and a harvestable tree.

It was wondrously peaceful under the massive walnut trees. Little undergrowth succeeded in the deep shade, and with the toxic substance the roots exuded. It was squirrel heaven, and jays scolded raucously at her presence. When she neared the big house, both Martin and James emerged from the barn to greet her. James was a veterinarian and usually had a sick animal or two housed in his barn. His greeting was warm and friendly, the greeting of an old friend rather than a simple acquaintance. She was glad that Martin appeared to be more relaxed than he had been in Eugene. His welcoming smile revealed what seemed to be an awful lot of very white teeth.

"You didn't tell us we'd be housed in a little paradise," he said. "This is great."

"Come on in," James said, heading for the house. "I think Tawna is using Binnie as a model for earrings or something. What's with women and jewelry? I don't get it."

"What's holed up in the barn?" Barbara asked. "A sick goat or pig or something. And you think jewelry is hard to get. Hah!"

Inside, Tawna and Binnie indeed had been trying on jewelry. A table was covered with it. Tawna's welcome was as warm as James's had been, and Binnie smiled shyly at her.

"She's so tiny," Tawna said, indicating Binnie. "Most of my earrings are ridiculous on anyone so small and delicate."

She was neither. Both she and James had struck Barbara as tall, handsomely built athletic types when she met them. They had shrunk down a bit next to Martin, but everyone in the room dwarfed Binnie.

"Well, you didn't come to buy jewelry, so to the study with you three," Tawna said. "Barbara, James and I are plotting on how to keep them here forever. He's a genius in the kitchen and her pastries are downright sinful. I never want them to go away, although I could start waddling."

She led the way to a study as she spoke, glanced around, and added, "Do you want something to drink while you talk? Wine, beer, coffee . . . ?"

"Not for me," Barbara said, and both Binnie and Martin shook their heads. Tawna nodded and left them.

There was a leather-covered sofa, side chairs, coffee table, and a large desk covered with papers and books. They arranged themselves in the chairs and on the sofa.

Binnie signed to Martin and he said, "She has copies of all her notes in our room. I made Xeroxes of everything for you. We'll hand it over before you leave."

"Good. I have an agreement for you both to look over," Barbara said, taking it from her briefcase. "It's an attorney-client agreement recognizing me as your attorney of record in this matter. It allows me to act on your behalf. Binnie, Martin, I have to say this so you'll understand our relationship. I told you I'm not an expert on immigration matters, and I'll try to find someone who is but, with your permission, I'd want to use such an attorney as a consultant, not ask anyone else to become your primary attorney. I'd oversee the case."

Binnie's eyes filled with tears and she nodded vigorously, and Martin said huskily, "Barbara, we couldn't ask for anything better. We'll be forever in your debt if you handle this for us, however you want to do it."

She watched them read the letter, sign two copies, one for them to keep, one for her. "Okay," she said. "On to a few questions. Who has access to your kitchen at the restaurant?"

"We've been thinking about that," Martin said. "There's a new guy making deliveries, he started early last week. Everyone else has been there about as long as we have. A couple who come in the mornings to clean. Guys with deliveries of drinks, things like that, and that's just about all. On busy nights we have a busboy, a neighborhood kid, but he hasn't been there for a week." He gave her names and she made a note of them. He had pegged it, she thought. A new deliveryman whose deliveries included more than just drinks, timed to coincide with when the tip would have been passed to the immigration people.

"Next," she said. "Martin, did you pay off Domonic Guteriez? Did you pay him anything?"

"No. I never even heard from him directly. It was the Coast Guard guys who told us there was a kidnapping charge, and there was one short item in the Miami paper, that's all I knew about it."

"You told the first attorney you talked to in Chicago?"

He nodded.

"Have you mentioned it to anyone else?"

"No. We haven't talked about this with anyone until we came to you."

"Have you asked Tawna and James to keep it quiet that you're houseguests here?"

Martin's look was reproachful. "Barbara," he said slowly as if taking care with his choice of words, "black folks don't generally talk about their trouble with the government. Like preaching to the choir, just no point in it. In any case, they know better than to talk about us. The fact that we asked for asylum is enough said about the matter."

She brought up Nell and her two children and he shook his head. "Tawna told us about them, but she said they've gone over to Bend to spend a week with the kids' grandparents. Spring break starts tomorrow. The Greshams have a daughter at Juilliard, but she won't be coming home until summer."

She had more questions. Had any of the other football players suspected Binnie was aboard the yacht? He said no, that he kept hanging out with them as usual, and they all took food to their staterooms. No one paid any attention to that. Binnie signed rapidly and he added, "I never touched her on the yacht, Barbara. I think I was scared to death of her, most girls but especially her, so little and afraid and all."

Barbara turned to Binnie then. "Did your mother talk about her father? What he was like, anything about him?"

She signed and Martin said, "A little, not much. She was running away from him and a marriage he wanted to arrange. She had fallen in love with Binnie's father. She was attending the university when she met him, and hated the man her father was trying to make her marry."

And finding her pregnant scotched that, Barbara thought. She asked Binnie how and when she had learned to swim well enough to jump off the yacht and swim to shore at Miami Beach.

This time Martin answered without waiting for Binnie to sign. She nodded as he told how Domonic had made her and her mother dive for abalone and conch for the restaurant trade. Her mother and Anaia had swum a lot in Belize, sometimes down deep by the reefs. Her mother had taught Binnie.

After she asked Binnie a few more questions, Martin said, "Barbara, she's written a lot of the things you're asking about. Pretty much all she can remember about her mother. How Domonic used Binnie as hostage whenever he sent her mother out to shop or anything. After her mother got sick, she became the hostage and Binnie was sent out to the market. It's all in the notes she made for me, a notebook full of them."

"Okay, fair enough. I'll read the material, and if I have more questions we'll get back to them. One more for now. Binnie, do you resemble your mother?"

Binnie looked taken aback by the question, surprised and very unhappy. It was a tough one, Barbara knew. Few people saw their own resemblance to family members, likenesses others recognized at a glance. But it was more than just that, she realized, watching Binnie struggle with the question.

She started to sign, stopped, and looked at her hands miserably. After a moment, she signed again, not looking at Barbara or Martin. When her hands became silent, Martin reached out for one and held it.

In a low voice he said, "She doesn't know. Her mother had turned into an old, destroyed woman by the time Binnie reached puberty. They were about the same size, that's all she can tell you." His voice dropped even lower. "Her mother died, probably of AIDS, before she reached forty."

Tears were on Binnie's cheeks, and Martin said, "Why don't you go up and get that notebook for Barbara?" He kissed her hand before releasing it. Without a glance at either of them, Binnie rose and walked rapidly from the room with her head lowered

"She needs a couple of minutes," Martin said.

Barbara could only agree. "When she's ready, I'd like to take some pictures," she said. "I'm going to try to get in touch with her grandfather and hope he's more humane with his granddaughter than he was with his daughter. I want to try to enlist his help in establishing her identity, her right to refuse deportation to Haiti."

Hope flared in his eyes but faded quickly. "There's not enough time, is there? Find him, send him pictures, write or telephone him. Just not enough time."

"I'll prepare another document, a letter to the immigration office in Eugene. It's a request for an extension of the deadline in which to locate the necessary documents. I'll use my father's office stationery. As imposing as that is, and as prestigious as the firm is, it should make them hesitate to deny the request. Or at the very least make them decide to pass it on to superiors for a response."

He nodded and then said, "You'll be buying some time, maybe. Barbara, if nothing works, if they come after her hard, I won't let them take her. I won't let her go to that hellhole and suffer what her mother suffered. I'll kill her first, and then turn the gun on myself. That's just the way it is."

"We won't let her go back, Martin. We're in this together and we won't let them send her back."

He studied her face, then stood and held out his hand to her. When he released her hand, Barbara reached into her briefcase for her camera.

Binnie returned with her hair brushed, her face washed, and without a trace of tears. She had put on lipstick. She looked ready to do battle, ready to swim to shore again.

6

Barbara did not linger at Frank's house any longer than good manners and her conscience demanded that night. She wanted to get home in time to call Bailey and to read Binnie's notes. As soon as she arrived, she checked her windows and the back door. Bailey had installed new locks, and he had left a small piece of Scotch tape on each of the old sash windows. If the window had been raised, the tape would reveal it.

Developing paranoia? she asked silently, and her answer was swift: You bet I am. All the tape was intact. It was not yet ten and she placed her call to Bailey.

He grumbled when she asked him to come around as early as he could. "Barbara, give me a break. Stuff takes just a little bit of time, you know."

"I have a roll of film I want developed and prints made as soon as possible. Your guy can do it. One-day service, same-day service, in fact."

"Jeez," he said. "Nine o'clock."

She made a pot of coffee and took a cup to her office to read Binnie's notes, more a journal than just notes, but in no particular order, no chronological order. She had written about various incidents and memories as they occurred to her or when Martin asked questions. As Barbara read, her stomach twisted and her head began to ache. Over and over, she stood, walked from her office to pace the cramped rooms, and returned, resumed.

What was portrayed in the pages was a life of degradation, humiliation, deprivation, pain, and fear. It was also the story of an intelligent woman with formidable courage and determination to save her daughter.

For several minutes after turning the last page over Barbara sat with her eyes closed, trying to banish the images that had forced their way into her head. She didn't blame Martin. Death would be better than such a life.

Finally she turned on her computer and began to write a narrative, a chronological reordering of the jumbled account.

The pirates had sailed the freighter around Jamaica to an isolated stretch of the coast, where they anchored the ship offshore and began to unload crates into several small boats that went ashore. They were at it when there was gunfire ashore. Domonic and another man, Louis, pushed Shala into a small boat and headed out to sea with her. They ended up in Haiti.

There was a shack, one big room with a kitchen at one end, a bedroom, and another closetlike room that had shelves as if at one time it had been a pantry. Shala and Binnie were to inhabit that room until Shala's death. The two men often fought and at some point the fight got violent and afterward Louis was gone. Shala had not known if he had been killed or if he ran away.

Domonic was obsessed with newspapers for weeks, until there was an article in an English-language paper that he made Shala read to him. The pirates had been ambushed onshore that night, and they had all been killed. Seven tons of marijuana had been seized by the government. No mention was made of Domonic and Louis, or of Shala. It was assumed that everyone aboard the freighter before the attack had been murdered. Soon after the article appeared, Domonic made Shala write to her father and plead for her rescue. When the man sent by her father denounced her, Domonic beat her severely.

The other newspapers were in Spanish, *The Caribbean News* and *Island News.* The English-language one had come from Jamaica.

Domonic began to exploit Shala, charging men to have sex with her in his bed. She had become a domestic and sexual slave. One of the men gave her a little extra money each time, and she hoarded her coins until, when Binnie was about three, she took her stash of money to a nun and begged her to buy a book of ASL. Few nuns would even talk to her, but treated her as a dirty, diseased whore until she finally found one who listened and agreed. As soon as she had the book, she began to teach Binnie to sign. She taught her to read the newspapers she managed to scrounge, and used the margins and whatever scraps of paper she could find for Binnie to practice writing and do math. Along the way Binnie also learned Spanish although Shala taught her English. When Domonic sent Shala to market, he kept Binnie locked in their room. Shala was afraid to go to the police. They were corrupt and she feared that they themselves might seize her and rape her. Domonic's threat to kill Binnie if she didn't return promptly when she went outside the shack was enough to keep her imprisoned. At night, he sent Shala into the room and locked them both in. There, in the dark, whispering so he would not hear, Shala taught Binnie all she could remember from her own education at a convent and two years at the university.

There had been a large plantation, where she and her sister had lived, and there had been a house in Belize City. At the plantation there had been servants and many orchids on a wide verandah. After their mother died, when Shala was ten and Anaia twelve, their father sent them to a convent boarding school. The sisters had inherited money from their mother, enough to leave the school and their father's house when they were seventeen, and to attend the university. He had denounced Anaia when she married an American, and he had tried to force Shala to leave school and to marry the man he had chosen for her.

When Shala became too ill to carry out Domonic's orders, he locked her in the room and made Binnie go to the market and to continue diving for the abalone and conch. It wasn't in the notes, but Barbara added: After Shala died, he no longer had a hostage to force Binnie to do his bidding and, believing in the curse, he was afraid to touch her or to let others touch her in his house. He decided to sell her.

Barbara shuddered and left her desk again, refilled her cup, and reluctantly returned. When Binnie's accounts swam to mind, she shook her head and said under her breath, "That part's over and done with. Let it go, damn it."

There were a few clues to follow up on in the notes, in her reordering of them. Shala was seventeen when she went to the university, and Anaia was nineteen. Shala attended for two years, and was nineteen when she fled with her lover. And Anaia had been married by then, between the ages of seventeen and twenty-one. Probably closer to twenty-one, Barbara decided. If Shala had known the American very long it seemed likely that she would have known his surname well enough to remember and include it in the message to her daughter. A possible starting place was to find the American's name.

More, Barbara continued, jotting notes as she reasoned. Binnie had swum to the yacht three years ago. Domonic had claimed his kidnapped daughter was a minor, and she might have been. So the three years since her escape plus sixteen, seventeen, possibly eighteen years put the piracy from nineteen to twenty-two years in the past. And assuming that Anaia had married during the year of Shala's departure meant that the wedding had taken place between twenty and twenty-three years ago. Between 1960 and 1963. The marriage had to be on record somewhere. How many young Belize women had married Americans during that period?

She had to find that sister, Barbara decided. If the father was still the tyrant who had rejected one daughter and believed the other one dead, the sister might be Binnie's only hope of finding an ally in Belize. Or Anaia and her father might have become reconciled over the two decades. She might have some influence over him, or influence of her own to wield.

If they could demonstrate that Shala was already pregnant when Domonic enslaved her, that Shala and her child had been citizens of Belize with relatives still in Belize, it would quash any charge of kidnapping made by Domonic. But would it be enough to put a hold on deportation? Would they deport Binnie to Haiti or to her legitimate family? Her status as an illegal alien would not be changed. Call her grandfather, Augustus Santos? Plead for help? Reluctantly she nodded. She had to try, even if it was a long shot.

Barbara paced until she was exhausted. She needed expert help, she knew, and there wasn't enough time. Martin was right. There wasn't enough time. Just get a delay, she thought tiredly at last and got ready for bed.

It was a few minutes before nine the next morning when her door-bell rang. Expecting to see Bailey when she opened the door, she was surprised instead to see Nicholson. She did not open the door wider to invite him in.

"Ms. Holloway, may I have a few minutes of your time?" he asked, glancing up and down the street.

"I'm afraid not," she said. "I'm quite busy this morning. I delivered your message to Mr. Owens and I don't believe we have anything further to discuss."

"You said something that I took to heart, Ms. Holloway. You

asked why I didn't make my proposal to Mr. Owens myself, and at this desperate time for him and his wife, I think you're absolutely right. My problem is that I don't know where to find them." He smiled and spread his hands wide apart. "If you would be so kind as to give me an address, or even a phone number, that would be most helpful."

His high-pitched voice irritated her as much as it had before, and now it had acquired a whining tone that made it even more hateful.

"Sorry," she said. "I'm sure he'll be in touch when they've made up their minds. Now, if you'll excuse me, I'll get back to my own work."

He held the door open. "Ms. Holloway, it is the duty of law-abiding citizens to assist government investigations if asked to do so and especially officers of the courts, as attorneys are, are even more obliged to render such assistance. It is not a good idea to antagonize any federal agency, to have it recorded in your file, which is shared by all agencies."

"I'll keep that in mind, Mr. Nicholson. Good day." She closed her door hard against the resistance of his hand, then went to her window to watch him walk to a parked car, get in, and drive away.

A few minutes later when the bell rang again, she checked at the window before opening her door to Bailey. There was no car parked at the curb except her own this time. Bailey was carrying a beat-up duffel bag partly over his shoulder.

"What's that for?" she asked when he came in.

"My gear," he said. "Junior detective kit. Cost me twenty-five cereal box tops. I smell coffee."

"Come on," she said, going to the kitchen table where she had the carafe and cups ready. "Did you see Nicholson? He wants to know how to locate Martin Owens."

"Is that who he was?" He pulled his notebook from the duffel bag and made a note.

"You got his license plate number?"

"Sure," he said. "Guy shows up at your door, you don't let him in, he's trying to hold the door open or push it open, then off he goes, looking pretty sore. Interesting. I parked down the street, walked back in case he wasn't gone far. I'll run a check just for fun. And," he said as she poured coffee, "I have some dope about piracy from 1960 to '65 in the Caribbean and Gulf areas. Four incidents. The accounts." He put photocopies on the table. "Plus a pretty good article about the Santos Shipping Company of Belize. It's a biggie. The guy will have plenty of influence."

"Great," Barbara said. "Good work, and fast, the way I like it. I'll look over the piracy stuff while you look over this." She gave him the summary she had made of Binnie's notes. "Her originals are there if you want to see them." She pointed to a folder with the roll of film on it.

The third piracy attack was it, she knew, as she read through it, then put it aside to look over the fourth account. In one instance, the pirates had been caught and imprisoned. In two cases they were not apprehended, and in the one she had set aside, they had been killed in a gun battle in Jamaica. That one was dated May of 1961.

Bailey helped himself to more coffee and pushed her summary aside. He shook his head at the folder with the full accounts. "I get the picture," he said morosely as he pocketed the roll of film.

"I need the sister," Barbara said. "I think she married the American in 1960 or 1961. I need a name for her and a way to locate her. They could have come to the States, been divorced by now, or are living happily on an estate in Belize. Can do?"

"And she could be dead," he said. "I don't know. Not in a day or two. Those newspapers could be helpful maybe, if they haven't gone belly-up. Or a Belize newspaper might be, but I'm not going to Belize to start running down a news story from twenty-two years ago that might not even be in the paper."

"Why would an American have been in Belize that long ago?" Barbara said. "Government work? State Department minion?

49

Probably not a tourist, not if he hung around long enough to get married to a local girl. A trade agreement? Buying mahogany? Sugar? Chicle? Chicle, for chewing gum," she said when he raised his eyebrows questioningly. "Belize exports it. Get help if you need it. Lawrence somebody, married in 1960 or '61, most likely to Anaia Santos, whose daddy owns Santos Shipping. There's a record somewhere."

"You left out drugs," Bailey said. "And the name he used might be an alias. Maybe a CIA spook without a name to call his own."

"I know," she admitted. "A Peace Corps guy, exchange student, instructor. Probably a lot of others we don't have a clue about. God, I know that. Fishing for a particular minnow in the ocean, but give it a try. Do you know people who would be good for this kind of research? I'm thinking of the time element," she added. "There isn't any to spare."

"From the looks of it, there isn't any, period. Yeah, I can round up some people and sic them on it. It's going to cost a lot." Then, pouring himself more coffee, he said, "I ran a credit check on Owens. You know, just part of the drill. He made about four and a half million playing football, and he spent a lot of it on houses and cars for his mother and sister. Other things. But he kept a lot. Like you said, he's good for it. He paid cash for his own car, the house, gutting and remodeling it to be a restaurant, and everything in it. No real debts, just current expenses. He probably still has a bundle left over."

"He was saving to buy a restaurant," Barbara said. "Okay. Anything else?"

"Just a thought," Bailey said, his gloom not at all diminished. "The government already knows how much he's got, and to them it might look like he held out enough so he could make a run for it without leaving a paper trail."

"And Nicholson already wants to know where he is," Barbara muttered.

Bailey shrugged, got to his feet, and slouched to the door, where he saluted and said, "I'll get those pictures to you later today."

Barbara waited until eleven o'clock to call Herman Krugman at Columbia. She got as far as his teaching assistant. "Ms. Holloway, I'm sorry, but Dr. Krugman is out all this week. You know, spring break. But he left two names for me to give you if you still want them."

Better than nothing, she thought. "I'd appreciate that."

She made a note of the names of two Los Angeles attorneys and thanked him. After getting telephone numbers from directory assistance she dialed the top name only to be told that he would not be in his office until mid-May, and if she wanted to leave a message. . . . She hung up and dialed the second one, with no better success. He was simply unavailable and there was not even a suggestion that she might leave a name or message.

God was telling her something, she thought, regarding the telephone and wishing it were a voodoo doll she could use as a pincushion. There were many immigration attorneys, she knew, but to consult any attorney without knowing something about him or her first was often foolish at best, and a catastrophe at worst, with a costly mistake somewhere in between.

She sat at her desk and considered what to do next. Even if she kept searching and found someone else, that person would most likely do exactly what she had done, tell the client she needed a little time to look into the matter, and use that time to try to verify as much as possible about what the client had said. She shook her head. They didn't have time for that.

"I just saved you a bundle of money, Martin," she said under her breath. She would skip the expert advice altogether, assume that both Krugman and the Chicago attorney had already given it by saying the INS would win, in the short run at least. No need to go for strike three, she decided, and pulled the article about the Santos Shipping Company forward to read.

After reading the article Barbara sat thinking about Santos, Binnie's grandfather. He would have influence in his own country, she knew. A prominent businessman, important in a small economy. The question was, Would he help his granddaughter? Finally she dialed the number given in the article.

A pleasant woman's voice came on in a recorded message: "*Santos Shipping. I'm sorry. The offices are temporarily closed. For information regarding shipments please call—*"

Carefully, almost gently, Barbara hung up, cursing under her breath. Another door slammed in her face.

7

On Tuesday afternoon Barbara opened her door to admit Bailey, whose long face probably mirrored her own, she thought, with a sense of foreboding.

"No beer, a little wine that might or might not be decent enough for human consumption, and a pot of coffee that's been sitting all day. Name your poison," she said, leading him to the kitchen.

"Let's nuke the coffee," he said. "You're going to need it."

"In that case I'll put on a fresh pot. Tell me the worst while my back is turned."

She busied herself with the coffee, listening to a rustle of papers, his reports, no doubt. His chair scraped, creaked a little bit, followed by a long silence.

"Get on with it," she said impatiently, going to the table to join him. "Get it over with."

"Right. Okay. No point in trying to find a guy named Lawrence at this end. No place to start. State Department, CIA, a university somewhere . . . I started in Belize. My team, headed by a research librarian, had a go at it. First the newspapers. Nada.

Nothing easily found from the time we were after. Then public records. It's a wash, Barbara, no matter where they start. In October 1961, along came a killer hurricane that wiped out a lot of the country, including Belize City. That was the capital in those days. They moved it inland later on. Anyway, the old city was flooded to the rooftops of anything left standing, and there wasn't much. But that's where public records were archived, in the courthouse in the capital. Ninety-nine percent of them destroyed. Who knows where they've been since then, or how many were restored?"

"So we can't find out whom Anaia married," Barbara said after a lengthy silence. "I think it's coffee." She went to get cups and the carafe and took them to the table.

After a moment, Bailey rose and crossed the space to the counter, where she had left the sugar and cream. "We can't find him now," he said, returning. "A crew of hundreds with unlimited time might do it eventually. Might never." He fixed his coffee to his liking and again there was a lengthy silence.

"I've been thinking," he said. "Maybe if they send her back to Haiti, Martin could go first and meet the plane. Meet all the planes until hers gets there."

"She isn't going back!" Barbara said. "I'll think of something. She is *not* going back!"

Bailey shrugged. "The pictures and various attempts to get information," he said, indicating papers clipped together. "And a little about that car Nicholson was driving, the plates I ran. Private car, registered to Rondell Emerson. Since it wasn't reported as stolen, seems he must have lent it to Nicholson. Emerson's in real estate and he's a partner in the Marcos Import store. Scuttlebutt has it that Marcos is dealing in more than just trinkets and doodads, stuff like that."

"He's dealing drugs?"

"Not sure, but that's the rumor. Never charged, never really investigated maybe. Rumor."

The coffee was foul. Barbara added sugar and cream to her own and made it worse. She pushed her cup back. "I spent yesterday and most of this morning cramming on immigration law," she muttered. "No loopholes that I could find." Although, she added to herself bitterly, an expert in the field might have known a dodge unavailable to her.

"Bailey, will you be around later? I need to think."

"Until ten," he said. "Phone rings after ten, we let it."

"Sure," she said. "Before ten."

But walking and thinking were not helping, she admitted to herself later, sitting on a bench staring blankly at the river. She should not have told Martin that, she thought then. She should not have told him they wouldn't let Binnie go back. It amounted to a promise and she had no way of fulfilling such a promise.

A flash of memory rose in her mind. Not the incident that sparked it, something she had wanted as a child, something she had insisted on being promised in advance. Whatever that something had been was lost in time.

"I can't promise," Frank had said. "I'll do the best I can, but I can't promise."

"Just say it," she had insisted.

"Honey," he had said, "never make a promise you don't intend to keep, and never make a promise that you know you can't keep, or that you don't know if you can keep. Your promise is your word of honor and it's sacred. Promises should be very rare."

Her words to Martin had constituted a promise, one that she could not keep.

God, how long ago was that little lesson? she wondered. She had been small, six, seven at the most. And there it was, stashed away in her memory to come back and shame her now. Slowly she rose and started to walk again. The air was cooling and she was getting chilled, but there was something important nagging her. Frank might not even recall that incident, he had no reason to recall it, but it had been faithfully stored away in her brain to come back now.

Memory seemed to be a bottomless purse, or the magic salt-shaker that contained all the salt in one's personal universe, waiting to be tapped. Who knew how many memories anyone stored away, how relevant they were, how to access those you needed? She suspected the answer had to be nobody. Maybe every minute of a life was there in the memory bank, irrelevant for the most part, and mostly inaccessible. She stopped walking. Relevance, that was what she was searching for.

Someone, more than just one person in Belize, would remember whom Anaia Santos had married, what her married name was.

Abruptly she turned and headed back to her car. It would take a human being talking to another human being to find out Anaia Santos's married name, to find out where she was, and to plead with her on behalf of Binnie. Not Bailey. She could not send him to plead with Augustus Santos, the tyrannical parent, or with Anaia, either. Bailey had his uses, but this was not one of them. He could sum up pages of reports succinctly and thoroughly, but then he withdrew, and this could take pleading, special pleading even.

You're tilting at windmills, she told herself, making a meaningless gesture because there simply was not enough time. She started her car, checked the rearview mirror, but her inner critic was still demanding a voice. Immigration would win because time would run out. Going there would be no more than another blindfolded stab at an impossible target. A waste of time, of Martin's money. It would be no more than an attempt to soothe her conscience, to try to make herself believe she had not taken on a case with zero chance of helping her client. To try to justify making a promise she had not known she could keep.

She shook her head as if to quiet that other voice. She had to try anything and everything she could think of to prevent a murder-suicide. Martin's words spoken quietly, and with absolute conviction, had elicited her promise, and now she had to go to Belize. That other voice was silenced.

She drove home too fast, hurried inside, and was dialing the travel agent used by the law firm before she had her jacket off. It was late, but the agency was used to handling emergency situations for the firm. An hour later she called Bailey to come by between one and two the following afternoon.

"Don't give me a hard time," she said irritably to Bailey on Wednesday. "I already know all the arguments against it. And I don't see anything else I can do. They can't survive as fugitives, not with the government after them, and that's what they face. That creep in immigration is salivating over having a celebrity on his hit list to make an example of. He's practicing his strut for when he demonstrates that not even the rich and famous can get away with concealing an illegal alien. I know how that goes."

The letter demanding, not requesting, Binnie's presence on Friday had irked her beyond reason. As a consequence she had prepared two letters, one for a Dennis Linfield in Eugene, and one for his superior, Walter Sokolosky, in Portland. She handed them both to Bailey. "Mail that one tonight and this one tomorrow. I want them both delivered by Friday and that should do it. Certified, return receipt on both of them."

"Barbara, you don't have a clue about what you'll be stepping into," he said morosely. "If your pal Nicholson is Marcos's pal, drugs are probably involved. People get shot nosing around in the drug trade. Did you read that stuff about Marcos?"

She had read it, and she had even been in his shop that featured imported clothes and handcrafted items from Central America. Bailey's report had also said again that he was likely a drug dealer, never charged, but rumored to be the one to go to.

Ignoring his words, Barbara handed him another sheet of paper. "My flight schedule, going and coming back. I'll drive to Portland this evening, catch that crack-of-dawn flight in the morning, and by evening be in Belize."

"By way of L.A. and Mexico City," he said with deepening gloom as he looked over the schedule.

"If I'm not back by next Thursday, send in the marines," she said. "Or at least tell Dad where I was last seen."

"He doesn't know?"

"I told him I have to research some old records, that I'm off to L.A. in the morning." Did a part lie qualify as a total lie? She didn't want to answer her own question. She thought a moment, then said, "I called Martin and told him to sit tight until he hears from me. No problem there. I guess that's it for now. I have a ton of stuff to Xerox, and I have to pack, then drive to Portland."

"Okay," he said. "You have any idea where to start when you get down there? I could give you some pointers."

"Good," she said. "As much as you can in five minutes. Shoot."

"Schools, high school and college for old friends. Santos employees, current and retired. That convent school where they were sent. Priest. Library."

He went on with several others, and each one felt like another weight tied to her neck when she was already thrashing around in deep water. Too much for such a short time. But she listened and added the possible information sources to those she had thought of herself.

"How about a private investigator?" she asked, interrupting him.

He shook his head. "If you knew the score, maybe. But you don't. For all you know the guy could already be in someone else's pocket, ready to blow you out of the water. You go in there, start asking questions, hire a PI, bingo, you're a target."

"Okay, I get the picture. Now beat it. I have a lot to do before I take off."

His gloomy expression did not lighten as he pulled on a wind-breaker that had been designed for someone a size or two bigger than he was. He picked up his duffel bag and slouched to the door where he paused to shake his head at her before leaving.

"All I need," she muttered, locking the door. "Mr. Doom and Gloom to wish me a bon voyage."

8

On Thursday evening, after Barbara had showered and changed her clothes, she eyed her bed longingly but resisted. The dining room opened at eight thirty, the desk clerk had told her. And she could not wait until eight thirty or later for something to eat. She went down to the lobby, looked in on the pool area, and bypassed it. Too many people, too much music, too many loud children. The bar was dim with fewer people, but she wanted air and went on to the terrace adjoining the bar.

She had been cooped up all day, had breathed in the air others breathed out in airplane cabins, or had been assaulted by an incessant din of voices and music, and too many odors of hot oil and fast food in terminals. She sat down and took a deep breath, gazed at the waterfront where boats gently rocked, then closed her eyes, savoring fresh ocean air, unfamiliar plant and flower fragrances, air different from any at home. The air felt good, not too warm, not too windy. It smelled good, clean, not recycled through countless lungs.

"Miss, would you like to order?" A voice roused her. A waiter stood at her table. He was very dark and had a friendly smile.

Skin color seemed to range from light Mediterranean or Spanish warm tones to the deepest black, and so far everyone had spoken English.

Barbara picked up the menu on the table, but after a moment, she put it down again. "What would you recommend in a dry white wine? Most of the wines on the menu are unfamiliar to me."

She saw a man rise from a nearby table and approach hers. "Henry, hold on a second," he said. Then he smiled genially at Barbara. "He'll push the most expensive French wine on you and it will be near the bottom of what's actually best. May I recommend one? It's an excellent white from Argentina, somewhere between a fume blanc and pinot gris, the best of both. And less than half as expensive as the one Henry would have you choose. You are a weary traveler, having had the most atrocious food possible all day, and you should not be faced with a difficult decision on your arrival."

Barbara grinned at him. That was exactly right. He was six feet tall, trim, well tanned with sun-bleached hair and a charming smile. Probably mid-fifties, she guessed. Presumptuous, but not aggressively forward, and meanwhile he seemed to know the menu, and he certainly knew the waiter. Henry was laughing quietly with a chagrined expression, waiting for her decision.

"I'll have what the gentleman suggested," she said. "Thank you," she added, nodding at the man still standing by her table.

"May I join you?" he asked. "Share a bottle of wine?"

Her hesitation was brief. "Of course," she said.

"Good. And, Henry, a platter of sizzling shrimp and empanadas."

Barbara picked up the short bar menu, which did not include shrimp.

"He can see that it happens," her companion said lightly. "Can't you, Henry?"

"Yes, sir," Henry said. "Will there be anything else?"

Barbara shook her head, and so did her new companion.

"Gabe Newhouse," he said, extending his hand. "Fellow American."

She said her name and shook his hand.

"Now we're officially introduced," Newhouse said. "Excuse me a second, I left a few things on my table." He went to the other table and returned with some pieces of mail that he put down before pulling out a chair and sitting to the right of her, in such a way that they could both look out over the waterfront.

"You live here?" Barbara asked, nodding toward the mail.

"No. Just a mail drop. Actually I live out there." He pointed to the bay. "Third boat from the left." The boat he pointed to was a yacht at anchor. "I make it a point to put in here frequently to pick up mail, provision the boat, buy a book or two, just spend a little time on land to remind myself why I prefer to be out there. If I ever decide I want to be a landlubber again, someplace like Belize would be my first choice, however. Quiet, laid-back, not overrun by tourists or gambling casinos. One major drawback. It's hurricane-prone. And the bouncing broncos most likely will eradicate the other attractions, if they have their way."

"That's too fast for me," Barbara said in protest. "What are the bouncing broncos?"

Henry arrived then with a wine bucket and opened the wine. He offered Newhouse a sample for his approval, poured for them both. "The shrimp will be along in a minute or two," he said.

"The broncos are one of the reasons I've delayed my departure past time," Newhouse said. "That and provisioning the boat. Who was it who said she wasn't ready to die yet because she wanted to see how it all came out? Tallulah Bankhead? Dorothy Parker? I forget. The broncos are very enthusiastic young men with too much time on their hands, and with very rich daddies. At least two of them qualify as such. The third one is a working stiff, a photographer they hired. They have an agenda to develop one of the offshore

63

islands as a tourist destination playland, a water wonder world. That's the first delaying playlet.

"Also," he continued, "there's an amusing little scandal going on, involving a government official, his mistress, his wife, and a former mistress who is demanding money she claims he promised her. Every day I change my mind about who will win that one.

"And finally, there's a real Shakespearean drama coming to a head soon. I want to see how they all end."

"Oh, my," Barbara said. "I understand about the development. California, here we come. And lovers and philandering government officials hardly even make the tabloids any longer. But what drama?"

"It has all the right elements for great drama," Newhouse said. "Brothers who were bitter enemies until one was murdered. Gunned down on the road on his way home. A fortune in land and holdings of various sorts. A beautiful princess. Her uncle has seized the property to which she is the legitimate heir, and she has vanished in the wilderness out of fear for her life."

Barbara nodded gravely. "Shakespearean to the core. Is there a handsome prince ready to come to her rescue?"

He shook his head. "It doesn't seem likely. The elusive Mrs. Thurston might be very hard for such a prince to find. Her wall of brambles is the jungle itself. She's been teaching out in the jungle for years, and she knows where and how to hide. No doubt she has a multitude of people out there to help. I believe that Uncle Julius is hard at work trying to find her."

"My," Barbara said, smiling. "If you could weave all three stories into one novel, add a touch of magical realism, it sounds as if you'd have a major bestseller."

"No way. I'm not a writer. Just nosy."

Henry came back with a serving cart. He set plates on the table, finger bowls of water with lime slices, and towels at the side. Carefully handling a metal dish, he put it on the table and lifted the lid. Shrimp were sizzling with an aroma that made Barbara's mouth water. He put a platter of empanadas down and poured more wine.

"Finger food," Newhouse said, picking up a shrimp by the tail.

The wine was excellent and the shrimp, redolent with garlic, lime, and something undefinable, was almost sinfully good. Barbara drew in a long breath of contentment. "This is wonderful, Mr. Newhouse. Thank you for your advice."

"You're most welcome. Just one more bit of advice and then I'm done with that. Before you stroll around in daylight, do get a wide-brimmed hat, and use sunscreen. Pale from a northern climate without much winter sunshine, you'll burn without realizing how fierce the tropical sun can be."

"Noted," she said.

"The first week on *My Bettina* I nearly burned to a crisp," he said, nodding toward the yacht at anchor. "And I'm from Southern California."

Barbara was taken by surprise by his words. "You're G. M. Newhouse? The director?" Bits and pieces of discordant memory came to mind. There had been a scandal involving him and his wife at the time. She was Bettina, his leading lady in several films. Drugs had been involved, an affair or more than one, threats. . . . It was too fractured, and she had paid too little attention to find a coherent narrative now.

"Retired director," he said with a broad smile. "But tell me, and please say no, do you happen to have a play tucked away in your suitcase?"

She laughed. "Nope. And I have no aspirations whatsoever toward becoming an actor."

"Whew! God is merciful."

"You still think in cinematic terms, don't you?" she said. "The bouncing broncos, the official with too many women, the damsel in distress with an uncle who may or may not be murderous. Wanting identifiable endings."

"Afraid so," he said. "Habits are so easily acquired, so hard to break. But tell me about you. You're a professional woman, I assume. Not a medical doctor, unless it's psychiatry. Not a teacher. What?"

"Attorney. Why did you assume professional?"

"Everything about you; an air of competence, independence, traveling alone to a foreign country, no hint of coquetry, curiosity. That all spells professional. Corporate lawyer?"

"Defense attorney." She sipped her wine, then added, "I just finished a difficult case and needed a few days away, someplace warm and sunny and not touristy."

She recalled Bailey's warning that she did not know what she was stepping into, and now this friendly man, who had gone out of his way to talk with her, to choose her wine and snacks, turned out to be possibly involved, however indirectly, with drugs. At least her incomplete memory of past scandals might indicate such was the case. He apparently had the freedom to cruise among the islands, anchor wherever he wanted. Moreover, she thought, he seemed to be fishing for information perhaps a bit more than casual strangers chatting in a bar warranted.

"Did you win the case?" he asked.

"My client was innocent and was acquitted," she said. "I've enjoyed your films immensely, Mr. Newhouse."

"Thank you, but, please, it's Gabe. In Los Angeles, it's first-name basis instantly, and on the second encounter, it's 'darling.'" He was eyeing her closely. "You're not from New York, Northeast, or the Midwest. Not the South, of course. That seems to leave the Northwest, but not where the sun shines in the winter. I believe it does in Idaho and Montana. Am I getting warm?"

She laughed and sipped her wine. "How long do you stay out on the yacht at any one time?"

"Days, weeks, months. Until we run out of water or wine or something else. It varies. I threw away my day planner when I retired." He twisted around to glance at the bar. "I think the bron-cos will join us soon. They come to report their adventures of the day, just as if I'm the uncle who demands an accounting. Or to show off a little. Possibly both."

She heard the voices then. Several men seemed to be talking at once in a rapid-fire dialogue.

"Hey, Gabe!" one of them called out before they came into sight. "You'll never guess what."

"So it would be futile to try," he said.

They came to the table. Two of them looked to be under thirty, one a blond with intense blue eyes, and tanned to a deep, rich ma-hogany color. The second young man, equally tanned, had dark brown hair and dark eyes. They both were muscular, athletes to all appearances. The third man looked a few years older, dark-haired with dark blue eyes, and heavier than the other two without being overweight, just more filled out. They all looked her over with interest as Gabe Newhouse made the introductions.

"Bobby Tyson," he said, indicating the blond man. "Ben Bol-linger and David Grinwald. Barbara Holloway. She arrived to-day," he added.

Without waiting for an invitation, the three newcomers pulled chairs up to the table and sat down. "Henry's bringing beer," Bobby said. "May I?" He picked up a shrimp as he asked.

"Barbara, do you scuba dive?" Ben asked, leaning toward her.

"No. Never have."

"We could teach you in a couple of hours. You have to see that reef out there. It's fantastic, second only to the Great Barrier Reef in Australia. Fish like out of Disneyland. It's an underwater fairyland."

"Would you be interested in getting in on the ground floor of our enterprise to develop a world-class playland?" Bobby asked, picking up another shrimp.

"No," she said. Gabe Newhouse was smiling faintly, leaning back in his chair.

"It's the chance of a lifetime," Bobby said. "Charter member, all that kind of thing. Wait till you see what we have in mind. Mayan ruins for day tours. A stupendous waterfall, where we were today," he said in an aside to Gabe. "Botanical gardens, monkeys in the wild, jaguars, also for guided day tours. We'll have glass-bottomed boats, windsurfing, fishing trips, the best beaches on earth, scuba diving and snorkeling . . ."

Gabe's mouth was twitching, but he suppressed the smile and gazed out at the water.

Barbara held up her hand. "If I upended my piggy bank I might be able to come up with two dollars and some cents. So I'm out of it." She glanced at her watch, prepared to return to her room.

"What was it that I could never guess?" Gabe asked then.

"Oh, yeah," Ben said. "We get to go see the orchids tomorrow. Santos said okay, since his brother gave permission, he would honor that decision." He turned to Barbara again. "Come with us. It's the world's best and biggest collection of orchids. At the Santos estate. Julius Santos agreed to let us photograph the flowers for the brochure David's going to put together." He nodded toward David Grinwald, who had not said a word.

Barbara picked up her wineglass, more to have something to do than because she wanted more wine. Julius Santos, Uncle Julius, Mrs. Thurston hiding in the wilderness, a murdered father. . . . She felt almost light-headed as the pieces fell into place. The Santos Shipping Company closed temporarily. Because Augustus Santos had been murdered? Anaia's father murdered? Anaia Santos Thurston? Her uncle searching for her? She put the glass down again without taking a sip.

As Henry approached with a pitcher of beer and steins, she reached into her purse for her room key, with her room number visible on a plastic tag. Gabe shook his head at Henry, motioned toward the shrimp and wine, and then toward himself.

"Barbara," he said, "it has been delightful chatting with you for even this short a time. It will go on my tab."

He was regarding her with the same amusement he had shown toward the broncos, but also with an intensity that had not been evident before.

"I'd rather not," she said, holding up her room key, but Henry was already walking away. "Thanks," she said to Gabe. She looked over the three younger men and nodded to them. "Good luck with your project."

"David, how long will it take to get out to the Santos plantation?" Ben asked.

"Hour and a half probably," David said. "Maybe a little longer. It's not clear how far off the highway the place really is."

"Barbara, if you decide to come along, we'll meet in the lobby at around noon," Ben said. "How can you resist? A fabulous collection of orchids!"

"You should go, Barbara," Gabe said. "A once-in-a-lifetime opportunity. Something to tell your friends about back home."

"I'll decide after a good night's sleep," she said as lightly as she could.

She thought she could feel Gabe's eyes on her as she left the terrace and the bar. She stopped at the front desk where she asked the clerk if there was a telephone directory for outlying areas.

"It's all in one directory," the clerk said with a smile. "There should be one in your room. The areas are separated by districts, but it's easy to navigate. If you want an outside line, just dial nine first."

She thanked him and went up to her room, telling herself it couldn't be this easy. There was a catch. She was kidding herself thinking pieces could fall from the sky for free. "Like manna," she muttered as she unlocked her door and entered her room. The problem was that she didn't believe in manna, or any other miracle, she added to herself.

She found the directory in a drawer, sat at a table by the wide sliding door to a balcony, and started searching. In a place called Belmopan, Anaia S. Thurston was listed. Belmopan, she repeated to herself, then remembered it was now the capital of the country, in the western area, nearly to the border with Guatemala.

She pulled the telephone close enough to dial. She felt almost dazed by this development, unbelieving, waiting for the catch to blindside her.

She got an answering machine, and after hesitating only a moment, she said, "Mrs. Thurston, my name is Barbara Holloway. I'm from Eugene, Oregon, in the United States, and I must talk to you about the death of your sister Shala. She died three years ago in Haiti."

She added the hotel name and her room telephone number. "I'll wait here for your call," she said and hung up.

It was a long wait. She ordered a pot of coffee and sat on her balcony for a short time as it became dark. Lights reflected in water, lights in windows, advertisements, another hotel canopy, traffic, everywhere lights began to come on. She felt too exposed on the balcony and went inside again.

The room that had seemed almost spacious on her arrival seemed to be shrinking minute by minute as she paced from the sliding door to the bathroom by the opposite wall and back, over and over. And she might not even call back, she told herself many times. Wait all night? All the following day? She emptied the coffee carafe into her cup and drank cool coffee.

It could even be the wrong person, she told herself. For all she knew Thurston was not that uncommon a name here, and Anaia might be every third girl's name. She was too prone to leap to conclusions. Hasty decisions were too often wrong decisions. The phone rang. It was ten minutes past nine.

"Hello. Barbara Holloway speaking," she said, sinking onto the side of the bed.

"Who are you? How do you dare talk about my sister? Tell a lie about my sister? What do you want?"

The voice was low-pitched, not quite a whisper, and it had a mixture of indignation, hostility, outrage, possibly even fear.

"Mrs. Thurston, please listen. Your sister did not die on that freighter twenty-one years ago. She was taken to Haiti where she lived as a captive until her death. When you both were very young, after the death of your mother, you were sent to a convent boarding school where you remained until you were seventeen, when you came into an inheritance and could live independently. You attended the university, and two years later your sister also attended. You married Lawrence Thurston, and your sister fell in love with Juan Hernandez, and fled with him to Jamaica to go to his parents. Please, Mrs. Thurston, I can offer proof of what I'm telling you."

"Stop!" Anaia said, and now it was a whisper. "No more on the telephone. Yes, we must talk. Stay where you are. I'll call back in a few minutes." Without waiting for a response she hung up.

Barbara felt weak as she replaced the phone in the cradle. She could sense warning flags waving all around her. Too easy. Too fast. There was a catch. It couldn't be this easy to find a stranger in a foreign country, to have falling manna practically bury her.

When the phone rang again, she snatched it up. "Holloway."

"Listen carefully. On Saturday morning leave your hotel and turn left. Walk to the intersection and keep going to the next block. Enter a shop called Mary's Clothing. Be sure to come out at ten o'clock. A young man will be leaning against a Jeep. He'll be holding a tourist folder advertising Mayan ruins, and he will ask if you want to see them. You ask him his name and he'll say Philip. You ask how much, and he'll say ten dollars American. Take the folder and put it in your handbag and get in the Jeep. Then follow his instructions. Do you have all that?"

"I have it," Barbara said.

"Unless it goes exactly the way I've outlined, don't get in the Jeep," Anaia Thurston said, and she hung up without another word.

Bailey's words of warning arose in Barbara's head as she replaced her phone. *You don't have a clue about what you're stepping into.*

9

Barbara had a short list of necessities to buy on Friday morning. First, a hat. Just nine o'clock and the sun was already fierce. Almost as important was a bag of some sort large enough to carry the manila clasp envelope locked in her suitcase with Binnie's material ready to take to Anaia. She had planned on spending days in official buildings, talking to businesspeople, dressed for business, in places where such an envelope would not have been unseemly. But as a casual tourist such an envelope would be out of place. She also wanted sandals, and to get out of the damned panty hose that had her itching from crotch to toes. She walked from the hotel toward the shore, window-shopping.

Souvenirs. Toys, kites . . . and finally a beach accessory shop. She entered and was satisfied that she had found the right place. A profusion of wide-brimmed hats was on display.

Half an hour later she left, wearing a lightweight hat and carrying a matching beach bag, both made of linen decorated with embroidered orchids in rainbow colors. That seemed appropriate since she had decided to go with the broncos to see the orchids, and to meet the man who might or might not be a killer, who might or might not be Anaia Santos Thurston's uncle Julius.

A short walk later, she found a shoe store. She added sandals to her purchases, and moved on. Sunscreen and sunglasses would complete her list, and a notions store provided both. A few souvenirs would be appropriate in her role as a tourist, she decided, and wandered through several shops before she settled on a jaguar and a monkey carved in a lustrous green serpentine stone.

She examined the blouses, skirts, and shorts on display in the window of Mary's Clothing shop, but did not enter. "Tomorrow," she said under her breath, and turned to go back to her hotel.

At twelve o'clock when the broncos showed up in the lobby she was standing before the display of tourist attractions, reading about the zoo. She stuffed the folder into her big bag along with the others already there, and turned to say hello. David was carrying two camera bags, and under his arm a tripod and something white rolled up.

"Hey!" Bobby said. "Great, you're coming with us? Add a little class to our act."

"If you're sure Mr. Santos won't consider it an imposition, since I haven't been invited as you guys have been."

"I'll say you're my assistant," David said. "And you can start now, if you will. Want to carry the screen and tripod for me?"

She put on her hat and took the tripod and screen. "Now I'm official, I guess."

"I'll bring the Jeep around," Ben said, and trotted off.

"We have to use a Jeep," Bobby said. "You wouldn't believe some of the so-called roads we've been on. They don't believe in guardrails here, or in paving roads, either. You should have seen the one we were on yesterday, going to the waterfall. It's a sixteen-hundred-foot drop and that so-called road is without guardrails, or even a shoulder. Just the road and straight down. And some of those ruins don't even have roads going to them, just a little clearing of jungle and a track."

He was still talking about the roads or lack of them when Ben drove to the hotel entrance and blew the horn.

"Barbara, why don't you sit up front with me," David said after stashing his equipment in the Jeep. The camera bags were in the front. "I think your feet will have room enough."

There was little traffic, and Barbara recalled that Belize City, the only real city in the country apparently, had fewer than fifty thousand residents.

"We'll make one stop at a grocery store down the road a bit," David said. "Bottles of water. It can get pretty hot out in the countryside."

"And this is the cool season," Bobby said. "But the people who come for the water fun won't care how hot it gets in the jungle. We'll tell them it's part of the adventure, jungles, heat, a cooler with drinks with every guided tour . . ."

"Trekking through the jungle to the ruins will be another part of the adventure," Ben said. "Something to write home about. We've been to three so far and not through yet. More trekking, more jungle. Way it goes."

David evidently paid no attention whatsoever to anything Bobby or Ben said. And he also did not volunteer much of anything. A hired hand, Barbara thought. Neither of the other two had offered to help with the camera gear, and his taking the wheel had been accepted without question.

They stopped for the water, and soon were on the road again. The commercial sections were left behind, giving way to residential areas with blooming trees and bushes along with more varieties of palm trees than Barbara had known existed. The neat gardens and yards were replaced by shantytowns, shacks and huts, and then mangrove swamps and wetlands with low-growing grasses and scrub palmettos.

"They call them lagoons," Bobby said from the backseat. "Swamps is what they are. I guess in the rainy season they could be lagoons. Alligators in there, water moccasins, and God knows what else. Bats, vampire bats, mosquitoes, horseflies as big as birds . . ."

"Jesus, Bobby, you got to quit bad-mouthing everything," Ben said. "We want to sell a dream vacation package, and all you do is bitch."

"I just was saying . . ."

Barbara tuned them out and watched the changing landscape. Soon dense forest—jungle, she corrected herself—bordered the road. Then cleared land where cattle were grazing. Or land in agriculture. More jungle, more clearing to reveal an extensive orchard. Orange trees or lime trees. She couldn't tell. There seemed to be no people, but it was the hottest part of the day, too hot to work out in the sun. She reached into her bag for tissue to wipe the sweat from her face.

"Let me do the talking," Ben was saying. "Just let me handle it, will you? And don't babble about the water and the reef. He knows about them already, for Christ's sake."

Barbara glanced at David and he gave her a fleeting grin, then faced the road again without a word. She wondered how long it had been since he had paid any attention to a thing either of the broncos said.

"You know how long before we get to the turnoff?" Ben asked after a few more minutes, leaning forward on Barbara's headrest.

"Probably twenty minutes," David said. "It's a paved road, the only one on the right. A settlement called Orange Walk."

"I thought I saw that on the map north of here," Barbara said, visualizing the map she had studied.

"This one may be just a signpost," David said. "The other one's a real village."

"You'd think in a country small enough to stuff into the corner of a real state back home, they could come up with more names," Bobby said.

"Stop that!" Ben said. "Jesus, you drive me crazy!"

How long will that marriage last? Barbara wondered. Bobby's complaints and whining would drive her crazy in one day. How long had David put up with that petulance? They must be paying him well, she decided. She took a sip of water.

"After we finish at the Santos finca," David said, "we'll go on into Belmopan for some lunch before we start back to town."

"It's a curious mix of Spanish and British, isn't it?" she said.

"More Caribbean than Central American," David said. "And more British than Spanish. The best tea shops have excellent coffee. A real mix."

"We'll play up the British part," Bobby said. "Americans feel less threatened by the Brits than by the Chicanos."

"If you say anything like that in front of Santos, I'll strangle you with my bare hands," Ben muttered.

The jungle seemed to be getting denser. Occasionally a gravel road vanished in the greenery, or even a track that simply had been cleared and possibly bulldozed. It looked as if a wall, perhaps a sound-deadening wall, had been constructed along the sides of the road in shades of green dotted with brilliant bursts of colorful flowers from the ground upward until a canopy of foliage closed in.

"It looks impenetrable," Barbara said.

"So did the fir forests of the Northwest, according to accounts written by the first sailors who made it up the coast," David said. "A big difference is that you couldn't hack your way through that wall of trees with a machete. Here you can. And in places it thins out considerably, not quite a savannah, but not like this, either. Near the road, with more light, everything grows and grows."

Somewhere along this road, Barbara was thinking, Augustus Santos had been gunned down. Where had his assailants hidden?

How had they known he would be along? Or was it a common-place, random event on this jungle-enclosed road?

David slowed down a bit and said, "Let's all keep an eye out for the turn. It might be hard to spot in advance."

No guardrails, and no road signs, either, Barbara thought with-out commenting on it. The broncos stopped their ongoing chatter and helped watch. Suddenly there were ear-piercing screams, howls, roars.

Barbara jerked away from her door. "My God! What is that?"

The howls continued, gradually died down, only to be echoed from a greater distance.

"The goddamn baboons," Bobby said in disgust when the noise subsided. "They're not baboons, no matter what the bozos here call them. They're just fucking monkeys screaming their asses off."

"Black howler monkeys," David said. "Little guys, ten, fifteen pounds at the most, indigenous here. They say they have the loudest cry of any land animal." Another howling started, this time from a different direction, somewhere behind the Jeep. "If they scream and no other bunch picks it up, it's probably a male dominance contest. If it gets repeated, it probably is an attack. Jaguar, snake, guy with a gun, whatever, they can tell the difference and repeat the warning."

"I think for the brochure we should include something like if you're lucky you might hear the famous howler monkeys, and if you're really lucky you might even spot a group of them," Ben said.

"If you're lucky enough, they'll all drop dead of monkey plague or something," Bobby muttered.

"We have to include them," Ben said. "You can't spring some-thing like that on people not prepared for it. You saw how Barbara jumped. It scares the crap out of people the first time they hear it."

"I think that must be the turnoff," Barbara said, squinting at a break in the foliage. It looked more like a deep shadow in the greenery than the entrance to a road, but a few seconds later, it proved to be the road they wanted. Paved, narrower than the one they left, with a small sign that said, ORANG W LK in lettering so faded as to be almost illegible. There was a ramshackle, abandoned building and the remains of a gas station with a concrete post for a pump, a ruined bit of concrete that might have been a driveway, and nothing else.

"Three miles and then left onto a gravel road," David said, after making the turn.

It was much hotter on this road. The canopy closed in like a ceiling, then opened to admit a shaft of brilliant light, closed in again, and no air stirred. If two cars approached each other, one of them would have to brush against the jungle. Late in the day, early morning, whenever the sun was not high enough to shine almost straight down, it would be perpetual dusk in here, Barbara thought uneasily. At night, it would be a child's worst nightmare, especially if the howler monkeys started screaming.

She realized that she was beginning to feel a bit of sympathy for Bobby. This was not her kind of forest.

The broncos apparently shared her unease. Their endless chatter was silenced until David turned off onto the gravel road.

"If we can sell him, we've got it made," Ben said in a low voice then. "He said one hour. That's how long you can take, David. Use it all, the whole hour. I just hope and pray he meant that we'll have an hour to talk to him while you're doing the pictures. Bobby, remember, we go for the economic benefits, not the fun part, not the diving or how great the reefs are. Just the economic benefits. He's a businessman. He'll understand that even if he hates the idea. People. Tourists. New businesses. He'll dig that."

He was talking himself into his role as salesman, Barbara thought, hearing a note of near desperation in his voice. She felt sorry for him, tackling a job he had not trained for, had not studied, or even wanted. Just a job that had to be done.

"Light at the end of the tunnel," David said in a low voice then.

Ahead, there was brilliant light, as if stage lights had been turned on, or as if the jungle had died and a sunlit desert lay ahead. Barbara took another sip of water and wiped more sweat from her face.

The vista ahead that opened was of a broad, grassy plain, studded with palm trees in clumps, oasislike in appearance. The gravel road turned into a paved driveway. Birds were flying, and bird cries and songs could be heard over the engine noise. Three parrots flew in a straight line into the jungle. The road curved and before them the plantation house appeared, a low, sprawling building with a red tile roof, shaded by tall trees with scarlet blooms, surrounded by blooming shrubs and low-growing trees heavy with flowers. A beautifully maintained lawn, one that might have been found on an upscale golf course, surrounded the building. A short distance behind it, and on both sides, the green wall of jungle rose. Nearer, a flock of parakeets erupted from a group of trees as a single body, milled about, and descended again.

"Jesus!" Bobby muttered. "It's a fucking Hollywood setting!"

As they drew closer, more house details became clear. The building was in deep shade with a wide covered verandah that appeared to encircle it. A man stood on the verandah and watched their approach. He waved, indicating a parking area near the verandah where two Jeeps and a dark sedan were parked. David pulled in and turned off the engine.

"Here we go, kiddies," he said. "Barbara, want to help me unload some gear?"

"Sure thing," she said.

"Come on, Bobby," Ben said. "Let's get started." He might have been saying let's face the music from the sound of his voice. Side by side they walked up to the steps leading to the verandah as

Barbara and David hauled the camera cases, tripod, and screen from the Jeep.

David laughed softly. "Two scared kids not yet ready for prime time."

"Do you think they'll succeed?"

"Probably. They reek of money and, as Ben said, Santos is a businessman. Big-time money just walked into his neighborhood. I'd expect him to carve himself a piece of it before he says why not. We'll see how it plays out."

For the first time, she sensed a crack in the indifference he had shown the broncos and their project. There was a note of contempt in his voice.

10

The man who met Barbara and David on the verandah was no more than five feet five inches tall, and very wide. His face was as brown and deeply folded and furrowed as a pecan nut, with the same kind of shiny high spots. His hair was thick, straight, and black, showing a touch of gray at the temples. His broad smile revealed uneven teeth that never had been near an orthodontist when he was young, although how many years ago that might have been was impossible to guess.

"Miles Ronstadt," he said. "I'm delighted that you will photograph the orchids. Delighted."

"David Grinwald, and this is my assistant, Barbara Holloway," David said.

"My dear Ms. Holloway, please allow me," Ronstadt said, taking the tripod from her. "Come, meet Mr. Santos before we get started."

The broncos and Santos were standing at a table farther down on the verandah, waiting for them. Ben and Bobby looked like two college students facing an oral exam they had not prepared for. Santos was tall and slender, dressed in a fawn-colored silk shirt and close-fitting trousers of the same color. He reminded Barbara of pictures she had seen of the conquistadors, with sharply chiseled features and a rather haughty, disdainful expression. His hair was brown and wavy, with a strand on his forehead in what looked like a carefully arranged coif, as if he expected the photographer to pose him along with the orchids and had assumed the right appearance, the right expression, the right hairdo.

Barbara knew he had to be in his sixties, but his demeanor, his stance, everything about him was youthful.

At the table, Ronstadt introduced Barbara and David to Julius Santos. He bowed deeply to her.

"I am charmed, Ms. Holloway, to have the opportunity to meet such a lovely photographic assistant. Please, join us. May I offer you a cool drink? A mixture of local fruit juices? Lemonade? Iced tea?" His voice was velvety smooth, seductive. And his eyes were as cold as black ice, Barbara thought.

"Thank you, but no," she said. "I understand our time is limited."

"It will go faster if she assists me," David said. Then to Barbara, he said, "Ready to go to work?"

"In my country a man would be considered very foolish to rush to conclude any activity that involves such a lovely companion," Santos said, continuing to focus his attention on Barbara. "But as you wish. I'm sure Dr. Ronstadt will offer every assistance possible. He is our expert."

"Ready," Barbara said, placing her beach bag on the floor near the verandah rail. "I'm really eager to see more of the orchids." She nodded to Santos and turned away, aware that he was continuing to watch her.

"Dr. Ronstadt," David said as they started to walk down the verandah, "why don't we begin with the ones you consider the most beautiful or the most startling, something like that."

"Good, good," Ronstadt said, smiling even more broadly. "My

own favorites. Of course, that's a difficult task, to pick favorites. I daresay parents would voice the same objection in having to choose the favored child, but we do have favorites, don't we? Built-in prejudices, largely unconscious ones."

"We won't need the scientific names," David said. "These shots are for a brochure, just an indication of the beauty and variety. I'd like pictures of at least half a dozen individual orchids, and several more general shots of the verandah, to show the whole, overwhelming effect of so many rare flowers in one place."

The orchids were incredible, Barbara was thinking as they walked and David and Ronstadt talked about the photo shoot, the best way to get the effect David wanted. She had nothing to contribute, and examined the verandah and the stunning array of flowers. They were in hanging pots that looked ridiculously small for the number of leaves and the blooms. They were on the verandah railing, and in pots on the floor. Dazzling colors, with strong whiffs of perfume now and again, flowers growing in sprays, uprights, in sizes ranging from no bigger than her little fingernail to mammoth blooms eight inches from top to bottom, or even larger.

Even as she admired the display, she was aware that behind some sliding glass doors to the verandah, men were standing, keeping an eye on them. Maybe they were afraid David would pull a gun from his bag and start shooting, she thought. Or maybe they suspected she might try to steal a bloom, or a whole plant.

"This is a special flower," Ronstadt said, stopping to indicate a hanging orchid that at first glance looked almost transparent. One of the single large blooms, it was a pale violet pink, with two parallel streaks of bright red on the petals.

"We'll start with it," David said. He opened his case and brought out a camera, took the tripod from Ronstadt, and set it up, then took the screen and unrolled it.

Barbara had thought he wanted it behind the flowers, but he asked her to hold it to one side of the one he was studying. "The idea is to diffuse the light, soften it. Let's have a look," he said after positioning her with the screen.

He returned to the camera and peered at the orchid through his viewfinder, motioned her to move to the left. "Just an inch or two," he said, and looked again. He made adjustments, motioned her to move again, and finally he snapped four or five shots. Then he started the whole process over from a different angle. He was meticulous, painstaking, maddeningly so, she thought after several more shots had been taken. Her arms would be sore, were already protesting with warming muscles. His concentration was so intense that she felt she had become no more than another tool of the trade, a variation of his tripod, and she doubted that he was even aware of Ronstadt any longer.

The next orchid Ronstadt selected was so dark it was almost black, a velvety dark red, sensual, with an elusive fragrance, mildly spicy.

"We have at least two hundred and fifty native orchids here," Ronstadt said. "I mean in the country. This collection contains most of them, and we find and add more from time to time. Mrs. Santos was a collector, you know. She spent days at a time out in the forest and never failed to bring back a rare and beautiful plant. Never."

David appeared oblivious to his monologue.

"Mrs. Julius Santos?" Barbara asked.

"No, no. Augustus Santos's wife. She died years ago, but she started the collection. And she brought me in to identify some of her plants, although she was very good herself. Never trained, but self-taught and dedicated. She found that one." He pointed to the dark red orchid that apparently was giving David a hard time as he arranged and rearranged the screen, adjusted his camera and readjusted it.

"So you've been tending them for all those years?" Barbara asked. What she wanted to do was put the damned screen down and relax her arm, but she continued to hold it exactly where David told her to.

"Yes. I was teaching at the university and she called and asked me to come have a look. I was stunned. Stunned. It was already the finest private collection possible, and she said she had only recently started. We explored the forest together often, running down hints that one or the other had overheard, or had suggested. Often, she brought her two little girls along, and they both became very adept also, very knowledgeable."

Jesus, Barbara thought, she wanted to get this man alone and ask a thousand questions. He knew the history. He had been part of the history. Now he worked for Julius Santos. Did he know his history, also? What did he know about Augustus Santos's death?

David snapped a dozen or more shots and they moved on down the verandah. The next spray of flowers was twelve inches from top to bottom, gold and copper colored, with an extravagantly frilled edge.

"We found this one together," Ronstadt said happily. "It was on the edge of a lagoon, and it continues to be a water hog. It requires watering three times a week."

"After Mrs. Santos's death, it seems that Mr. Santos continued to maintain the collection," Barbara said. "Was he a connoisseur also?"

"No. Actually he had little interest in them, but when she was so ill, near the end, she asked him to allow me to tend them just as I always had, and he honored her request. I fear that Mr. Julius Santos, without that sentimental attachment, will no longer do so, and may actually sell off the whole collection. It is worth many thousands of dollars, of course."

He continued to talk as David focused his camera and took his shots. Ronstadt, retired from the university, was the director, he said, of the botanical gardens in Belize City, and he was trying to find funds to make the acquisition, if it materialized, as he assumed it would. "But we are a poor country," he said, his voice tinged with sorrow, "and I fear it will not happen and they will leave the country, perhaps go to a millionaire's estate in France, or even in the United States."

They moved on to the next favorite of his, and he continued to talk about the orchids, David continued to work, and Barbara continued to struggle to hold the screen.

Then, her gaze wandering past David, she glimpsed, peering out from one of the glass doors, the man who had called himself Nicholson in Eugene, and who had represented himself as an official from the Drug Enforcement Agency. He vanished almost as fast as she caught the glimpse.

She nearly dropped the screen, and she ducked her head, hoping the wide brim of her hat had shadowed her face enough to make him doubt his recognition of her.

"My dear Ms. Holloway, are you all right?" Ronstadt asked.

"Barbara, what's wrong?" David said, leaving his camera. He took the screen and studied her face.

"I'm fine," she said. "My arm muscle cramped for a second. It's fine now."

"No, it isn't," David said. "You're too hot, and that's a punishing position to hold in this heat. I have enough of this one. I'll get some wide-angle shots while you rest a few minutes. You and Dr. Ronstadt move back away from the rail, where it might be a little cooler."

"I'll bring you a glass of water," Ronstadt said. "One not yet acclimated doesn't realize how dehydrating and debilitating this heat can be." He hurried away, and Barbara stood close to the house, where she was not visible to anyone looking out the windows and doors. Although her gaze was fixed on watching David remove the lens from his camera, open the second bag, and bring out a different lens, her mind was racing with the implications of what she had seen.

Nicholson must have recognized her, or why would he move

out of sight so quickly? None of the other men who watched had cared if they were seen, but he had vanished in a flash. He knew whom he had seen. But why here? In Santos's camp apparently. Working for him? A double agent of some kind? Simple corruption? *You don't have a clue what you're stepping into.* Bailey's words of warning came to mind again. He got that right, she thought. He damned well got that right.

And Ronstadt. What was his position here? Apparently he believed that Julius Santos was master of the estate, in charge, that it would be his decision to sell the orchids. Was Ronstadt a faithful retainer, loyal to the Santos name, unaware of the problem with Anaia? Barbara felt as if she was whirling about in the dark without a clue about an exit.

Ronstadt returned with a tall glass of cold water and assured her it was safe, bottled water. He still looked concerned, as if he wanted to hold the glass for her, to fan her, or escort her to a chair or something. He was behaving almost exactly the way her father would have in this situation, she thought with both surprise and confusion.

"Dr. Ronstadt," she said, thinking of the pleasure Frank was finding in writing his book about cross-examinations, "I'd like to make a suggestion. Since you are so intimately aware of the history of so many of the orchids, and as someone professionally qualified to write a book about them, why don't you do so? Write a book, giving the history of various orchids, who found them, where, with complete scientific identification concerning taxonomy, of course, but a more personal account than just that. Your personal account. I assume you have taken many pictures of your own over the years and certainly they would be included, or perhaps a professional photographer such as David could supplement your own photographs."

He looked bewildered and even intimidated by her suggestion. "But who would purchase such a book? Who would publish it? Why would a publisher want to publish it?"

"There are niche markets," she said, remembering a similar conversation she'd had with Frank. "Professionals in the field, of course. Supplementary reading for classrooms, and a small but significant lay audience. Not a massive bestseller, of course, but a steady seller for what is called the backlist for enthusiasts. It certainly would be a beautiful book, ideal for gift-giving to like-minded people." More slowly she added, "It would not make much money, I imagine, but there is compensation that has nothing to do with money. It seems that a labor of love communicates exactly that message to others, who reciprocate in a like manner. I believe doing such a book would bring you great happiness, Dr. Ronstadt."

He looked away from her, and for several minutes neither spoke again. David was kneeling, evidently taking shots of the orchids in pots on the verandah floor. He had ranged back and forth, shooting upward, straight down the verandah, in many different positions, snapping fast, moving on, again with the same kind of concentration he had shown in the close-up shots. He had gone the short distance to the corner of the verandah and had aimed his camera down the west side, and then returned.

Finally Ronstadt looked at her again, and he said, "I'm an old man, Ms. Holloway. Seventy-two. Such a work should not be rushed. I'm afraid there would not be time to do it properly."

"Then perhaps you should start right away," she said.

He studied her intently, the many folds and creases of his face seemed to have deepened, or his face was reflecting his inner conflict. He nodded. "I should start," he said softly, wonderingly. Then he smiled the same big welcoming smile that had greeted their arrival. "Yes. I should get started. Ms. Holloway, thank you. Thank you. I must get started right away."

David came to them shortly after that. "Ready for a couple more?" he asked Barbara.

"Of course. Arm's all rested up. Which way?"

"Let's try the east side. It's too hot over there. The sun's blazing down on the west verandah."

He changed the camera lens to the original one, and they walked back toward the table where the broncos and Santos were talking. The broncos had bottles of beer, and Ben was leaning forward with a very earnest expression. Bobby looked a little bored, and Santos was leaning back in his chair with an unreadable look on his patrician face. They walked past without speaking and went around the corner to the east side of the verandah, where the same kind of overwhelming profusion of orchids awaited.

This time Ronstadt insisted on holding the screen, and Barbara was glad to let him do it, content to be an idle observer. She did not look again at the sliding doors. They seemed to open to every room in the building, and they were all screened. Depending on how much the air cooled after sunset, it could be quite pleasant even without air-conditioning, if that were the case.

David took close-ups of three more orchids that Ronstadt directed him to, explaining a bit of the history of each one as David made his adjustments, took the shots. At last David stepped back from the camera and stretched.

"I guess that's it," he said, glancing at his watch. "We've gone ten minutes over the hour. Not bad. Let's see if it's time to skedaddle."

Santos rose and glanced at his own watch when they returned to the table. Again he bowed to Barbara. "Please, you've done your work, now perhaps you would like a cooling drink?"

She was still holding the water glass, emptied, and put it on the table. "No, thank you," she said, retrieving her beach bag. "Dr. Ronstadt was kind enough to give me a drink of water."

The broncos stood and Bobby drained his bottle of beer. "It's really good local beer," he said to no one in particular.

"Mr. Santos, we appreciate this opportunity to talk to you and explain our project," Ben said. "Thank you very much. If you'd like a copy of David's photographs, we'd be happy to send them."

Santos shrugged. "Perhaps Dr. Ronstadt would like copies. It's been my pleasure, gentlemen. I trust we shall meet again."

He did not accompany them to the Jeep, but remained standing by the table and watched. Ronstadt carried the tripod and Barbara the screen, again rolled up. He opened the door for her as David put the camera bags on the floor and the broncos settled into the backseats.

"Ms. Holloway, it has indeed been a pleasure to meet and talk with you. And, Mr. Grinwald, I would very much like to have prints of your photographs. I learned a great deal today about how to take photographs and I am indebted. Thank you."

"I'll need an address," David said, standing at the driver's side door.

"The botanical gardens in Belize City is sufficient. I don't have a card with me, but the hotel has the proper address, if that isn't too much trouble."

"I have a folder with the address," Barbara said. "I'll give it to David."

Again he thanked them, and then to Barbara's surprise he took her hand and kissed it. He backed away from the Jeep as David started the engine, and he continued to stand watching them as David made a U-turn and drove back out the driveway.

"What the crap, Barbara," Bobby said, "I thought Santos was going to sling you over his shoulder and haul you off to the nearest bed. And now Ronstadt falling all over himself like that. These guys down here must really dig American women,"

"We're wasted on American men," she said lightly.

The narrow road was as deeply shaded as she had suspected it would be without direct sunlight, and it was more ominous than ever, darker, more menacing. At least the howler monkeys weren't screaming. No sooner had that thought reassured her than the howling started in the distance. It was not echoed this time, and it was far enough away not to be ear-piercing, but it was even more uncanny in the gloom than it had been with brighter light.

At the highway, David turned to the right, toward Belmopan, and after a mile or two there was another ORANGE WALK sign, this one quite legible, and with an assortment of small houses designated.

"Probably housing for the workers at the finca," David said. A few children were at play in the shade of palm trees.

"I didn't see any sign of a real farm, fields, or anything else except the house," Barbara said.

"Behind the hedges all around the fields, I expect," David said. "It's a farm, all right. Sugarcane, they say. Who knows what else?"

"Who cares?" Bobby said. "That guy Santos wanted to know our business plan, for Christ's sake. How much we planned to spend on a hotel, cabanas, equipment, staff, shit like that."

"I kept telling him we're just trying to test the water for support," Ben said, sounding almost as sulky as Bobby. "He said no one's going to offer support for just a dream. We need a business plan first, then support. Not the way we see it. What's the point in going through that if the support isn't there?"

Babes in the water, Barbara thought, gazing at the landscape, thinking about what David had said: fields screened from view. That wall of green had not been random jungle growth, but a planted screen? It had been too regular, she realized, for the kind of exuberant growth everywhere else, especially the edges of roads where sunlight hit. But why screen off the producing part of a plantation? She gave it up when no answer came.

The landscape they were driving past had changed again, had become agricultural in nature. There were more houses, farm and field equipment, pastures, cornfields. . . .

In the distance she could see hills, or low mountains, as green and dense-looking as any of the jungle.

"Maya Mountain off to the left," David said. "That's really rugged country, hairpin curves in the road, white-water rapids and falls."

"And no guardrails," Bobby muttered.

It was only ten miles to Belmopan, which turned out to be little more than a village, even though it was the capital of the country. There were several churches, the capital building, and a few other official buildings, a street of apartment buildings, a scant residential section, and small houses that seemed to be temporary, Quonset huts or similar buildings such as she had seen before, often for student housing. She knew they had moved the capital inland after a particularly destructive hurricane. It didn't appear that a lot of residents had followed.

"Okay, a coffee shop, restaurant, something like that, and cold water," David said, driving slowly through the main part of town.

They settled on a tea shop, where the coffee was excellent, and the waitress did not seem to find it strange when Barbara asked for iced coffee. David asked Ben how receptive Santos had been, besides asking for a business plan.

"I couldn't tell," Ben said. "He wasn't giving away a thing. He did tell us to get in touch with a local attorney that he recommended, one who knows what we'd need, permits, stuff like that."

Barbara sipped her coffee and found herself shaking her head. "Don't do it, Ben. Let me give you a little advice. You do need an attorney, and in fact you'll need one stateside, and another associate here in Belize, but not one that Santos or anyone else here recommends. Your stateside attorney should be the one to find a local associate, and he should vet him thoroughly and make certain that your interests are protected. You can't count on anyone Santos recommends to do that."

"Why not?" Bobby said sulkily. "You guys are supposed to take care of the one who pays the bill, aren't you?"

"We are, but you can't know who else might be paying him," she said slowly.

"You just didn't like him," Bobby said, sounding more peevish than ever. "You wouldn't even accept a cold drink from him. I thought that was pretty rude."

"Let me tell you a little lesson I learned a long time ago," she said, surprised at the memory that had surged with his words. "My dad's a defense attorney, too. I was in court once when I was about twelve or thirteen and he was questioning a witness. That night he asked me what I had thought of the part of the trial I had watched, and I said the guy on the witness stand was scary. He made me explain what I meant and all I could come up with was that his eyes were dead. My father didn't say anything for quite a long time, and then he said I was exactly right, his eyes were dead. His soul was dead and it showed. Santos has dead eyes and he's every bit as frightening as that witness was. I would not trust him to recommend anyone."

11

For the most part the drive back to Belize City was a quiet one, as if they all had private matters to think about. Barbara was trying to place Ronstadt in the drama of Julius Santos versus Anaia Santos Thurston, and having little success. If asked why she had advised him to write a book, she would have had no real answer, except that he had reminded her of Frank. Following the death of Barbara's mother, Frank had stopped taking capital cases, compounding his loss. She had seen him sink into almost an apathetic state, during which he had said he planned to retire altogether. Retire and prepare to die, had been her thought at the time. But Frank had found a new life-sustaining purpose and pleasure. He had returned to the law in a different guise by writing a book about it. Ronstadt had had that same kind of resigned acceptance but had shown her the same kind of solicitude and concern that Frank would have shown. Recognizing that, responding to it, did not in itself help place Ronstadt on either side of the Santos versus Thurston drama, however. He continued to hover somewhere between Julius and Anaia.

At one point on the drive back to Belize City, Bobby said

plaintively, "Let's hang out on one of the islands a couple of days. Do a little diving."

"Sure," Ben said. A few minutes later he broke another silence, saying, "I want to talk to Gabe. Maybe we've been going at it all wrong from the start."

"He might not even be around anymore," Bobby said. "He's getting the boat ready to take off again. He's just waiting for some books or something."

No one responded, and they all resumed their silent contemplation.

When they reached the outskirts of Belize City, David said, "You guys can get out at the hotel entrance while I take the Jeep to the parking lot. Barbara, join me for a drink on the terrace? Compensation for your work today."

"You're on," she said. "But only after I shower and change my clothes."

"Good enough. I have to stow away the camera gear."

She stayed in the Jeep when he pulled up before the hotel. "I'll go with you, help carry stuff," she said.

Ben and Bobby were out of the Jeep before she finished speaking. Pointed as she had been with offering help, neither one had picked up on it, she reflected. Too much money, too used to having people wait on them, serve them, it showed in ways they weren't even aware of.

Driving around the block to the parking area behind the hotel, David said, "Bobby isn't the dope he appears to be, not entirely at least. If they make it work, Ben will end up as business head of the enterprise, and Bobby will be the water sports guru. He's good at anything to do with water, maybe the best, and it's his passion. He could teach rocks to swim and dive."

"And he'll never go inland at all," she commented.

"He'll make damn sure of that," David said with a laugh.

He parked near the rear entrance of the hotel, and they unloaded his gear. As before, Barbara carried the tripod and screen. His room was on the second floor, as was hers, and she went to his door with him, where he took the tripod and screen and thanked her.

"An hour? Enough time?" he asked.

"An hour," she said. She planned to stay under a tepid shower for most of the hour. Hot and sweaty was not a condition she had ever grown used to, and one she did not like.

In her room, she eyed her suitcase, locked but breachable. Anyone determined to open it could do so. She unlocked it and gazed at the manila envelope. Now that Julius Santos knew who she was, he could easily find out where she was, and he could decide to see what she had brought with her. She considered the hotel safe and shook her head. Unknown security, unknown access. Finally she removed the envelope and put it in her beach bag. She would keep it in her possession until she saw Anaia Thurston.

When she walked out onto the terrace, she was not at all surprised to see the broncos and David at Gabe Newhouse's table. She realized with a bit of surprise that she had removed David from the bronco camp. Gabe waved her over.

"Join us," he said, standing, pulling out a chair next to his. "David said he owed you a drink, but I preempted that by ordering a bottle of wine. I've been hearing about your day."

He also had ordered a cold plate of shrimp, fish escabeche, thin slices of what looked like tuna, and a loaf of a crusty, dark bread.

"Just a little snack to tide us over until dinner," he said, pouring wine for her. "Friday and Saturday nights dinner never even pretends to start until ten or later. Shops are open, stalls on the streets, music and dancing in the square, paella in the square, but later." Then he added, "And, of course, pickpockets are also in the square." He was eyeing her big bag.

Barbara put it on the floor at her feet. "Nothing in there to tempt a thief," she said.

"Ah, but does the thief know that before he grabs and runs?"

"I almost forgot," she said. "The folder for the botanical gardens." She brought it out from the bag and made certain that the bag was securely fastened afterward. "Ronstadt's address," she said, handing the folder to David. He thanked her.

"Oh, you met Ronstadt," Gabe said. "I'm afraid he does not approve of American filmmakers. No doubt he believes we're all rather frivolous."

"He insulted you?" Bobby asked with interest.

"Not at all. He was polite, exceedingly polite." Gabe laughed. Then he said to Barbara, "They told me what advice you gave them about attorneys, and I second it wholeheartedly. Good advice." Thoughtfully he said, "I know the forest can be dangerous for inexperienced wanderers, and I believe many locals who appear to be quite charming can also be dangerous. I've never met Julius Santos, but if you consider him to be less than trustworthy, I'd accept that judgment without hesitation, unless and until proven wrong."

"Everyone is local somewhere," Barbara said. "I've learned that charm and good manners wherever encountered can be a facade that masks a lot of intentions, some of them quite evil."

Gabe nodded and sipped his wine.

"Okay," Ben said then, "so we need to get an attorney back home. Make a real presentation, the whole MBA thing. We'll have to bring someone aboard who knows how to do that. Make the presentation." He sounded resigned and morose.

"Not my thing," Bobby said. "Count me out."

"What do you mean, count you out? This whole thing was your idea."

Bobby stood and said, "I'm going to go shower and take a nap."

He walked away, and Ben jumped to his feet and followed.

"You're in this," he said furiously. "So it won't be all fun and games! No way am I going to count you out."

Gabe laughed and poured more wine for Barbara and David. "I think the forest is wearing Bobby down," he said.

"You call it forest," Barbara commented. "So did Ronstadt. But I kept thinking of it as jungle, and my idea of forest is the fir forests of the Northwest."

"She advised Ronstadt to write a book," David said. "Made his day."

"Really? Why did you?" Gabe asked.

Barbara was surprised that David had overheard that brief conversation. He had appeared to be concentrating so much on his camera, the orchids, his technique, that she had assumed he had tuned everything else out. Wrong, she thought, and again considered the question: Why had she so advised Ronstadt?

"I think that when anyone no longer does the one thing he or she has loved, whatever it is must be replaced by something else equally compelling, or that person starts the downward spiral into a life without purpose that leads to depression and despair," she said slowly. "He has tended those orchids for years, they are his passion. And he believes that Julius Santos plans to sell them. He's already in mourning."

For a time Gabe did not speak. Then he said softly, "I think you are wise beyond your years, Barbara."

"It also seems to imply that he believes Julius Santos has the right to sell them, or that he soon will have that right," she said. "I wonder, does he know about the ongoing drama you described?"

Gabe was watching her closely. He looked away, toward the boats at dock. Still speaking softly he said, "He knows. Most people around here know."

"Do they all think that Julius Santos will have the right to sell the orchids, or anything else from the plantation?"

He continued to watch the dock. He sounded almost mocking

when he said, "I don't believe a poll has been taken. But, Barbara, I think they would agree for the most part that Julius Santos would be a dangerous enemy."

"I'll try to keep out of his way," she said, and helped herself to the escabeche.

More and more people had come out to the terrace. Another waiter appeared to help Henry, and music was started in the bar. Strolling musicians with guitars wandered among the terrace tables, and Gabe began to tell funny stories about Hollywood. It was a pleasant hour, Barbara thought later, but she wanted to be alone, to think about the day, and especially about the coming day when she finally would meet the elusive Anaia Santos Thurston.

"You might take a little walk," Gabe said. "Friday evening into the late hours is a fine time to pick up souvenirs, sample some of the local food."

"And watch out for pickpockets," she said gravely.

"But you've been warned and would naturally use caution," he said.

"Perhaps I will later," she said, collecting her bag. "Once again, thank you for food and drink. Good night."

Pleasant, yet strange, she thought, back inside her room with the door locked. Strange that David had spoken so little, or else that was his usual behavior and he had no small talk, while Gabe just as naturally took center stage and held it. And just whom had he been warning her about? The broncos had told him that she did not trust Santos, such a warning would have been redundant. That left Ronstadt, the broncos, or David. Possibly someone she had not even met. Or Gabe himself, she added after a moment. Had he sensed her wariness concerning him, was amused by it, mocked it? Unknown territory, she told herself, then turned off her lights and went out to the balcony in the dark in order not to be exposed to anyone below.

No way was she going to go for a solitary walk that night, she thought, watching lights on the water, listening to music drifting in along with food smells and the sound of laughter. She regretted that. She felt a need to walk, but more, it would be fun to go out and mingle with people, see the local artisans' work, pick up a few things, but not fun enough to risk it. It had been a mistake to go to Santos's plantation, a mistake she could not undo, and she would take great care indeed to keep out of Julius Santos's way.

Later, she decided, she would have room service deliver dinner to her room, and she would review all the papers and photos she had brought to show to Anaia, perhaps to give to her. If things worked out, she added. Only if things worked out.

12

Barbara left the hotel at nine fifteen on Saturday morning. She shook her head at the several drivers lounging by Jeeps and a single sedan. Jeeps were the vehicles of choice, she thought, walking in the direction of Mary's Clothing shop. Window-shop leisurely, she had decided, pause outside Mary's shop, enter at nine forty-five, and leave promptly at ten. When she arrived at the set time, there was no Jeep waiting. When she walked outside again at ten, a young man was standing by a Jeep. He looked to be no more than sixteen, possibly as old as eighteen. He waved a tourist folder.

"See the famous ruins, miss?"

"How much?" she asked.

"Ten dollars, American," he said with a big grin, evidently enjoying playing by the script.

She accepted the folder he was holding and said, "Okay. What's your name?"

"Philip."

He opened the front passenger side door and she got in.

This drive was through a different section of Belize City, with bigger buildings, some that appeared to be for civic matters and offices, and there were more shops that were not beach and tourist oriented.

"Is it true that streets in New York City are canyons?" Philip asked.

"No. Some of them look a bit like that, but not many."

"Oh." He seemed disappointed. "Do you live in New York City?"

"No. I'm from the West Coast."

He was silent for a moment, then asked, "California? Disneyland? Hollywood?"

She laughed. "Afraid not. Oregon. It's north of California."

He gave her a reproachful look, as if she had let him down purposely, or had presented him with a place-name he had never heard of before.

"In Hollywood," he said, "everyone has a swimming pool and movie stars walk around on the streets. You should live there." He was silent for a short time, then said, "Movie stars never get old. They have a secret formula no one else knows about."

Everything he thought he knew about her country, Barbara realized, had come from movies and television. No doubt he believed that cowboys rode around shooting guns or fighting Indians, or both.

They passed a modest shopping mall that he pointed out with pride. "Just like your malls," he said. "Many American shops. You should go there and see for yourself."

"Another day," she said.

Soon they were on the outskirts of the city, with the same kind of deteriorating neighborhoods as on the Western Highway, and then the jungle was the predominant feature on one side and mangrove swamps on the other. This was the Northern Highway, and how sensible that was, Barbara thought. Yesterday they had traveled the Western Highway, today the Northern. She had seen a Southern Highway on her map. It made life easier than remembering a lot of numbers, and highways that abruptly changed their names from numbers to proper names honoring this or that person, usually a politician. The countryside here seemed much wetter than on the Western Highway, with more extensive swamps as well as open water here and there.

Philip continued to tell her things about the United States that she had never known before: It took a month to travel across it by automobile, and one out of four cars ended up in an explosive crash. Everyone had a gun and no one really cared if people shot one another. All the kids were given their own cars as soon as they reached the age of sixteen. . . .

Occasionally she tried correcting him, but she soon realized that he thought her refutations were false. He knew what he had seen. She let it go and he prattled uninterrupted.

She had brought her own bottle of water and sipped some as he drove and talked. "There's a bird conservation place over there," he said, pointing. "Thousands of birds. All kinds, all colors. You should go there and see them."

As before there had been narrow clearings for driveways or rough roads, or more often simple tracks into the jungle, and then an unpaved road to the bird refuge. Twice she heard the howler monkeys in the distance. The morning got hotter and more humid. It was nearly eleven when Philip slowed down and turned onto one of the unpaved roads or driveways. It was hardly wider than the Jeep, with dense growth on both sides. Another Jeep was parked on the road, heading out, and Philip stopped.

"Here we are," he said cheerfully. A man was approaching them. If Santos looked like a conquering conquistador, this man looked like an unconquered Mayan. Aquiline noise, straight black hair, deeply bronzed skin, and very muscular. He was wearing jeans and a T-shirt, running shoes.

He came to the passenger side and nodded to her. "Ms. Holloway, my name is Robert Aquilar. I'll escort you the rest of the way. May I please see your bag?"

Silently she handed it to him and watched him examine the contents. He handed it back and opened the door. "Please, we'll take the other Jeep from here." He turned to Philip. "You did well, thank you."

They both watched Philip maneuver his Jeep back and forth until he had it turned around and drove off. Barbara said, "I didn't pay him."

"He has been paid," Robert said. "Now we'll leave here. I have water, but I see you also brought some. That's good. It is very hot today. You'll want water."

They got in the Jeep and he drove out to the highway and turned, continuing in the direction Philip had taken. Far ahead Barbara could see the other Jeep. After a minute or two of silence she asked, "Those tracks into the jungle, where do they go? Who uses them?"

"Different people," he said. "Sometimes there is a small community, three or four houses, and a little bit of farming. Those don't last long, and the people move on. Sometimes just a single cabin or camp, often with a poacher. Bird feathers, baboons, once in a while a jaguar hide, or alligator skin. And sometimes a planting of marijuana is there. Some of the tracks are simply trails from one place to another."

"I don't see how anyone could do farming in such wet country," she said, gazing at another lagoon. "This land is so low it must flood often."

"It does," he said. "And farming is difficult unless one has the patience and skill to care for the land. It is poor land, with nutrients leached out quickly if the forest is cleared, and then you end up with lateritic soil that can grow nothing for a very long time."

She looked at his profile with interest. It might have been one carved on stone two thousand years earlier. "You've studied soil, agriculture? Earth science?"

"Yes. The University of Belize, and then UCLA. Anaia and I

are working to educate our people about soil, what it needs, how to provide it. Most of them cannot afford fertilizers, and chemical fertilizers are, in fact, the worst thing they could do to our soils. It's a struggle to reeducate people when tradition is challenged."

Barbara felt as if she had tumbled down the rabbit hole to find the most unlikely assortment of misfits. A conquistador, an environmentalist-scientist who looked as if he would fit into the role of a high priest sacrificing a virgin, a botanist with a passion for orchids, an ex-Hollywood director, the naïve broncos, a crack photographer. All of them seemed out of place in this tiny country she had not been able to find on a map two weeks earlier.

A second, more sobering thought occurred to her: was Robert another one she should be wary of? Quickly she told herself that the warning had been generic, with no particular person intended, and, besides, Gabe Newhouse could not have known she would meet Robert.

"Do you, others who live here, find it dangerous to go on foot in the jungle here?" she asked, thinking again of the tracks that led into the greenery that appeared impenetrable.

"Our forests," he said, "can be dangerous to those who are careless, or who stray off the trails and get lost. It is easy to get lost, of course, but so is it in the great redwood forests of California, or the deep forests of Oregon and Washington. There are dangers there, too. Cougars, bears, some say Sasquatch can be a menace."

She glanced at him. He was smiling. "Some say Paul Bunyan might step on you," she said. "But I'm perfectly at home in the woods in Oregon. I've never felt threatened there, while here I think I would be frightened."

"Because you are not in familiar territory," he said. "We are, those of us who live here."

They had come to a crossroad, and he made the turn onto a narrower road. She had thought they were going all the way to the other Orange Walk, but it lay straight ahead on the main highway.

There was a toll bridge presently, and the road became narrower after that. Barbara had not studied the map for the land on the other side of the river, and was surprised to find it higher and drier than it had been before.

"A Mennonite community is over there," Robert said, motioning to the left. "They brought good farming practices with them, but unfortunately they are practices better suited for a more northern climate."

He made another turn onto an unpaved road after a few more minutes, and it seemed that with each turn, the jungle pressed in closer, with fewer and fewer clearings for roads or tracks or anything else. Although she tried, Barbara had not been able to bring herself to think of the dense growth as anything but jungle. Also, she realized that she was hopelessly lost and would never be able to trace their route on her map.

"You can't tell from here," Robert said, after making another turn onto a road much like the one they had left, "but no more than ten to fifteen miles ahead there are mountains. Not like your Rockies, but mountains nevertheless. Guatemala is over there on the other side of the river."

Whether it was due to the higher ground, or because of mountains ahead, the air felt less humid and thick, the heat less enervating. Barbara could see brighter light ahead, the way it had been going into the Santos plantation. They were coming to a clearing, an open space.

They arrived at a village with a dozen or so small houses and tended fields behind them, children playing, a group of women in a yard. They all waved to Robert as he passed. He kept going to a church and pulled up behind it.

"Here we are," he said. "Come, there will be cool water inside. Yours must have become quite warm."

It had, and also it was mostly gone. As she got out of the Jeep, a man came from a rear entrance to the church. Like Robert, he was dressed in jeans, but he wore a loose shirt printed with scarlet and yellow flowers. He was portly, with a red face, as if he never tanned, and pale hair that might have once been red. His eyes were very blue.

"Barbara," Robert said, "this is Father Patrick." He added her name, and Father Patrick seized her hand and pumped it vigorously.

"Ms. Holloway, I am indeed glad to meet you, another American. Welcome, welcome." He had a thick Brooklyn accent.

Why not? she thought when he released her hand. Down the rabbit hole, why not a priest from Brooklyn who looked like a hawker on a midway?

"Anaia is inside," he said. "And I have orders to go home and wait to be called. I trust and hope we'll have a few minutes to talk. Fill me in on American gossip and the latest jokes from *Saturday Night Live.* New slang. Little things." He started to walk away, turned, and said, "What I really would love is a hot dog from a street vendor."

Robert was smiling, but he didn't comment. "This way, Ms. Holloway. Anaia has borrowed an office where she'll meet with you."

The church was so small, it was surprising that it even had an office, which turned out to be hardly bigger than the one in Barbara's house.

Anaia was standing with her back to a window, her features so shadowed as to be indistinguishable as Barbara's eyes adapted to the dim light. Then she came forward the few feet the office allowed.

"Who are you? Why are you here? How dare you speak of my sister as you did?" Anaia said, stopping at the side of a desk, one hand gripping the edge of it.

Barbara caught her breath. For a moment it was as if magically Binnie had been transported here to this office. The moment passed and her second thought was that Anaia Santos Thurston could have been Binnie's older sister. She had the same café-au-lait coloring, the same big, beautifully expressive eyes, hair. . . . She was how Binnie would look in a few years.

"Mrs. Thurston, I think we'd both better sit down," she said. "I have things to show you, and things to tell you, things for you to read."

"You said she died three years ago," Anaia said in a harsh whisper. "I don't believe you."

Barbara glanced around the office, the desk with a few papers on it and a sweating pitcher of water with glasses on a tray, a shelf of books, a file cabinet, one desk chair, and one other chair. She moved the chair closer to the desk, opened her beach bag, and brought out the manila envelope.

Still standing by the open door, Robert said, "I'll be outside, Anaia." He left, and after a moment, Anaia sat behind the desk opposite Barbara.

"I'm an attorney," Barbara began, "and last week a couple came to me for advice. . . ."

"Binnie gave me this letter written by her mother," she said, concluding her account of the first meeting with Binnie and Martin. Anaia had not moved throughout. Her hands were tightly clenched on the desk, and she had looked ready to spring to her feet and run away as Barbara told the story of Binnie's escape from Haiti, her marriage to Martin, and finally her trouble with immigration. Barbara handed her the sheet of paper with the copy of Shala's letter to her daughter.

Anaia gasped as she read the letter quickly. She jumped up from the chair, clutching the letter. She moved to the window and with her back turned to Barbara, she read it again, then stood with her head bowed. After several minutes, she faced around again and said in a near whisper, "Lavinia was my mother's name. Shala and I agreed that whoever had a daughter first would name her after our mother."

Barbara brought out the photographs she had taken of Binnie and passed them across the desk. Anaia looked at them, at Barbara, back at the prints. She reseated herself and separated the four pictures, staring at them fixedly, then gently touched first one then another.

"She is beautiful," she whispered. "So like Shala, just like Shala."

And so like you, Barbara heard her own words in her head.

"What are you going to do?" Anaia asked after another minute or two.

"Following the law of the United States, the immigration department must deport her since she is undocumented and entered the country illegally. I came here to enlist the help of her family to press her case that she is a citizen of Belize, that her mother was Belizean, held captive in Haiti, and that Binnie has a right to be reunited with her real family here. To demand that they deport her to Belize, and not to Haiti."

"No!" Anaia cried. "She can't come here!"

13

Do you understand a word of what I've been saying?" Barbara said furiously, jumping from her chair, leaning forward on the desk. "She is Lavinia Santos Owens, and if she is deported to Haiti she will be seized by that man Domonic, or someone just like him, and she will vanish from the face of the earth! She can't cry out for help! She probably will be dead in ten years if she isn't beaten to death sooner."

Anaia had risen also, and just as furiously cried, "And if she is sent here she will be dead within a week! You come here from your safe country and don't understand anything. Protect her. You have courts, judges, officials. Plead her case for her. Be her advocate, but don't try to manage a situation here that you can't comprehend."

For a moment they glared at each other. Barbara straightened up, then resumed her seat. She poured water into both glasses on the tray and passed one across the desk, sipped from the other.

"Why don't you tell me the situation, explain what it is I don't understand," she said levelly.

Anaia sat down again and, looking at the photographs, she said in a low voice, "I can't protect her if she is sent here. I doubt any-one can. Coming here today puts me at risk. Every day the risk increases, until one day someone will betray me. These people are desperately poor, and they can be intimidated, or manipulated, bribed. Sooner or later one of them will yield. My father was mur-dered, Ms. Holloway, and I'm next on the list. Lavinia is safe in your country. Here, she would follow me, or perhaps precede me, on that same list. I have many friends, but there is always the pos-sibility that someone will reveal my whereabouts. She would be in a strange country and friendless, unable to move about in the forest, unable to hide in any of the villages among friends."

"Start further back," Barbara said coolly. "You're telling me the endgame. Where does it start?"

Anaia raised her gaze from the photographs and regarded Bar-bara for a moment. Then she said, "There is a vast estate, fifty thou-sand acres, and there is a shipping company at stake here. My father inherited it all on the death of his father. My uncle Julius was left a generous annual allowance. It was never enough to sat-isfy him. Although over the years my father increased it several times, it never was enough. When my mother died, Uncle Julius came from Spain for the funeral, and he and my father fought, physically fought while he was here. He was driven away and told never to return. My sister and I were sent to a convent school and never lived at home again, but visited from time to time, and I never saw Uncle Julius after Mother's funeral until three years ago when he came back."

She paused and drank water, then drew in a long breath. "That isn't the real beginning. My mother's death was the real begin-ning. Before that, Father was a loving, caring father, and he adored my mother. She caught influenza that led to pneumonia and killed her within a week. He died, too, I think. Everything in him that had been good and caring died at that same time. He could not bear to look at us, at Shala and me, and he sent us away.

When I married Lawrence, Father said he never wanted to see me again. He said I had disgraced him. I thought he had disowned me entirely. After we were notified that Shala had died at sea, there was a memorial service. He came to me afterward and said he was glad she was dead, that she had brought more dishonor to our name, and it was better that she was dead."

Anaia lifted her water glass again. Her hand was trembling and she put it down without taking a sip. Then, clasping her hands on the desk, she continued. "From that day until Uncle Julius came eighteen years later I never saw my father."

She began to speak in a brisker tone as she continued talking about the more recent past. When Julius returned he had found her in Belmopan, where she had been teaching, and he told her that he had heard from friends that Augustus was demented and no longer capable of running the finca and the shipping business. He said Augustus had to be properly cared for in a psychiatric hospital, that it was their duty to place him there, and he proposed that Anaia and he form a partnership to oversee the entire estate. She could continue as the visiting teacher of the outlying areas as she had been doing and he would be the active manager.

"He was persuasive, solicitous, concerned about Father, and about me. I told him no and he became an iceman instantly. He said my decision was regrettable, that he had proposed a humane solution to a problem, and he left. I visited my father a short time later and found him to be as vigorous and mentally capable as he ever had been. I told him what Julius had said. Father asked me what I would do with the finca if it were mine. I told him truthfully that I would convert it to a farm using the methods Robert and I had been teaching for many years. The house would become a school, an agronomy, earth science college, with classes for the workers' children. He laughed until I had to wonder if he really was demented."

She looked at Barbara and said slowly, "Father told me that day that the estate was to be my inheritance, and also that if he died in anything that appeared to be an accident, or if he was murdered, my life would be in danger and I should take every precaution until my uncle was gone, arrested, or dead. He knew, Ms. Holloway, that his brother intended to murder him. For nearly three years he escaped that death, but then it came. He, two bodyguards, and a driver were murdered on the road from Belize City to the finca. It was made to look like a robbery, but it was exactly what my father had been afraid would happen. Uncle Julius moved to the finca the following day, and I have been in hiding ever since the funeral."

"Why don't you use whatever legal measures there are to claim your inheritance?" Barbara asked.

"There is a survivor's clause in the will. I must survive my father's death for thirty days before I can claim the estate. My attorney said that such clauses are common."

Barbara nodded. They were in the United States also.

"If I don't survive for thirty days, everything will be passed on to Julius Santos," Anaia said. "No one knew there was another possible heir, Lavinia."

"Someone knew," Barbara said. "When will the thirty days be up?"

"Next Tuesday at midnight." She looked again at the pictures. "Why do you say someone knew?"

"There wasn't any reason for immigration to look for her. They must have had a tip, and since there was no reason for anyone to suspect she was an illegal alien, it must have come from someone who wanted her found and deported."

"Can't you prevent that?" Anaia asked. "Are your laws so rigid that it can't be prevented?"

"I can't prevent it," Barbara said. "There are people who would gain from her deportation, bureaucrats who would benefit. Martin Owens is a high-profile, somewhat wealthy celebrity. For a minor cog in the great wheel of government to bring down a man who is also a rich celebrity would do a lot to demonstrate that wealth and fame can't protect anyone from justice. In this case trying to prevent the deportation of an illegal alien. It would look good in the personnel file of the official who brought it about. He likely would get a promotion and a bonus.

"I may be able to stall them for a short time, but not for long. If there are witnesses to testify that Shala was pregnant when she sailed, I could possibly make a case. I was hoping you, and perhaps a doctor, could make statements to that effect, that she was pregnant already. Binnie doesn't know her birth date and there's no way to prove such a date, in any event, but I could raise it as an issue. Mrs. Thurston, there is absolutely no documentation available to indicate that Shala Santos was captive in Haiti, or that Binnie is not the daughter of that man Domonic Guteriez, as he claimed. There is nothing to prevent her deportation to Haiti."

Anaia shook her head. "No one knew except me. We were both afraid Father would kill her if he knew she was pregnant before her marriage."

"The person your father sent to Haiti to ransom her knew that she was pregnant," Barbara said. "The question is, what did he tell your father?"

Anaia looked stricken and bowed her head. "If fleeing in order to marry Juan brought dishonor, a pregnancy would have been cause for her death," she said, hardly above a whisper. "But they are both dead now, Father and his lieutenant. There is no record of that meeting."

"Well, unless I can provide documentation proving that she is a Belizean citizen, due to her mother's origins, she will be deported to Haiti. She will be deported in any event, I'm afraid, the only question is to where. If she had been born here in your country, and her birth registered, that would make a case for deportation to be to Belize. Yet you say she would not be safe here."

She took another drink of water and leaned back in her chair. "From what you tell me, and what I know, it seems that there isn't any place she could be safe."

For a time neither spoke. Finally, knowing it was futile, Barbara asked, "Is there any possibility of enlisting the help of your husband? Lawrence Thurston?"

Anaia shook her head again. In a strained voice, she said, "He came here as a consultant in a government exchange program. He was an expert in soils, in managing tropical land, and he taught at the university for one semester. Robert and I were in his class. The three of us went out into the countryside many times to collect soil samples, to set up test plots, to do his bidding in his work. Lawrence and I married after four months." Her voice became almost dispassionate, remote, and without inflection as she continued. "A year later he said he had been recalled, but he would be back. I never heard from him again. My letters to Northwestern University, where he had taught, were returned with no forwarding address. My letter in care of the State Department was never acknowledged, much less answered."

"What about your own law enforcement agencies here? Can't you appeal for protection?"

Wearily Anaia said, "There's little point at this time. There's no way for anyone to know how trustworthy anyone else is, who is paying whom, who answers to whom. Ms. Holloway, my father was growing hundreds of acres of marijuana, using the Santos Shipping Company to send it to his customers. Your own government has been spraying marijuana fields in my country, using a defoliant, what they call paraquat. My father's acreage never was sprayed. There is massive corruption and how high it goes is anyone's guess. Julius apparently has been working for the last few years to increase ties to others, possibly to become a shipper of even more drugs, probably from Colombia, possibly from Mexico, and he has enlisted people to become his allies. My father told me this when I went to see him. He was opposed to broadening his illegal activities, which he readily admitted that day. He didn't believe marijuana was as addictive as tobacco or alcohol, he believed that it was relatively harmless, and he saw no harm in growing it or selling it. He said that the men Julius was dealing with would destroy this country by shipping or even growing much more dangerous drugs. For all his faults, his dishonesty, breaking the law by growing an illegal crop, his prejudices, and his damned honor, he loved Belize, and he and Julius were in a deadly struggle over its destiny. Julius is winning. I stand in his way."

Door after door kept closing, Barbara thought despairingly. Whatever she had hoped to gain by coming to this jungle land seemed to fade away like a series of mirages the moment she turned toward it.

Almost as if in an afterthought, Anaia said vehemently, "I pray to God that they don't spray those fields! They would poison the land for generations with their filthy defoliant. Many of those people grew marijuana, a few acres here, there. It was their livelihood and they saw no harm in it. With their fields gone, nothing to replace them, they are destitute. Not even subsistence farming is left for them in many cases. The Santos land could feed many of our own people, teach them a different way of farming, sustainable farming, provide cash to buy the things we can't produce for ourselves. And free us from the need to import so much of our food."

"Does your attorney have instructions about how to press your claim on the estate? Is that likely to succeed?"

"Yes. We inherited the British legal system in which protecting property rights is a religion, more highly valued than life itself, it often seems," she said with some bitterness. "The will is valid and the land and the shipping business were bequeathed to me. The courts will order Julius off the land, and if he resists, he could be arrested and charged with trespass. As soon as I have the deed, and the right to do so, I shall write my own will and set up a foundation to take charge of the estate in the event of my death. I have already discussed the foundation with my attorney, laid the groundwork for it. It will become the farm and the school one way or the other! I shall designate Robert and Patrick as the overseers, managers, and codirectors. Julius will not get that property, if I can manage to stay alive a few more days, possibly a week. Then, when I'm recognized as the owner, with my own resources, then I may be able to help Lavinia. Now, there is nothing I can do."

Barbara drew back, defeated. She looked at her bag and said, "I have a few more items to give you. The newspaper reports about the piracy. And a journal Binnie wrote over the past three years. As Martin asked questions and she remembered incidents, she wrote them in a journal in no particular order. I have my summary of what she wrote, and a copy of her original writings. You should have them."

She put the newspaper clippings on the desk, along with her summary and Binnie's journal. She found a packet of tissues in the bag and placed it on the desk also, next to the manila envelope.

"Perhaps you would like to be alone when you read these," she said. "I can step outside and wait, if you'd like."

Anaia was gazing fixedly at the papers. She nodded. "I should read them by myself," she said faintly. "Robert can show you to Patrick's house. You must want lunch."

Barbara rose and went to the door, where she paused and glanced back at Anaia with pity, remembering how the journal had affected her, and she was just an observer. Anaia was going to go through hell reading about the hell her beloved sister had endured. The same hell, it appeared, that Binnie inevitably would face.

She walked through a short hall to the back door and out into brilliant, blinding sunshine and heat.

14

Barbara was groping in her bag for sunglasses when Robert touched her arm.

"Come," he said. "It's only a few steps to get out of the sun."

Shielding her eyes with her hand, Barbara walked the few steps with him and entered a house where Father Patrick met them.

"Isn't Anaia coming?" Father Patrick asked, looking past her.

"She needs a few minutes," Barbara said.

Father Patrick looked disappointed but he cheered up quickly and, smiling, he said, "Well, come into the kitchen and we'll have lunch. Anaia can catch up when she arrives."

As Barbara's eyes adjusted to the dim light inside the house she looked about with interest. A crucifix on the wall was only to be expected, she thought, and a stack of comic books on a low table did not seem out of place, since the room she had entered could have been found in myriad modest houses throughout the United States. Comfortable old easy chairs, a very worn sofa with a red woven cover that didn't quite cover it, scuffed bare floors, book-shelves overfilled . . .

She followed the priest into the kitchen, which was the width of the house with a dining table that could seat a dozen people, a stove, an ancient olive green refrigerator, and a sink at the far side. A few cabinets that needed paint flanked the sink and that was all. On one wall there was a calendar, and on another a beautiful wooden plaque. She moved closer to read what it had painted on it.

The plaque was lacquered, intricately painted in brilliant colors, with gilt scrollwork and the words "Heaven is high, and the emperor is far away."

"A reminder," the priest said, busying himself at the stove. "This is a very remote parish, isn't it? In China, it is told, the remote, local officials often made decisions that might not have met with approval of the central authorities. And heaven indeed is very, very high." He chuckled. "Just a reminder. The original was in silk, but moths ate it."

"Ms. Holloway," Robert said, "I imagine you'd like to freshen up a little. Let me show you the way."

She nodded and followed him through a short hallway to a bathroom. It was spartan, but there was a clean towel and washcloth on a rack, obviously meant for her, and there was running water. It was a relief to let the cool water run over her hands and wrists, and it felt good splashed on her face. When she rejoined Father Patrick and Robert in the kitchen, there were place settings for four, a plate of tortillas, a block of cheese, and bowls of soup waiting.

"I didn't make the soup," Father Patrick said, holding her chair for her. "One of the women, Margarita, comes in to cook now and then. She thinks I live on whatever is fast and at hand." He patted his ample stomach, belying whatever Margarita thought, and seated himself opposite Barbara as Robert took the chair at the end of the table.

Robert poured tea, and Barbara waited, thinking the priest might say a blessing, but he began to eat and she did also. The soup was delicious, tomato-based, thick with vegetables and bits of fish.

As they were eating, two little boys came to the screened back door, peered in, and one said, "Papa Pat, we have more comic books."

"Well, put them on the table with the others," he said, motioning them in.

They edged around the table, keeping a distance, eyeing Barbara with curiosity, then ran the rest of the way. A few seconds later there came the sound of the front door slamming.

"They're shy," the priest said.

"They call you Papa Pat?"

He nodded. "I seem to be in charge of a regular lending library," he said. "I go in to Belize City every few weeks, take all the comic books to a used bookstore and exchange them for a new bunch. The children take very good care of them," he added. "They know I can't exchange any that get torn or dirty."

"He takes a box of real books, too," Robert said. "He and others from the area get together in a book club to discuss them. As he said, he runs a library." There was affection in his expression as he nodded toward the priest.

"You know what else I miss?" Papa Pat said with a faraway look in his eyes. "A McIntosh apple. A cold, crisp McIntosh."

"How long have you been here, in this village?" Barbara asked.

"Sixteen years. I came for two, and it's been sixteen. That only seems strange when I say it, not when I live it. It seems funny to think back about how it was when I first arrived here. Arrogant. I was arrogant, young, and so sure I had all the answers." He laughed. "I learned that I had not yet asked the right questions. Ms. Holloway, would you like more soup?"

"No, thank you. It is wonderful, and very filling. Are the vegetables all local? Is the fish?" Twice during that meal she had heard the howler monkeys, and neither of the men had paid any attention. Was it really something one got used to? she wondered, and remembered how startled her father had been at the sound of

125

trains coupling just a few blocks from her house. She had paid no attention to them.

"Yes, we grow our own vegetables," Papa Pat said. "And the fish was caught this morning in the river. Not by me, of course. I don't seem to have the knack for it. They feel sorry for me and bring me fish and things."

He removed the soup bowls and cheese as he talked. Robert poured more tea and in a moment Papa Pat returned with a bowl of fruits, small red bananas, a papaya and a mango, two bloodred oranges. Robert went to the cabinet and brought out small plates, forks, and several sharp knives.

"We peel as we go," he said with a smile, putting a plate, knife, and fork before Barbara.

"The funniest day," Papa Pat said, reseating himself, "was when Robert and Anaia came strolling out of the jungle. About the last thing I expected to see just out taking a walk. Peripatetic teachers, no less." He laughed again and started to peel a mango. He ignored juice running down his hand until he had it peeled and cut into slices that he divided among the plates. "The next one you peel yourselves," he said with a laugh. He got up again and went to the sink to rinse his hands, talking all the way. "The thing that made me jump out of my skin was the first time I heard the howler monkeys. I'd read about them, but it's not the same thing, is it? Demons? Banshees? Forest spirits? Escaped lunatics? It was hard to associate monkeys with that roaring and howling. Anyway, I never asked for the transfer that could have been mine after two years."

She glanced at her watch. Twenty minutes after two and still no Anaia. Was she praying? Had she walked back into the jungle, away from the misery Barbara had brought her? Papa Pat returned, cut off the end of a banana, and placed it on her plate.

"The children use the table here for classes," Papa Pat said. "Not on Saturday, of course, but weekdays. These days I'm learning a little geography."

He talked on as they ate the fruit. No one mentioned Anaia, and his talk ranged from the village people to the Santos finca and how they planned to farm it.

"We'll section off the marijuana acres," he said, "start clearing the plants and burn them, then spread the ashes over the ground and cover it all with heavy layer of green matter for mulch. After a few months we'll plant leguminous trees, and as soon as they achieve enough height, plant coffee trees. In time that entire acreage, a thousand we think, will be in coffee. The market is turbulent at times, but there is always a market, and for shade-grown coffee it is a very good market. That will be the major cash crop."

Startled by his words, his apparent assumption that she had known about the marijuana, she glanced at Robert, who was watching her. He nodded slightly, as if to say it's all right if you know about that.

"The idea is to never let the ground be exposed to direct sunlight and the pounding rains we get for months at a time," Robert said. "The reason the forest grows so luxuriantly is that there is a constantly renewed mulch being put down and the ground itself is never disturbed, never plowed, and never left idle and bare. We will emulate that process."

"Of course," Papa Pat said, as if there had been no interruption, "there is still sugar being grown there, and we'll keep it, even though with sugar so heavily subsidized elsewhere, it has small value as an additional cash crop."

As he talked about plans for the farm, he sounded as fervent as Anaia had sounded when she declared that the finca would be a productive farm. It was surreal, Barbara thought, this red-faced priest with his thick Brooklyn accent, howler monkeys in the distance, stifling heat, giggling children not far away, oranges that looked as if they had been dipped in red paint.

Papa Pat went off into another direction abruptly. "I've learned a lot here, Ms. Holloway. I went from a know-it-all to an ignoramus in my first two years, and for fourteen years now I've been in continuing education classes. Six ethnic groups here, you know, and maybe a dozen different approaches to spirituality. Paganism, animism, my own Catholicism, the Mennonites, some mixture of voodooism and mysticism . . . It's all here. Many paths to the same destination is how I've come to think of it all. Many paths. I've learned," he said, "that the path is less important than the arrival, and seeking the right destination more important than adhering to a predetermined path not visible to others."

This was starting to feel like the Mad Hatter's tea party, Barbara thought, and sipped her tea. Perhaps she should suggest that she go back to make certain Anaia was all right, that she would join them eventually. And how long should she wait before asking to be taken back to Belize City? She did not want to be on any road through the jungle after dark, with Robert or not.

"Speaking of paths," she said to Robert, "when you first met Father Patrick did you and Anaia really come through the jungle on foot?"

"Yes. We often find it faster and easier than keeping to the roads. During the rainy season many of the roads are under water, marked on the map as seasonal."

She heard the front door open and close at that moment, and both Robert and Papa Pat stood up. Anaia came into the kitchen.

Her eyes were red-rimmed and slightly bloodshot, and her nose was reddened.

"Anaia!" Father Patrick said in an agonized voice, "You're ill! You've been crying!" He gave Barbara an accusatory look and hurried around the table to Anaia.

"I'm very well," Anaia said in a firm voice. "And yes, I have been crying. Barbara brought me news today that was overwhelming." She nodded to Barbara, who was surprised by the use of her given name since they had been so formal before.

"She told me," Anaia said, "with proof, that my sister and my child were not killed when the ship they were on was seized by pirates twenty-one years ago. My daughter is alive and well in Oregon."

15

No one moved. Outside sounds that Barbara had previously ignored, filtered out, became audible: children's voices, a woman's laughter, distant howling monkeys, a rustle in palm fronds, and inside, a silent moment frozen in time. Then Anaia touched Papa Pat's hand on her arm, patted it. She pulled out the chair at the head of the table, sat down, and put the manila envelope on the table. Looking at Papa Pat, she asked, "Is there any tea left?"

"Tea," Papa Pat said. "Tea. Of course. I'll put on water. Fresh tea." He almost snatched up the teapot and hurried across the kitchen.

Barbara replaced on her plate the segment of orange she had been holding, marveling at how red it was, inside and out, and Robert sat down again without a word.

"I told you about Barbara's phone call the day before yesterday," Anaia said. "Her message that Shala died only three years ago. I didn't believe her. I was suspicious, fearful that she had been sent by Julius with a fantastic story to lure me out of hiding, or even that she herself was an assassin. She said she had proof, and she told me a few things that made me decide to talk with her."

The teakettle made a whistling, rattling sound, and from where Barbara was sitting she could see Papa Pat pour steaming water into the teapot. Anaia paused as he crossed the room to put the pot on the table and resume his seat.

"Today," Anaia said then, "Barbara brought me the proof of what she said on the telephone. She brought me documents describing incidents that only Shala and I knew about. No one else on earth could have related those things. My sister did not die at sea. She was taken to Haiti and forced into slavery and prostitution there. And she took my daughter with her and protected her over the next eighteen years until her death."

Her hand had rested on the manila envelope as she spoke. Now she opened the envelope and withdrew the photographs Barbara had given her. "I can't share the written words with you," she said. "That is too personal, but these are pictures of my daughter, Lavinia Santos Thurston."

She reached down the table far enough that Papa Pat could take the photographs. He laid them out between him and Robert and drew in a long breath as he studied Binnie's face. He looked from a photograph back to Anaia, then to the picture again.

Robert also looked up from the photographs to Anaia and back to them. He spoke first. "She is very like you," he said. "Very like Shala. She is beautiful."

Anaia nodded. "She is very like both Shala and me, and she is even more like our mother, for whom she was named."

"You never mentioned a child, a daughter," Papa Pat said in bewilderment.

"No. Those were turbulent times, Patrick. My father had disowned me. My husband had been recalled to the States. Robert was in California. Shala and I lived in the Belize City house in those days. She was enrolled in university, and I discovered that I was pregnant. My father, others, some I had considered friends, thought Lawrence had toyed with me, a native girl, naïve and innocent in many ways, and then abandoned me. I could feel their scorn, their mockery, their pity, and I was humiliated. I came to accept that same opinion. I told no one of my pregnancy, knowing they would only scorn me more, laugh at me. Shala was my only confidante. My pride would not permit me to suffer the humiliation if others should learn of it."

She shook her head. "I know I could not have concealed her very long, but I was not thinking clearly, only minute by minute. Lawrence did not answer my letters, they were returned with no forwarding address. I was confused, bitter by turns, heartbroken, furious, and I was deeply ashamed. I became reclusive, refused to go out or to see anyone. And my child was born. I named her after our mother, Lavinia, but Shala and I called her Binnie from the day of her birth. She was born mute and with a birthmark on her breast. That year a terrible hurricane hit Belize. Shala and I gathered what we could and fled inland to high ground, and when we were able to return, it was to find that our house had been destroyed. Much of Belize City was destroyed. Thousands died during the storm and the months that followed."

Robert poured tea into the fourth cup and took it to Anaia. He refilled Barbara's cup and resumed his seat without speaking. The surreal tea party had turned into a boardroom meeting, Barbara thought distantly. Anaia was chairman of the board, telling lies that only Barbara might dispute, and she remained silent, waiting to see where this was going. As Anaia talked, she included Barbara when she looked at those seated at the other end of the table, and her gaze was level and unblinking.

Anaia addressed her next remarks to Papa Pat, saying, "That was when the decision was made to move the capital inland, to Belmopan, several years before your arrival."

He nodded. "Belize was considered a hardship mission, the

reason I could have moved on in two years. It was still very much devastated when I got here. But how did your child end up in Haiti, in America?"

Anaia sipped her tea, then, with her head lowered, her gaze fixed on the cup, she said, "When the rainy season started, months after the hurricane, a new calamity struck. Cholera. It was widespread and it was deadly. Shala had become engaged to Juan Hernandez, and they arranged to sail on a freighter to Jamaica, to go to his parents where they would marry. Our father had been trying to arrange a marriage between her and the son of another landowner. We kept it a secret that she would leave with Juan out of fear that Father might have seized her and taken her to the finca. The cholera epidemic kept spreading, increasing in virulence, and I was terrified that Lavinia might be infected. A day before the freighter sailed, Shala and I decided that she would take my child to Jamaica with her, and I planned to take the first flight available to join them. In those days, with our airport in disrepair we didn't know when that would be, but we were told it would be within a month. She was delighted to be a surrogate mother to my child for that time. We smuggled Lavinia aboard, after learning that the freighter captain refused to accept infants as passengers."

She looked directly at Barbara as she continued. "When the pirates attacked, Shala was taken by one of them. She clung to Lavinia, claiming that if her daughter was injured she would kill herself. Evidently he accepted that the child was hers, and he took them both to Haiti, where he kept them until Shala's death three years ago." Her gaze held Barbara's for another few seconds before she turned to Papa Pat and said, "My daughter escaped immediately after Shala's death. She fled to America."

Papa Pat rubbed his forehead and looked at Robert as if asking for help. Robert might have been a carved wooden figure with an unreadable expression. "But the memorial service," Papa Pat said.

134

"It was for Shala with no mention of a child. She was not listed among the victims. I read about it."

"Father arranged the service," Anaia said. "I was in a state of shock. My mother dead, abandoned by my husband, my sister, my child dead, disowned by my father. I felt that I had no friends. Even Robert was gone, studying at UCLA. I was numb with shock. No one knew about Lavinia. My father died without knowing about her. No one knew. I was just going through the necessary motions for weeks, months, grieving, in shock, alone. Later there seemed little point to reopen such wounds."

Helplessly Papa Pat turned to Barbara. "How did you get involved? How did you come to arrive here at this time?"

Barbara glanced at Anaia, who nodded. "Tell him about meeting her and her husband," she said.

Barbara kept it brief, sticking to the barest of facts. After telling of the meeting, and the subsequent visit by Nicholson, she said, "We were able to find an account of the piracy since it's on record, and I came here not knowing that Augustus Santos had died. I planned to appeal to him to help his granddaughter, as well as to appeal to Anaia. I was trying to prevent her deportation to Haiti, and hoped they would both come to her assistance."

"They'd deport her back to Haiti?" Papa Pat said in alarm. "They'd do that?"

Barbara nodded. "I'm afraid so." Quite deliberately she added, "Binnie grew up believing Shala Santos was her mother. She has no documentation whatsoever, and she is an illegal alien. The law is clear. She will be deported."

"But you can prove she is your child!" Papa Pat said to Anaia.

She shook her head. "I can't prove that. The midwife who delivered her died years ago. There is no hospital record since it was a home delivery. When the capital was destroyed, almost all the public records were also destroyed, including Lavinia's birth certificate.

I didn't know that until years later since I had no reason to inquire about it. I learned about it only when a woman in Belmopan tried to obtain the certificate for her own child in order to get a passport. It took her many months to straighten out the matter. I had no reason to go through the process."

Barbara had to admire her. She was covering all the bases with well-thought-out answers. Admitting that, however, did not inform her about Anaia's intentions, and she continued to wait to see where it was going.

Papa Pat, clearly confused and troubled, asked if Lavinia had been christened. There would be a record. Anaia said gently that they didn't do that. A child was baptized at puberty, at the age of reason. No surprise there, Barbara thought, since Anaia did not address him as Father Patrick. In frustration he said that no one could hide an infant for a whole year. Someone had seen her.

"Many people saw her," Anaia said. "You don't understand how it was, homeless people looking for shelter, moving whenever they heard of anything available. We moved several times during those months, an emergency shelter, an apartment, a hotel room, sharing a house with two other families. Strangers moving in shock, that's how it was for months. Who would recall one infant, two desperate women, when everyone was desperate?"

"You could have gone to the finca," he said after a moment.

She shook her head. "No, Patrick. I could not have gone to the finca. When I married Lawrence my father had said he never wanted to see me again. Shala might have gone, but only to a forced marriage, and she would not leave me and my child."

He looked down as if shamed by not recognizing what she had gone through.

The monkeys howled closer to the village, and in spite of herself Barbara gave a start. No one else appeared to notice.

After another lengthy silence Papa Pat looked at Barbara beseechingly. "Can't you explain the true situation, make them understand that her only relatives are here in Belize?"

"They demand documents, proof. They don't accept anecdotal testimony. There may already be an arrest warrant for Binnie. She was ordered to present herself yesterday. I wrote a letter pleading for more time to locate the necessary documentation, but I didn't wait for a response. I booked a flight to Belize instead. I don't know if additional time was allowed or not. If not, and with her failure to appear as ordered, they have the legal right to arrest and deport her."

"She could already be in detention?" he said in an agonized whisper. "Is that what you're telling us, that she might have been arrested already?"

"No. She is in a secure place, in hiding, exactly the way that Anaia is. Also," she said, "I believe Binnie is in the same kind of danger that Anaia is. Not only the danger of deportation, but possibly she has been targeted for murder."

She repeated what she had told them about Nicholson's visit. "My suspicions were aroused. Why would the DEA be watching them, how could he have known they had come to me for advice? There was no connection between the girl Domonic Guteriez had claimed was his minor daughter and Lavinia Santos. He probably gave her name as Binnie Guteriez. I doubt that he even knew her name was Lavinia. But on her marriage license she signed Lavinia Santos and that's the only official document that bears her name. Only a tip to the authorities could have made that connection. Someone wanted her deported."

Robert shook his head. "Why does that make her a murder target? Someone could have had a different reason to expose her status."

"Of course," she said. "But yesterday I went to the finca and I caught a glimpse of the man who called himself Nicholson in

Eugene, the Drug Enforcement Agency official. He seems likely to have been the source of the tip, and he obviously knew who she was. And he knows I have been retained to represent her interests. I think they wanted deportation because it is silent, no investigation into her background, no Santos name involved, no connection to Belize. Now, knowing none of their expectations in those regards are likely to be realized, they may well decide to simply eliminate the other possible heir to the Santos estate."

Robert's eyes narrowed with her words. "Why did you go there?" he demanded in a hard voice.

Anaia looked pinched and frightened. She drew back in her chair. "Yes, why did you go there?" she said. "What exactly are you doing here? Why did you go to see my uncle?"

Barbara explained about the broncos' invitation. "I had a lingering thought that the brother of her grandfather, her great-uncle, might be enlisted on her behalf," she said. "I was wrong. I didn't trust him and told him nothing, but Nicholson saw me."

Robert stood and walked to the back door, where he remained facing out. Papa Pat touched the photographs on the table, first one, then the other.

Abruptly he stood and said, "I think I'll put on coffee. Ms. Holloway, would you like coffee? Anaia? Robert?"

They both shook their heads, but Barbara said, "I'd like that very much."

He went to the other side of the kitchen and opened a cabinet, saying, "I drink coffee for breakfast, but not later in the day. Sometimes, not often, just now and then, I find I'm in need of strong coffee. Weak willpower, I suppose. I should resist. It's very expensive and available only when I go to Belize City. What they have in Belmopan is inferior. . . ."

His words were strangely inflected and spaced, as if he were thinking something altogether different, not about what he was actually saying. As if, Barbara thought, he was trying with empty chatter to deny all that he had heard, deny the implications, the possible outcomes of what he had heard. She turned her gaze again to Anaia.

"You have to keep her safe!" Anaia said harshly. "Keep her in a safe place. They won't hesitate to gun her down exactly the way they did my father. I can give you the documents you need. I will. But that's not enough. They don't care about proof, documents. She is in their way and they will kill her if they find her."

"How can you prove it?" Robert asked, swinging back toward the room.

"Patrick, help me!" Anaia cried. "You take birth certificates to have them registered every month or so. You can fill out a birth certificate for my daughter, have it registered with the others."

Barbara leaned back in her chair, watching Anaia, and she believed she knew where it had been heading from the beginning. Anaia had known exactly where she was going with her lies. A masterly performance, she said to herself, star performance, thought-out from beginning to this point, choreographed all the way. Of course, Patrick loved her. It was apparent in his every glance, his every halted motion toward her, his disappointment when Barbara had come alone from the church, the involuntary rush to her side when he saw her tear-smudged face and tear-reddened eyes. And Patrick did not believe her story. That was apparent to Barbara, also.

Neither did Robert believe the story, she thought then. Yet, like Barbara, neither of them had tried to question it in a meaningful way that would have repudiated it.

With Anaia's plea, Papa Pat had stopped moving, stopped spooning coffee into a French press.

More quietly Anaia said, "She is my daughter. There isn't enough time to go through the proper channels to have a new birth certificate issued, authenticated, registered. What difference can it make if it gets done now, instead of twenty-one years ago or six months from now? You can see from the photographs that she is my daughter. She has the birthmark. Barbara has seen it. And she is mute. I have written material proving it. And my word."

And that was the hard part, Barbara thought, her word. Could a man of the cloth pretend to accept what he believed was a lie? How much of a renegade priest had he become? Would he suffer more if he refused than if he agreed?

Slowly he resumed the task of making coffee, still not looking at them. "I think tea is actually as addictive as coffee," he said in a hollow-sounding tone. "You just have to drink more to get the same caffeine boost. Coffee grounds are quite good for the soil, high nitrogen content . . ." The irrelevant words trailed off.

He finished with the coffee but did not return to the table immediately. He faced the opposite way, looking at the plaque on his wall, the one that read: "Heaven is high and the emperor is far away."

At the table Anaia had her head in her hands, her elbows on the table, and Robert remained at the door, a silhouette against the bright light. They waited for Papa Pat.

The teakettle made its whistling, rattling sound, and he shook himself. He poured water into the press and took two cups from the cabinet, brought them to the table, then went back to the sink for the coffee press. "I'm afraid I don't have cream," he said to Barbara. "Not even milk."

"Black is fine," she said.

"We'll give it another few minutes," he said, nodding to the coffee press. Taking his seat again, he gazed at Binnie's photographs. Without looking at Anaia, he said, "I don't suppose it makes any difference at all when a birth certificate is registered and certified."

Anaia lowered her hands. Her eyes were glassy with unshed tears. "Thank you," she whispered, her voice husky. Robert moved from the door. He poured more tea for Anaia.

"What will you need?" Anaia asked Barbara after drinking a bit of the tea. Once again she sounded in control of her voice, her tears. She sounded like a chairman of the board.

Barbara reached into her bag for a notebook and tore out a page. "The birth certificate, certified. Do you have your marriage license?" At Anaia's nod, she added that. "A photocopy will be sufficient. Lawrence Thurston's passport, or the number from it? Is that available?"

"Yes. The number was required for the license. I have it."

Barbara added it to the list. "You should also make out a will, and make a photocopy of it. A hand-written will with your signature witnessed by two people, including their addresses. Don't wait until you can claim your inheritance. It can be rewritten later by your attorney, but he should have it as soon as possible. If you indicate that you are setting up a foundation, with details to be worked out, or something to that effect, also include something for Binnie, using her full name. It can be jewelry, a sum of money, whatever you decide, but include her, and identify her as your daughter. It should be a significant bequest if that is possible. I want to demonstrate that she is not penniless, that she has means here in Belize that she can draw upon. As I said, you can rewrite it, change it any way you choose later. Use my address for this purpose. As her attorney I can serve in that function. No one needs to know where she can be found." She added her address and telephone number.

"Something else," Barbara said. "The survivor clause in your father's will is fairly common. Often it's followed by another routine clause to the effect that if the heir fails to survive for the time designated, then the estate would pass on to any issue of the heir. Do you recall if there was such a clause?"

Anaia shook her head. "I don't know. It didn't seem relevant if it was there. But I don't know."

"Do you know when he wrote his will?"

"I think it was years ago. Why?"

"The clause would include any future children, not yet born. If that clause is there, then Binnie is automatically heir to the estate should you not survive for thirty days."

"Not Julius?"

"Not if that clause is in the will."

"I have a copy of the will," Anaia said. "It's at the house with the other things you need. I'll get it, too, and find out."

Barbara nodded. She made no notes of her next suggestions. "This is going to be a shock to Binnie, of course. If you think of anything that might lessen it, you might include that. Maybe pictures of you and Shala when you were young adults. Perhaps your mother's picture. If you would add a statement to the effect that you believed your sister and the child were both killed by the pirates, explaining why you never tried to find her, that would also be good.

"For the authorities," she continued crisply, "I have the newspaper story about the piracy as well as an official account. I may not have to use them, but they are available to use. Much will depend on whether the official documentation is sufficient, on how determined some minor official is to have her deported."

"I have our newspaper stories, also," Anaia said. "A notice of the memorial service."

"But they won't mention Binnie, will they?"

Anaia turned away. "No. They didn't include her."

"I can't use them," Barbara said. She looked over the notes and passed the paper to Anaia. "You should do this as soon as possible," she said. "I don't know if an extension of time was allowed, but I do know that it will be finite and at its expiration, she will be classified as an undocumented illegal fugitive if I don't produce her. I want to avoid that if I can."

"It must be done quickly for another reason, also," Robert said. "Barbara has to get out of Belize. I'm afraid her name might well have been added to the list of targets."

16

Barbara stood at the back-screen door drinking coffee while the others planned the next days. The coffee was strong and very good, exactly what she needed. Her thoughts were swirling and the saying on the wall plaque kept intruding: *Heaven is high and the emperor is far away*. True for Papa Pat, she thought, but for her? If she had heard Anaia's story for the first time here in this kitchen would she have believed it? Probably, she decided. But she had talked to Anaia in the church, and that made a difference. *Heaven is high* . . . Stop it, she ordered herself. Binnie was her client, the one she had to protect, and if a principal character in her story, or anyone else, had a story that didn't corroborate hers, who was to say which one was the truth? Contrasting stories were testified to all the time in court. . . . Shala might have become delusional, might have lied. . . . She might have decided it was better to continue to claim Binnie as her child than to cut her adrift. Or something else, she added irritably.

She was not responsible for what anyone else might say. If Anaia, by lying, could do what Barbara couldn't do, save Binnie from deportation, save her life, why was she even wrestling with it? *Heaven is high* . . . She knew she would never be able to support a client in a lie if she knew the client was guilty. She remembered the long discussions in classes about the ethics of duty to client and duty to the law, how if they clashed an attorney would be caught in a moral and ethical dilemma that was likely to be career-ending if the wrong decision was reached. But Anaia was not guilty of a crime, was not accused of a crime, and if her two stories were radically different, who was to decide which one was right? Who had the right to make that decision? How could it be wrong to claim your sister's child as your own if that was the only way to save that child's life? *Heaven is high* . . . She closed her eyes.

They were discussing the best way for Anaia to get into and back out of Belmopan without anyone being the wiser. She had to have enough time to write a will, to find the marriage license, pictures, find her father's will. . . . And Julius had allies in the capital. Corruption at the highest level, someone with authority responsible for protecting the marijuana planting. Corruption that extended to one or more in the United States government.

"Barbara," Robert said, "there will be publicity concerning a new heir to the Santos estate. We'd like to delay it for several weeks. Can you delay it in your country for a short time?"

She turned to face them. They all looked grim. "I think so. Are you going to tell Julius Santos?"

"Yes. It might give him pause to think there's yet another heir, another obstacle, but only if you think you can keep Binnie safe. He isn't likely to want to make noise about it immediately, I think. As long as he thinks there's a possibility of eliminating Binnie, he probably won't want publicity. Especially publicity that moves him farther down on the chain of heirs."

Barbara asked Anaia, "Will you be able to deal with the doubts and suspicions your newly found daughter is going to arouse? Your uncle could hire investigators, take it to court to disprove your claim."

"He was out of the country and has no firsthand information

about me or my child," Anaia said. "If we wait a few weeks, the birth certificate will be on file, just one of hundreds, thousands, and who will remember when it was placed there or when it was registered? No one knows how many were reregistered or when they were after the hurricane that destroyed the records. Today, currently, there are often, maybe most often, delays in registering births from outlying districts. The date of birth is of importance, not the date of filing. Patrick is a well-known figure in the registrar's office. In a few weeks he will register another one or two. It's a routine procedure for them."

Barbara shrugged. "When the story does come to light, you might want to say you didn't release the information until it had been properly investigated, which always takes time. And let me know ahead of time," she added. "Also," she said after a moment, "there will be questions about why you didn't go instantly to meet your newly found child. For Binnie, travel to Belize would be impossible. A lot of paperwork must be done, normalizing her status, getting proper identification papers, and so on. It's a lengthy process. Consider why you didn't make the attempt."

"The legal situation I inherited," Anaia said, "required my attention. And I, too, have to apply for a passport."

True, Barbara thought, on both counts. She certainly did have a legal situation to deal with. "Good," she said.

Anaia returned to the conversation about the near future, and Barbara turned toward the back of the property again. The shadows were lengthening at an alarming pace. Shadows of palm trees were grotesquely long dark lines, the foliage so far removed from the bases, they looked like kites on strings. It was four thirty, and they would still be in the jungle after dark. Philip was only a boy, a naïve and inexperienced boy. Disquieted, she wanted to leave, to get back to the lights of the hotel, to a glass of cold wine on the terrace with people around. Howler monkeys set up a clamor and she clenched her jaw.

"Barbara," Robert said, again drawing her into their conversation, "late Monday afternoon Papa Pat will send all the documents to you at the hotel. If you can get a flight out on Tuesday morning, you should do it. Is that all right with you?"

"Yes. I'll cancel my flight and book the first one out after Monday as soon as I get back to the hotel."

"It will be late in the afternoon," Papa Pat said. "I have to register the certificate in Belmopan, of course, then drive down to Belize City and make photocopies of everything. I won't bring them myself. Someone might get suspicious." His Flatbush accent was more pronounced than before, as if he had consciously checked it earlier and now, stressed, could no longer do so.

She nodded. "I'll be waiting for the courier."

"We should be going," Robert said, rising. "I'll take you all the way. I told Philip not to wait for us if we didn't show up by two."

She appreciated the fact that there had been a deadline for her to deliver something meaningful. Otherwise, the bum's rush out of Dodge City. Her relief that it would be he, not Philip, was followed instantly by alarm. "You shouldn't be seen with me at the hotel," she said. "Someone might be watching."

"Right. We'll stop somewhere else for you to take a taxi the rest of the way."

At the front door, she shook hands with Papa Pat. Then, to her surprise Anaia embraced her.

"Thank you, Barbara," she said. "I hope we meet again one day. *Vaya con Dios.* Go with God."

The light was dim on the narrow, unpaved roads, where in places the canopy solidified, blocking all light. At those times the jungle edging the roads looked like solid black walls. There were no other cars or jeeps on the roads until they reached the paved road to the bridge, where only two or three other pairs of headlights came into sight. The smell of the jungle, a pungent mixture of moist earth, decaying matter, fresh greenery, perfume, other odors without names, intensified as the evening darkness deepened. Then, it seemed without warning, the light failed and there was only the dark wall of jungle on both sides and beacons of light on the highway ahead.

Neither Robert nor Barbara spoke until after the toll bridge had been crossed and they were heading for Belize City on the Northern Highway.

"My grandfather lived up near the Mexican border," Robert said. "He was illiterate but wise in many ways. When my father was hardly more than a boy he became a mahogany cutter. The trees were very scarce by then, most had long since been found and cut, but he had a sense of where one might be, then another. One day he came home and said they were all gone, the mahogany trees had all been cut down. He became emotional about it, his role in cutting the trees to extinction. Guilt and necessity in conflict, something of that sort. I remember what my grandfather said. He talked about two rivers nourishing the land, bringing life dependably for all the people. But when the two rivers met and joined, a great turbulence occurred and they became dangerous, and often killed those who ventured upon the new river. I didn't understand. Now I do."

"You believe the price of what happened today will be high," Barbara said.

"Papa Pat will pay dearly."

Barbara turned her gaze to the black jungle they were speeding past. "I believe that Binnie's life might have been saved today," she said in a low voice.

He might not have heard. "My father spent the rest of his life working on the finca of a wealthy landowner, no longer free to roam the forests searching for a particular tree. He died a bitter man."

A long silence followed his comments. There were few other cars on the road, which was not surprising, Barbara thought. Where was there to go to at night? Once or twice she heard the howler monkeys over the engine noise. She started to make her own plans for the coming days. Fly back to Los Angeles, and from there call Bailey, first order of business. Tuesday would be too early to expect an answer from the immigration people, but have him check with Patsy.

She was startled suddenly by the monkeys' howling that was close enough to drown out the engine noise.

When they left the howling behind, Robert said, "If they do that in the daylight, it could mean a lot of things. Two males competing for a female. Warning encroaching baboons to get out. They're territorial, claim possession of their own fifteen acres or so, and try to keep others away. There could be a poacher. They kidnap the babies and sell them on the black market. Or they could do it for the hell of it, just because they can. But at night it invariably means a predator is on the prowl and the warning often spreads far and wide. Jaguars hunt them, and keep their numbers under control."

"No one here seems to hear them most of the time," Barbara said. "How long does it take to get used to it?"

Robert laughed. "How long does it take to get used to jets flying overhead? Or train whistles? Or traffic noise on a freeway?"

"Touché," she said.

"Barbara, just to let you know. I saw you react to what Anaia told us today. You were as surprised as I was, as Papa Pat was. I don't know what you two talked about and may never know, but it wasn't what she announced when she joined us."

She was surprised now at how much relief she felt with his words. She had hated to think that Robert and Papa Pat would assume she had come here in order to concoct a lie, to collude with Anaia to lie for the benefit of her client.

"Thanks," she said in a low voice. "I've been thinking about school," she said. "Some teachers graded on the curve. You know? If the highest score is eighty-five, the lowest forty, then take the average and make it passing, and so on. Sometimes, often, in fact, a very high score had to be thrown out or the results would have been skewed in such a way that most in the class would have been marked as failing. It's like adding a millionaire to a group of average-salaried people and deciding the average wage is much higher than it really is. The law is like that in a strange way. It serves the majority very well, but there are always a few who don't fit the pattern. What to do about those few can present a dilemma. Laws can't be written for the oddball individuals, yet to apply standard law to them is to do a great injustice."

After a moment Robert said, "Two more rivers come together to create a great turbulence."

"Your grandfather was a very wise man," she said. And afterward, she thought, accept the struggle with turbulence, the long hours of inner debate without ever arriving at a definitive answer. Neither spoke again until there was the glow of lights ahead. They were nearing Belize City.

"Late next week," Robert said, "we'll give you a call. After Anaia's attorney presses her claim on the property, after we know how Julius will react."

"I'll want to hear," she said. "And I'll keep Binnie informed. Robert, will Anaia be safe after the court proceedings? Julius won't have the pressing urgency to eliminate her, but is that enough? I'm very concerned about Binnie's safety, of course, but will Anaia be able to come out of hiding, assume ownership?"

He took his time in answering. Finally he said, "I think it depends a lot on Julius. And it depends on whether Binnie is kept safe. I don't know."

"Then keep her in hiding," Barbara said.

The diffuse lights ahead began to take on shapes and more cars were appearing on the highway, lights in the blackness of the jungle. Then they were in town. Robert drove to a hotel not far from the shopping mall Philip had pointed out as one she should visit.

"You can get a taxi there," Robert said. "I'll go down the block a bit and let you out, and I'll wait to see that you get in a taxi. Take care, Barbara. Be very careful. And get out of Belize as fast as you can."

When he pulled in at the curb he leaned over and kissed her cheek. "Godspeed," he said.

At her hotel, as she got out of the taxi, she saw Gabe Newhouse talking to a man on the sidewalk. Gabe waved to her, then came to her side. "Barbara, the broncos have invited us to a feast of lobsters they caught on the reef today. The kitchen agreed to prepare them for nine o'clock. Please join us."

"Thanks," she said. "It sounds wonderful."

He grinned. "See you later."

She entered the hotel and he returned to the conversation he had been having. She went to her room, scanned the room service menu, then ordered coffee and a scone. She was incredibly tired, she realized, eyeing the bed. It was twenty minutes before seven and a nap was out of the question. She would sleep just long enough to stay awake half the night. What she really needed was a shower, a cup of coffee, and to deal with an airline reservation person, who was bound to turn a simple transaction into a hassle.

She put that part off until the coffee was delivered. The airline business became as complicated as she had feared it would. There would be a charge for the change, she would have to check in an hour before boarding began to complete the purchase, and on and on, she thought with irritation. Finally she repeated her credit card number, which they already had, and it was finished. There would be a two-hour wait in Mexico City, followed by a five-hour wait in Los Angeles for her two connecting flights. Another hellish day was shaping up on Tuesday.

Scowling, she bit into the scone and found it dry and tasteless. She ate it anyway. It had been a long time since lunch, and would be a long time before real food. She had little faith in dinner at nine o'clock.

At eight that night Barbara stood at the entrance to the terrace, scanning the patrons. If the broncos were there already, she had decided, she'd skip it and have a glass of wine in the bar. She was in no mood to put up with their chatter. She had already decided to skip the lobster feast and have dinner in her room later, probably out on her balcony, where she could see the lights on the water.

David Grinwald came to her side and paused. "I don't think Gabe or the boys are here yet. Are you up for sharing a table for two? I won't talk if you don't."

"You too? Looking for a quiet time?"

"Yep. Let's get that one over by the potted whatever it is."

The table he pointed to was on the far side of the terrace, was dimly lighted and too small for a group of five. "That looks just right," she said.

A waiter who was not Henry came to the table almost as soon as they were seated. David ordered beer, chips, and guacamole, and Barbara the Argentinean wine Gabe had provided before. To her relief, David evidently meant it about quiet time. Neither talked while they waited for the drinks. The strolling guitarists singing about lost love wandered around, and she was grateful for David's presence. She suspected that the troubadours would have serenaded her endlessly if she had been alone.

They were served. The chips were unlike any she had ever had, and David said they sliced real potatoes and deep-fried them in palm oil. She said, "Yum," and silence returned.

Then, to her regret, Gabe came to the table. "Mind?" he asked.

"Not at all," Barbara said.

"I've been arguing with Fitz," Gabe said. "He wants to shove off and I want to wait a few more days. You don't want to argue with the skipper of your boat if you can avoid it. He can spot high seas miles away, and he'll sail into them in retaliation."

Their waiter came with a bottle of wine and a platter of steaming pastries.

"I caught him at the door," Gabe said. "Savories. Good stuff." He bit into one, then said, "Fitz thinks I'm planning on making a new picture, and he's dead wrong. Done with all that. I'm just curious about how that little Shakespearean drama I mentioned before will play out on Wednesday. Will the evil uncle hold off the sheriff of Nottingham with an arsenal and gallant fighters at his side, Alamo-style?" He laughed and shook his head. "Mixing stories. A director's prerogative. Do they have a SWAT team here? I wonder. Storm the barricades if he won't come out with his hands up? Lob in tear gas? Is the beautiful heiress still hiding out in the trackless jungle? Living in a tree house, à la Jane? Befriended by black howler monkeys? I guess that's too kitschy even for me. Skip that part."

David looked at Barbara and smiled apologetically, as if to say so much for quiet time.

"Maybe the beautiful heiress should confront the evil uncle herself," Gabe said. "Beat him to the draw and shoot him dead, crying, 'Take that! You're guilty of fratricide!'" He looked thoughtful, then laughed. "Guess not. Sounds ghoulish, doesn't it? Making a story for entertainment when there's real pain and suffering. But that's the grist for the mill for directors. And writers. Also defense attorneys," he added. "How many people would be out of jobs if they didn't use the pain and suffering of others one way or another?"

"Some people use others for little more than profit," Barbara said, "and some see the pain and suffering and try to ease it. Like doctors and nurses. And some defense attorneys."

She looked at David and asked, "Were you out diving again today?"

"Not me. I was shooting birds. At the sanctuary. Shorebirds mostly, but cockatiels and parrots, birds of paradise. Quite a few that someone else will have to identify for me. The hummingbirds are getting ready to head out, migrate back north. That's a miracle, far as I'm concerned. An eighth of an ounce of feathers, two, three thousand miles to go, and they grit their little teeth and just do it."

She laughed. "Giving them teeth is the real miracle." Glancing at her watch then, she said, "I'm off. Enjoy your dinner."

"You're not staying?" Gabe asked in consternation. "Barbara, I offended you. I'm sorry, truly sorry. Not my intention at all."

"No offense," she said. "I'm tired. I guess the heat is taking a toll. I didn't plan to stay any longer than it took to enjoy a glass of wine. Good night, Gabe, David."

In her room a few minutes later, she turned off the lights and went out to her balcony to sit and wait until it was late enough to order dinner from room service.

Gabe had baited her, she thought. But why? What was he after? And more important, whose side was he on? She watched lights that appeared uneasy on the water, never still, bobbing up, down, to one side, then the other. She frowned at a knock on her door, reentered her room, and turned the light on, then at the door she hesitated before opening it. A waiter holding a tray with a bucket of ice, a bottle of wine, and a wineglass was there. A card was propped up by the glass.

"Mr. Newhouse's compliments," he said. "May I open it for you?" At her nod, he put the tray on the table, opened the wine, and returned the bottle to the ice. He ducked his head in a bow, and left.

She read the card: "Barbara, my most sincere apologies."

She poured a glass of wine, turned the light off again, and went back to the balcony. "What the hell is he up to?" she muttered, and sipped the excellent wine.

17

Barbara nodded at her reflection in the mirror that Sunday. Wide-brimmed hat, sunglasses, sandals, big bag with water and a book, and to hold little things she might buy along the way, the perfect image of an American tourist. Today she was just that and nothing else, American tourist out sightseeing, starting with the botanical gardens. She might even buy a blouse, she thought, if the stores were open. At the rate she was going through the lightweight clothes she had brought with her, she would run out or have to find a Laundromat. Just until Tuesday morning, she told herself. One blouse for one more full day, then fly north like the hummingbirds.

She got a taxi outside the hotel, a real automobile, not a Jeep. On the way to the gardens, they passed a scene of mild chaos, with music, a lot of people, booths, awnings, children running around.

"What's going on there?" she asked.

"An open-air market. All day Sunday. Good music, food, art, all kinds of things. You want to stop?"

"No," she said. "What time does it close?"

The driver laughed. "No one knows. Eight, nine, when they get tired or no one comes. No rules."

Later, she thought. She would go there after a few hours at the gardens, where she planned to stroll about for a time, then find a place to sit in the shade and read. It was too hot to walk the way she did at home.

She had to admit that the gardens were beautiful, laid out in intriguing ways, with plants she never had seen before as well as familiar ones. The orchid display did not excite her. It was disappointingly meager compared to the abundance of orchids at the Santos finca. Paths wound about, with rock formations, water features, lotus blossoms with heady perfume, regimented plantings of colorful flowers, followed by a wild profusion of blooms whose order could be discerned with careful study but was not immediately seen. As lovely as it all was, what she really wanted was a bench in the shade.

She spotted such a bench near a small waterfall, and sat down gratefully. Enough sightseeing, she told herself, and opened *Four Quartets* by T. S. Eliot. It was a slim book, a reliable travel book, one she usually could open anywhere and get caught up in the language and the complexity. That day her mind kept straying from the page before her. She should have given Anaia a few more suggestions about the will. God only knew what she would come up with, how valid it would be. What if she had been spotted sneaking into her own house in Belmopan? If anything happened to her, would Barbara even know about it until days later, after she was back in Eugene?

No matter what, she told herself sternly, she was going to be on that plane Tuesday morning. There was nothing more she could do here. No matter what.

She persevered as long as she could sit still, then she strolled some more, until she could feel sweat gluing her shirt to her back. A gift shop would most likely have air-conditioning, she thought, and started back on the winding paths to find it. All tourist attractions had gift shops, she reassured herself, and in a climate like this, those shops would have air-conditioning.

But when she found it, tacked on to a tea shop, the air-conditioning chilled her thoroughly. She took a cup of coffee out to a covered area and sat down again, in full recognition of her failure as the typical American tourist.

She had known Sunday would be a long day, as would Monday until she had the Anaia papers in her hands, and a chance to go through them, to see if Anaia had left out anything, or had failed to sign anything, or whether anything else untoward popped up. She couldn't even plan her course of action concerning Binnie's status until she was sure of what documents she possessed and if she had enough to make a convincing case.

She was worried about Binnie and Martin. Would they stay put? If they began to feel that their presence was becoming too awkward for them to remain with Tawna and James, would they take it on themselves to relocate? Would they, like Anaia, find it necessary to go home, however briefly, and run into someone watching for them? She also had started to worry more about what Martin had said, that he would shoot Binnie and then himself before he'd let her go back. She would have been willing to bet any amount available that he had a handgun.

She told herself to stop borrowing trouble, but that never had worked in the past and it didn't work that day. She decided to have lunch at the tea shop and then go to the open-air market to kill a few more hours, if she could bear doing it.

Flea market, she thought several hours later. Giant garage sale. Open-air market. It was all the same, a place for local artisans and craftspeople to show their work, where farmers could sell some of their produce, although by the time she arrived little produce was left. Fortune-tellers had booths, countless shops displayed sandals, huaraches, thongs, boots. She even found a blouse that she immediately bought. Not her usual style, but a Belize-style blouse, ecru, made of a gauzy cotton, scoop-neck, not meant to be neatly tucked in and belted. It made her want to strip on the spot and put it on. There were cages crowded with live and unhappy chickens, booths and vendors without booths with food from all over Central America—tacos, enchiladas, tamales, ice cream, fish and chips, sausages on sticks, and even American-style hamburgers. . . . Everywhere, it seemed, there was music, guitars, pipes, horns, a steel drum band, accordionist. . . .

She walked up and down the loosely arranged aisles and rows of stalls and booths, crowded with shoppers and teenaged boys and girls laughing, flirting. Abruptly she stopped moving. Ahead, David was snapping pictures of young girls dancing, their wildly printed skirts flying.

He lowered his camera and turned at the same moment she decided to go back the way she had come. "Barbara! Wow, isn't this something!" he said, coming to her.

"For the brochure?" she asked, pointing to the camera.

"Maybe a few shots. Mostly for me, though. I'm ready to call it quits for the day. Look, there's a pavilion over that way with fish and chips that smelled great when I passed it a few minutes ago. Join me? Something cold to drink and the specialty of the house, fish and chips."

He looked almost as hot as she was, and she hesitated only a moment, then nodded. "Something cold to drink did it," she said. "I have water, but it's just about hot enough to make tea by now."

The pavilion was crowded, but they found a table and David flagged a passing waiter to place their order.

"What's a Belize cooler?" Barbara asked.

"Juices," David said. "I think whatever fruit is available, at least the ones I've had were all slightly different, all tangy and good."

She ordered it and he said beer, fish and chips. "You have to make sure you differentiate between a Belize cooler and Belize Breeze, by the way. Order Belize Breeze and someone could call the cops, or else direct you to a bong shop, depending on who you asked." He grinned. "I suspect the food and drinks will take a few minutes. No one seems in a hurry on Sundays here. Or any other day as far as that goes. It's a paradox. Belize, I mean. An overlay of British on pure Latino. And here, a place like this, the Brits lose." He gestured generally at the market. "The boys asked me to be their official photographer and I jumped at the chance to see another country and be paid for it. I'm glad I did. What made you decide to come to Belize?"

"No language barrier," she said. "Away from endless rain and cold. I thought there wouldn't be hordes of American tourists, and I was right about that. If the broncos have their way that might change."

He laughed. "Broncos is exactly right. Gabe's word for us. You chastised him thoroughly, by the way. Good for you. He keeps taunting us one way or another, and no one seems to notice."

"Apparently you do," she said.

"Nothing he says really applies to me. I work for a living. He may not see it that way. God knows my folks don't. They think I just run around the world and take pictures for the fun of it. They would have gone crazy for joy if I had become an attorney. What made you go that route?"

"My father. He was a good defense attorney. I used to watch him in court and I knew that's what I wanted to do."

"Was an attorney? No longer?"

"He's semiretired."

"I've been trying to think of what I know about defense attorneys," he said with a grin. "My info comes from movies and television, the tabloids, and so on. They take cases involving fraud, larceny, assaults, murder, drugs, divorces, immigration squabbles, the underbelly of society. Any truth to that?"

"I don't do divorces," she said. "Too messy."

They both laughed. Their waiter brought the drinks and food and she found the Belize cooler just right, tangy and exotic, and cold.

"Gabe is dying from curiosity about you," David said a little later. "He's one of the nosiest guys I've met, and makes no pretense about it. He asked me point-blank what we'd been talking about yesterday. I told him what you said."

Startled, she tried to recall anything she had told him.

"You said, 'Yum,'" he reminded her.

"And I say it again. Yum. That's good fish. What is it? Do you know?"

"Grouper. Gabe," he said, "is sure you're here on a secret mission of your own. Are you?"

She laughed. "I bought a blouse a while ago. Mission enough? Is he going to hang around long enough to ferret out anything else I might have on my mind? Will his skipper shanghai him, drag him aboard the yacht, and take off?"

"He comes and goes when it suits him, apparently. After the boys leave in a few days, I'm going to hang around for a time. Still things I want to see and shoot, like stumbling across the market here today. Who knows what lurks around the next corner? Maybe we can get together. Lunch, dinner, something like that. When do you leave?"

"In a day or two. I'll have to check my ticket when I get back to the hotel. Who knows how many murderers, assaulters, larcenists, et cetera, are lining up at my door back home?"

She realized that the archetypical American tourist had left, and she was again the attorney from Eugene, wary and alerted to something that had gone unnoticed until that moment. Subtly, carefully, and very cleverly David was quizzing her. And he had explained in advance that he would still be around after his employers left. She looked past him at a strolling guitarist, singing about his beautiful Isadora.

"I wonder why the term 'Latino' got attached to Central America," David said. "No Latin here. No Rome."

"There are a lot of phrases that bothered me along the way," she said. "Be that as it may. As it may what? As it may be another that? Why two?"

"No reference, no context," he said. "You'd have to know what the first that referred to."

She finished her Belize cooler and looked at her watch. Twenty minutes before five. She had managed to kill most of the day, after all. "Split the tab?" she asked.

"Of course not. Are you leaving already?"

"Yes. Time for another shower. I'm averaging two a day. If I keep it up I'll start growing moss. Thanks for the high tea." He was standing by the table as she walked away.

She left the market by a different entrance than she had used entering, and found herself on a mostly deserted street without a chance of finding a taxi. Vexed, she started to walk toward the corner where she could see a traffic flow passing.

He had not been following her all day, she felt certain, but how likely was it for them to have met accidentally at the market? And on the day before, when she stopped to make sure the broncos were not on the terrace, how likely was it to have had him appear suddenly at her side and suggest a small table for two? But he had not questioned her then. Just a holding pattern, waiting for Gabe to come along? She shook her head. Don't weave conspiracy theories out of thin air, she cautioned herself. Gabe had been the one to suggest that no one was to be trusted. How right that was, she thought then. No one at all. Almost instantly it occurred to her that if either Gabe or David was allied with Julius, he would already know that she was in Belize on Binnie's account.

Was a third party involved? Someone she was totally unaware of? She was frowning when she reached the corner and, to her relief, saw a taxi near the market entrance. Trust no one, she repeated to herself emphatically as she waved to the taxi driver.

18

She walked, window-shopped, entered shops and browsed when the sun was too hot to bear another minute, then remembered nothing of what she had seen. She sat in a café with a Belize cooler until it became warm, then walked some more. She was staying in tourist areas where there were others walking and shopping, where she felt that many people about afforded more safety and cover than other places would. The morning was interminable. Sleep had been elusive on Sunday night, and she had come wide-awake at some ungodly hour and was unable to go back to sleep. By noon she felt as if she had been up for at least twenty-four hours.

Lunch, she decided, not because she was hungry, but because it would take up another hour, and then she would return to the hotel and wait. Papa Pat had said late afternoon, she reminded herself, but what had he literally meant by late? Three? Five? Two? She should have asked. Wait where? Her hotel room was too pris-onlike, the balcony too sunny until late in the day, the lobby too exposed, too likely a place to encounter Gabe or even David, al-though she assumed he was out with the broncos. It was a working day for him. She envied that, a working day, a day of purpose, with things to get to, to get done.

At one thirty, back in her room, she packed her suitcase, leaving out only what she would need for the flight home: jeans, a T-shirt, sweater, jacket, sneakers. . . . She emptied the big bag and put what she needed in her purse. She planned to leave the beach bag and matching hat in the room, to be tossed out, or, more likely, for the maid to take. Neither would be of any use to her once she was back home. There was nothing else she could do in the room. Taking her purse and her Eliot, she went to claim a comfortable chair in the lobby and stay in it until a courier arrived with Anaia's papers. If Gabe, David, or anyone else came to talk to her, she'd tell him to buzz off.

When she walked into the lobby the desk clerk stepped out from behind the counter and said, "Miss Holloway, your driver is waiting for you in front of the hotel."

She thanked him and kept going through and out the front where she saw Philip standing by his Jeep.

"See the waterfall," he said, holding up a folder.

She nodded and went to the Jeep, where he was holding open the back door. Not the smiling, open-faced boy she had ridden with before, today he looked nervous, and did not meet her gaze.

Something's gone wrong, she thought with alarm.

She got inside the Jeep. He closed the door and got in front, drove away from the hotel without a word. There was no point in questioning him. He was a messenger, a driver, a useful for-hire kid. They were not likely to have told him anything more than to go get her.

She couldn't stop the scenarios of possible disastrous incidents from playing in her mind, overlapping one another, repeating with variations: Anaia had been captured, killed, had had an accident. . . . Papa Pat had lost the papers, had been stopped in Belmopan, had found it impossible to take part in this charade, had changed sides. . . . Robert had been compromised. . . . They had all been arrested. . . .

Philip was driving on the Western Highway, out of town, past the mangrove swamps, past the shantytown, driving faster than he had driven before, driving in silence, both hands tight on the steering wheel.

Were they going all the way to Belmopan? Possibly meet Anaia or Robert there? That meant going past the finca. Her unease was becoming dread and fear. "Philip, where are we going?"

He shook his head and did not answer.

She bit her lip and tried to relax, told herself that he worked for Robert, that he was just an innocent, gullible boy without an ounce of harm in him. But where was he taking her?

At last he slowed down and turned onto one of the narrow dirt roads into the jungle. After a minute or two he stopped. Ahead on the road was a black sedan, and by it were three men Barbara had never seen before. They walked to the Jeep and one of them pulled open the front door and yanked Philip out. He held a handgun. Another one opened the back and said, "Get out."

When she hesitated, he reached in, grabbed her by the arm, and pulled her out. Philip said something she didn't catch, and the man who had yanked him out of the Jeep hit him in the head with the butt of his gun. Barbara screamed and started to run toward Philip, but the one holding her arm jerked her around and to the sedan. He shoved her into the backseat. The third man got in on the other side, and both doors slammed shut. The one who had pushed her inside walked around the car to get behind the wheel. He turned on the engine and the locks on the back doors clicked into place as the Jeep began to back out the way it had come in. There was no sign of Philip.

At least they hadn't gunned her down on the highway, Barbara thought. Too many possible witnesses? Traffic was sparse, but there was traffic. The sedan windows were darkened, no one could see in, see her. Philip had been out of sight. No witnesses to an abduction. They could have shot her and Philip on the dirt road, but they hadn't. They were taking her to the finca. Put the gun to her head on the plantation? Bury her in a field of marijuana? She knew she was close to hysteria, and bit her cheek hard. *Think! Don't panic.* Her only thought was that there was nothing she could do.

They passed the decrepit, useless ORANGE WALK sign, then made the turn onto the narrow paved road. How far had David said it was, two and a half miles, three? Today the road was as dim as before. She could hear no howler monkeys from inside the closed sedan. The next turn was onto the gravel driveway, and soon the brightness ahead signaled their approach to the clearing, the beautifully landscaped grounds of the finca.

The driver stopped near the steps to the verandah. He got out and opened Barbara's door. She didn't want him to touch her again and got out. He took her by the arm and hurried her up the steps and down the verandah to where Julius Santos was seated, watching her approach.

"My dear Miss Holloway," he said in his silky voice, "how very nice of you to stop by again. Please, sit down."

When she didn't move immediately to the chair opposite Santos, the man holding her grasped her shoulder and pushed her down.

"It's most uncomfortable having to look upward when talking to one who is standing," Santos said. He had a tall, sweating glass of juice at hand that he lifted to take a sip. "Since you scorned my hospitality on our last meeting," he said, "I won't risk your disdain by offering you a refreshment on this occasion."

When she continued to be silent, his eyes narrowed a bit. "What? No protestations! No cries that I can't do this to you? That I can't get away with it? Not even any questions? You surprise me, Miss Holloway. You, an attorney without a single question."

"What do you want from me?" she said.

"Not a thing. Absolutely nothing at all. I had thought I might ask you a few questions of my own, but there's no need now. It matters not at all what you planned to do for the bastard pretender, what scheme you had in mind for her. And I accepted that you couldn't tell me where my dear niece might be found and questions in that regard would be fruitless. Again, no questions. Mrs. Owens failed to appear for her scheduled appointment, of course, and she will be apprehended and deported forthwith. No clever spokesman on her behalf appeared and she could make no meaningful appeal. So that matter is settled satisfactorily. And as for my dear niece, Robert has told me what I need to know. Another little matter will be settled soon. So, I need nothing at all from you. It's immaterial what your plans were when you embarked on this mission."

He took another drink. "You made a serious mistake by coming here, Miss Holloway. My American friend is dispensable, however it is convenient to have him remain where he is, and I'm afraid you have made that quite impossible. It crossed my mind that I might offer you a substantial sum to forget you saw him, but I'm afraid I find you untrustworthy, like so many of your fellow Americans. But you especially since you abused my hospitality by coming here under false pretenses."

When she continued to look at him in silence, his face darkened. He leaned forward and said coldly, "You look at me the way I was looked at in New York, in Los Angeles. Arrogant, uncouth, vulgar Americans treating me like a filthy Mexican immigrant, drawing away from me as if I carried a disease, expecting me to give way to them on the sidewalks. Checking to see if a law officer was nearby to come and drag me away if I so much as glanced at their women. You think you're so superior, all of you. You come here to my hacienda and act as if I'm not worthy of courtesy."

His voice became raspier, harsher as he said, "I've been cheated all my life. Treated like an ill-begotten beggar all my life. My father, my brother, all of them, treating me like a piece of dirt. I offered my brother a fair partnership and he treated me with contempt. My dear niece was contemptuous when I offered her a compromise. And you dare come here and regard me with the same kind of contempt."

He stopped and took a long drink of juice. When he spoke again, he had regained the smooth, silky tones as earlier. "It doesn't pay to treat me so, Miss Holloway. There is a certain honor to be closely held, protected. Those who treat me with contempt do not come to a happy ending. Still, you do not speak. No pleas for mercy even. But I am a gentleman and I extend mercy to you. Initially I had thought to let Manuel"—he nodded at the man standing by her side—"and his friends have sport with you. They would enjoy that, of course. But I decided no. Usually when one denies himself a pleasure there is a reason, and I confess my reason outweighed the pleasure I would have had watching you being possessed by Manuel and the others. But it was not to be. When they perform an autopsy on you in a few days, there can be no internal damage to cause an investigation. No, it must be seen as a simple accident. At daylight you and the boy will indeed go to the waterfall, where, unfortunately, there will be a tragic accident, clearly identified as such."

He spoke in rapid Spanish to Manuel, standing at her side. The man took her purse from her and handed it across the table to Santos. He looked inside, pulled out the Eliot volume and flipped through it, replaced it, then did the same with her notebook. He handed the purse back to Manuel, who dropped it into her lap.

"Still no words, Miss Holloway?" Santos asked mockingly, rising from his chair.

She stood and Manuel grasped her arm in a hard grip. "A few, Mr. Santos. If people regard you with contempt, it is because you are contemptible, a little man with others to do your bidding as long as they have weapons and you have money to pay them. You are a man who has fed on hatred and resentment for a lifetime, and such a diet has poisoned you and all you touch."

Santos came around the table and slapped her viciously. "Something to remember me by through your long night," he said. "Take her to her room," he ordered. He turned and walked into the house.

With a viselike grip on her arm, Manuel propelled her through a room, out the back to a wide covered walkway that encircled a courtyard where a fountain threw water high into the air. He took her around the corner, opened a door, and pushed her inside. The door slammed shut.

The room was a sparsely furnished bedroom, with only a bed, a stand holding a lamp by it, a dressing table, and chair. A second door was to a bathroom. A sliding glass door with drapes was open and screened, and on the verandah outside a guard had already been posted. He was stretched out on a chaise. She closed the drapes. Then she sank down on the side of the bed, shaking hard.

She did not move again until the shaking subsided. She crossed the room to look inside the bathroom where a tall bottle of water was on the counter. She opened it and took a long drink, even as she thought it would not do for her to be badly dehydrated when they performed an autopsy. That might arouse suspicions. He had thought of that. With a shudder she examined her face in the mirror. Her cheek was bright red, already swelling, and it ached. No broken tooth, no broken jaw, just bruising and swelling. That could be attributed to a fall. Her arm hurt where Manuel had gripped it so hard. It would be bruised, too, she knew, and didn't bother to inspect it.

Nothing was in the drawers of the dressing table. Nothing in the room could be used as a weapon of any sort. And it was getting hotter by the minute with the drapes closed. She returned to the sliding door and opened the drapes a few inches. The man in the chaise looked up and she stepped to the side, out of his sight.

Sitting on the side of the bed she tried to think of what she could do, if there was anything she could do. After a few minutes she stood and looked again at the chair by the dressing table. She turned it over and examined the legs, how they were attached to the seat. It was a little chair, the legs held in place by two braces with screws, and no doubt with glue. After considering it for a minute, she returned to the bed and dumped the contents of her purse onto it. A fingernail file might do, she thought, and searched for it. She brought the chair to the bed and worked at unscrewing one of the legs. When the file began to cut into her finger, she wrapped it in a bit of the sheet and returned to the screw, praying that the file would not bend, would not break. At last the screw yielded, and she was able to get it out. She started on the second one.

When both screws were gone, she began to work on loosening the glue that still held the leg in the bottom of the seat. It didn't move. After another drink of the water, which was disgustingly warm, she returned to the leg and continued to try to move it back and forth, back and forth, and finally she felt it move a fraction. She put it down to rest her hand, to run water over it, and splash water on her swollen face. Back in the bedroom, she continued to work on the chair.

Back and forth, back and forth. She heard a faint breaking sound and applied more pressure, back and forth, back and forth. At last the leg came free with a jagged edge where it had broken.

She held it and raised it over her head, swung it around. It was too lightweight to do damage, she realized, too short, but it was more than she'd had an hour earlier.

She replaced the chair by the dressing table where it looked all right, at least until someone tried to sit on it. She put the leg under the sheet on the bed.

Now what? she asked herself, sitting on the side of the bed again. It was four thirty, less than two hours until dark. She was drenched with sweat but unwilling to open the drapes wider to let any breeze in, unwilling to be under the gaze of her guard. When she glanced out the narrow opening she had available, she saw him on the chaise with a magazine. He was smoking a cigarette.

Now what? she asked again, looking at the things she had emptied from the purse. Comb, wallet, Eliot, passport . . . her notebook was there, and three pens. She picked up the notebook and a pen, opened to a clean page, and started to write.

"Today, my driver, a boy named Philip, and I were apprehended by three men. . . ."

She wrote a detailed account of exactly what had happened, what Julius Santos had said, included the slap, and her imprisonment. When done, she signed and dated it.

Then, after thinking a few minutes, she picked up the *Four Quartets* and started to flip through it, looking for a half page that was blank. She had annotated the volume at various times with margin notes, notes following text, crowding some pages to the margins. She found a suitable page at the end of "The Dry Salvages."

She copied what she had written in her notebook, signed and dated it, then closed Eliot. It had become too dark in the room to read any of the poetry, or even to proofread what she had written. She reached for the light switch but withdrew her hand and instead went to the bathroom, turned on the light there, and left the door partly open when she returned to the bedroom. It was enough.

Now what? From outside she could hear voices, men talking, laughing. In a few minutes silence returned. She smelled marijuana. Her guard was smoking. A bit of breeze was drifting the smoke into the room. When it grew darker, she decided, she would open the drapes wider, maybe cool the stifling room a little. Sweat was running down her back, down her temples, her arms and legs. Her hair was plastered to her neck.

A dim light came on outside the glass door. Between the light from there and the bathroom light, she knew she would not turn on the bedroom light to be watched by anyone. And so what? she asked herself derisively. To watch her sit on the side of the bed?

They had gotten to Robert, and he had told them where to find Anaia, she thought despairingly. Tortured first? Probably, but he had told enough to put a smug look of satisfaction on Julius Santos's face. No papers had been delivered to her hotel. Had Papa Pat been waylaid, the papers seized? Again she thought of the satisfaction Santos had shown, and she wanted to weep. And that poor boy, Philip. That confused, gullible boy who believed Hollywood stars knew how to keep age at bay. They had gotten to him, too. Intimidation, threats, bribery? It didn't matter. She doubted he had survived that savage blow to his head. All her efforts for nothing. Binnie, Martin . . . they would wait for her, hoping, praying for a miracle.

Did Santos know yet that she had petitioned for an extension of time? She shook her head. That didn't matter, either. In fact, it would make it worse for Binnie if an extension had been granted and she failed to show up at the new time. Even that ploy would backfire and make matters worse.

She should have turned them over to an expert in immigration law, she thought, cursing under her breath. The sensible thing to have done, what Frank would have advised, what her first thoughts had been, steer them to an expert and bow out.

She stood and paced the room for a few minutes, trying to quiet her recriminations, but it was too hot to continue, and she went to the bathroom to bathe her face and arms again, then stood regarding herself in the mirror. In the distance she could hear the howler monkeys. She nodded. Exactly what she wanted to do. Scream and howl. The howling was picked up by another group, closer. A predator was on the prowl; the warning system activated.

She thought of the dense black jungle, of the howler monkeys communicating trouble, poisonous snakes and spiders, bats, alligators. . . . And slowly she began to make a picture in her mind of exactly where she was positioned. Where this room was. Where the driveway and gravel road were. She returned to the bedroom and picked up her notebook and pen and took them back to the bathroom, where she lowered the seat on the toilet and sat down with her eyes closed, visualizing where Julius Santos had been sitting, how far she had been forced along the walk by the courtyard to this room.

This was the east side of the building, she decided, and she visualized the many orchids on the railings, hanging from the ceiling, on the floor of the verandah. She began to make a sketch of this end of the building, the verandah, and the driveway. She was in the first room around the corner of the verandah.

First, get out of sight of the guard. Go around the corner to the side with the steps. Go straight out that way, far enough to be out of the light from the verandah. Although the many orchids would help conceal anyone moving on the lawn, she wouldn't count on it. Out of the light, turn left to intercept the driveway. Follow it to the gravel road, and keep on it to the paved road. Turn right.

She stared at the sketch, shook her head, again thinking of the jungle, the warnings she had heard, her own sense of fear of it, then very slowly she nodded. She'd be damned if she'd simply sit all night and wait for them to come and manhandle her to a waterfall and toss her over. She would take her chances with the jungle first.

19

Eight o'clock. She was staring at her watch as if it were an alien artifact, she realized, and turned the face inward in order to make looking at it a conscious effort, not the compulsive reflex it had become. She considered taking it off, but that would be worse than knowing what time it was. Every hour on the hour, she decided, she had to exercise, walk, do knee bends, do something. The bed was tempting, but she didn't dare stretch out for fear she might fall into a deep sleep. She was very tired after a night when she had slept little, had awakened before daylight.

She should add a footnote to her previous account, she thought then, and was grateful that there was something she could do. She took the notebook and Eliot to the bathroom and added a few lines: "Later, if and when the guard goes to sleep, I plan to leave this room and try to make my way through the jungle to Belmopan and get help there." She signed and dated the additions.

Trying to read was futile. She could not concentrate on the words, even though a few lines seemed to leap out at her. When she came to "In the end is my beginning," she snapped the book shut and returned it and the notebook to her purse. She imagined carrying a purse through the jungle, then undid the shoulder strap, let it out full length, and put it over her head to let the purse hang down her back where it could not slip off, leaving both hands free. That was better.

At nine she heard conversation on the verandah and watched her guard and another man change places. Dinnertime, she guessed. The new guard had a bottle of beer and in a minute she smelled marijuana again.

Ten o'clock, changing of the guard, with the original guard returning to take the chaise. She hoped he had eaten a very large meal, one big enough to make him lethargic and drowsy, make him fall asleep. And she knew she was getting lethargic. She did knee bends, then splashed water on her face and arms again. As much as she wanted a shower, she was unwilling to undress and use it. She had no control over who might enter her room or when.

At eleven thirty she heard her guard's chaise make a scraping noise. She peeped out to see him walking back and forth. She took it as a good sign. He was trying to stay awake, exactly the way she had been keeping herself awake and relatively alert, through movement.

At twelve thirty the guard smoked another joint. She watched him stand by the chaise, no longer walking back and forth, and she watched him settle back down. He seemed to be having trouble getting comfortable, kept shifting, moving his legs, half turning over, grunting a little. At one o'clock, he stopped moving and gave a deep sigh.

Ten minutes later he began to snore. She looked at her watch. She would wait twenty minutes to let him fall into a deep sleep. It was a long twenty minutes, but her lethargy was gone, she was wide-awake, adrenaline charged. Without a sound, she retrieved the chair leg from under the sheet, slung her purse strap around her neck, and went to the screened door to start easing it open a little at a time, praying it would not make enough noise to rouse him. He continued to snore.

She slipped from the room and carefully eased the screen closed behind her, then, keeping close to the wall of the house, she made her way to the corner, around it, and down ten feet farther. She stopped there to peer both ways. No one was in sight and the dim light on the verandah was the only light. From where she stood, she could see the orchids on the verandah floor at the opposite edge. She would have to move at least one, get under the rail, and return the potted orchid. She didn't dare try to go the long way to the steps that led straight to the driveway. Someone might be out of sight on the verandah farther down, or wakeful in one of the rooms facing the verandah, and she would be in full view that way. Her new pale blouse would be a giveaway. She drew in her breath and crossed the verandah, then stopped moving again. When there was no outcry, she lifted a potted orchid and held it as she ducked and went under the rail, careful to avoid dislodging the orchid on it. On the ground, she replaced the orchid she had moved and hurried away from the verandah, away from the house, away from the light. It was too pale to extend very far out onto the grass.

Although it was not as dark as the gravel road would be, she still could not see the driveway when she turned left and began to walk toward where she knew it had to be. She held the chair leg out as a blind person might do, to avoid stumbling over a bush or running into a palm tree, now and then testing the ground ahead with it, feeling for the paved driveway.

When her stick make a tapping sound she stopped moving, listened, moved ahead again. She had come to the driveway. Now she used the stick to keep herself on the driveway, trailing it alongside the grass. The driveway gave way to gravel and she paused again, this time trying to see anything at all in front of her. It was like looking at a solid black curtain.

She had been aware of noises, the rustle of palm fronds in a slight breeze, scurrying sounds, the flap of wings, a loud bird cry, but as she started to walk on the gravel, into the jungle, the sounds faded and the silence was more ominous than even the flapping of wings that had made her shudder with the thought of bats. She felt that the jungle was holding its breath. And there was no longer even a slight breeze.

Keep the gravel underfoot, she told herself, and the jungle on the right. She held the chair leg out to her right until she felt the resistance of foliage, and she could feel the gravel through the soles of her sandals. She did not want to blunder into the jungle, risk falling over vines or feel the leaves of strange plants on her face and arms, risk breaking into and through a spiderweb. She moved ahead slowly, cautiously. The odor she associated with the jungle grew stronger, a smell of decaying matter, of soil, the fecundity of growth smothering other rampant growth, the perfume, sometimes sickeningly sweet, of blooms. . . . And she began to hear sounds she had not heard before, as if things unseen were moving abreast of her, keeping pace, measuring her.

Stop it! she ordered herself. She moved the chair leg, swept the air with it, took a step to her right, and again felt the resistance of foliage. She moved ahead.

She didn't know, and couldn't know, what time it was, how long she had been walking on the gravel that seemed to stretch endlessly. Jungle on the right, gravel underfoot, and ignore the noises, the smells. Ignore everything except the gravel underfoot and the jungle to the right. The gravel was bruising her feet through the thin sandals. Ignore that, too, she ordered herself, and tried to follow the order, but the bottoms of her feet hurt, and a blister had formed under one of the straps. She realized she was not feeling the jungle and stopped again, swept the air, stepped right, and swept empty air once more. She became afraid that she had crossed the narrow road and now the possibility was that she could blunder into the jungle on that side. She swept the chair leg to her left and was relieved when it encountered nothing. She bit her lip when it occurred to her that she could have turned around, that she might be heading back toward the finca. Denying that, she rubbed her eyes, shook her head hard, moved again to her right, and swept the air again. She took another step to the right and felt the foliage.

It would take too long, she thought in despair. They would come in their black car, find her on the gravel road and throw her in the back again, return to the finca, and on to the waterfall. Even as the thought lodged in her mind, she rejected it. No! If she saw even a glimmer of light from behind, she would plunge into the jungle foliage, out of sight. They would not find her on this gravel driveway. She walked faster and suddenly she brushed against leaves, and jerked back with gasp.

You're doing okay, she told herself. Making progress. Don't try to run, slow and steady, but keep moving. Gravel underfoot, jungle on the right, straight ahead. Keep moving. She moved ahead.

She heard a new sound, the crunch of gravel, and she froze. Something was on the road in front of her, coming her way. She raised the chair leg and didn't move while her heart pounded alarmingly. Whatever was on the gravel road would surely hear that drumbeat. When the crunching sound didn't repeat for what seemed a long time, she felt the jungle on her right, the gravel underfoot, and she took a step, another. It, whatever it was, must have gone into the jungle, she hoped, prayed. She moved forward.

Suddenly someone sprang on her, grabbed her from behind, grabbed her arm holding the chair leg, and clamped a hand over her mouth. "Don't make a sound," he whispered against her ear.

She struggled to swing the chair leg, to twist away, to bring her leg up to kick, but he held her fast. "We're getting out of here," he whispered again. "Not a sound."

She felt relief swamp her and she would have fallen if not for his grasp of her arm, his body behind her, and his hand on her mouth pressing her hard against him.

"David!"

"Shh. Come on." He moved his hand and released her arm, then took her by the hand and hurried her along the gravel road without another word.

He was moving as if in daylight, not quite running but close to it, and it was hard for her to keep up.

"We're here," he said a few minutes later. She could see nothing, but he held her hand out to feel metal. He led her around it, opened what had to be a car door, and guided her inside. She sank into the seat.

In a second she heard the other door open and close and felt his presence in the car. He didn't start it immediately, and she wanted to cry out, to urge him to drive, get them away from here before anyone noticed she had escaped. She heard a groan from the backseat but didn't have a chance to ask anything. The sudden sound of the howler monkeys very close by made any question or answer impossible. David started the engine under the cover of the screams and howls and she realized he had turned on a tape recorder. The howls were repeated, more distantly, then repeated again.

Without turning on the headlights, he drove slowly ahead into impenetrable blackness, turned onto the paved road. After a short distance, he switched on the headlights, and in the dashboard lights she saw him remove night goggles. Another groan came from the backseat.

"Who's back there?" Barbara asked this time.

"Robert. In a few minutes I'll stop on the highway and use your stick to splinter his arm. It's broken."

"Philip, the boy who drove me, is back there at the finca," she said. "He's injured, too."

"He's dead," David said flatly. "His body is in the Jeep. Did you kill your guard?"

"No. I knew I'd have just one chance, and I didn't think that chair leg would do it. He's sleeping."

"Let's hope he stays asleep."

"David, how did you know? Who sent you? What's going on?"

"Not now," he said curtly. He was keeping an eye on the rearview mirror and driving too fast for the narrow road.

"Santos knows where Anaia is," Barbara said. "She has to be warned, if they haven't already gotten to her."

"I lied," Robert said in a weak voice.

When David made the turn onto the Western Highway, Robert groaned again. David drove faster, heading toward Belize City. There was inky black on both sides of the road, no other traffic, their headlights like a path opening before them. Barbara was aware that he was keeping an eye on the rearview mirror.

"I'll stop long enough for you to get over behind the wheel, and bring that stick with you. I'm going to get in back with Robert to attend to that arm. When I do, just keep driving until I tell you to stop again," David said. Shortly after that, he slowed, then stopped.

"Now," he said. "Make it fast." He stepped out of the car and pulled off a long-sleeved black shirt as she clambered over the seat to get behind the wheel. She saw the glint of a knife. He was cutting his shirt into strips. As soon as he was in the backseat and said, "Go," she engaged the gears and drove.

She passed the chair leg back to him when he told her to do so, and moments later Robert screamed, then fell silent. She clenched her jaw tighter and concentrated on following the pools of light on the road ahead. Not long after that David said, "Pull over, don't turn off the engine, just set the hand brake, and get back to the passenger seat."

It took less than a minute to make the switch, and David was driving.

"Is he . . . is he alive?"

"Passed out. That arm was agony every time it shifted."

"How badly hurt is he?" she asked in a low voice.

"Don't know. Broken arm, beaten, possible internal injuries."

She closed her eyes hard and her hand moved involuntarily to her cheek. *He* would have watched, would have enjoyed seeing Robert being beaten, his arm broken. . . . The car sped up even more and, when she looked again at David, he was holding the steering wheel with both hands, watching the road and alternately the rearview mirror. She twisted around and saw headlights in the distance. They raced forward. The other lights kept pace. The jungle became tunnel walls as he sped past, faster and faster. Behind them the lights did not vary.

Finally, a more distant pale glow indicated that they were approaching Belize City. She watched the headlights behind them brighten and dim again as David sped toward the city, toward safety. They came to the shantytown, the shacks all dark with few streetlamps in this area, few lights anywhere. The following lights were keeping the same distance as far as Barbara could tell, but as David slowed driving into the city, they became brighter again.

"Hold on," David said a few seconds later. He turned off the car lights and made a turn onto a side street, throwing her against the door in spite of his warning. From the backseat Robert groaned and made a deep sobbing sound. David drove two blocks, then stopped at the curb and turned off the engine. "If they turn this way, duck down," he said, twisting around to watch the street they had left. She watched, too.

Very soon the other car drove past the street. David waited another minute, then took a walkie-talkie from his pocket and made a connection.

"I've got them both. Robert needs a doctor. We have a follower." After listening, he said, "Right." He clicked the walkie-talkie off and put it back in his pocket, turned the key, and started to drive again, still without lights. There was city light, a few house lights or yard lights, enough. At each cross street, he stopped long enough to make sure no other car in sight was moving, then drove on, keeping to residential sections of the city, as far as Barbara could tell. Then, at a wider cross street, flanked by office buildings or government buildings, he flicked on the high beams, turned them off again, and waited until there was an answering signal of lights on and off. He pulled ahead and into a parking lot. Two men rushed to meet him as he stepped from the car. They held a brief conversation before one opened the back door. With two of them on one side of the car, David on the other, they maneuvered Robert out. He was limp, unconscious or simply too weak to walk. They carried him to a waiting van, put him inside, and two of them got in and drove away. David returned to take his place behind the wheel.

He sat with his forehead pressed against the steering wheel for a minute or two, then started the engine again.

"David, will you please tell me what's going on? Who are you? Who you're working for? Something, anything."

"Not now," he said, sounding very tired. "Help me watch for that prowling car. Keep in mind that if they spot us, they'll start shooting and just be done with it. They might have turned off their lights exactly the way I did."

He drove as before, relying on the sparse lighting of the city, approaching intersections cautiously.

"At least tell me where we're going," Barbara said, watching parked cars, watching cross streets on her side. She dreaded going back to her hotel, to where they might come looking for her.

"I'm taking you to the waterfront where you're going to get in a rowboat and be taken to where you'll be safe," he said, pausing at an intersection. "That's where we'll have to move fast. There are lights all over the place down there and people moving around, fishermen mostly, getting ready to sail at dawn."

A few minutes later she said, "Headlights coming."

David backed into a parking space at the curb and they both ducked down out of sight until a black sedan drew near on the cross street and passed, moving slowly.

"Good," David said when the other car was blocks away. "They're still using lights."

He crossed the intersection and soon after that the tourist hotels came in sight. He kept going, and didn't stop again until they had reached the waterfront street. At last he pulled over, not at the docks, where the launches and pleasure boats were at anchor, but much farther down, and, as he had said, there were lights in the area, lights on boats, men carrying boxes, calling out to one another, loading boats, other cars and trucks pulling in. Some boats were already slowly moving out to sea.

He scanned the boats, then turned the headlights on and off quickly. A flashlight flicked on and off.

"Final act," David said. Before he opened his car door, he took a careful look around, then said, "Let's go."

Holding her arm, he hurried her across the street and to a wharf where small boats were tied. Almost at the end a man was standing by a post. He nodded to David, stepped into a rowboat, and held out his hand to Barbara.

"David," she said, "thanks. Just thanks."

"Sure," he said. "Now get your ass in that boat and beat it." He grinned at her, but he looked exhausted.

She took the other man's hand and stepped into the rowboat, which tilted alarmingly.

"Sit down," the man in the boat said. He took his place at the oarlock while David untied the boat. David gave it a push, and the boat glided away from the wharf.

Barbara watched David run across the street toward the car until he was lost to sight. She would never know more about him than she did at the moment, she suspected. Not whom he worked for or what his real mission was, or how he had learned that she and Robert were at the finca. He must have carried Robert to the car and left him there to return for her, and she was grateful for that much. That he had taken it for granted that she might have killed her guard suggested that he had left a dead man, possibly more than one, when he rescued Robert.

And now she was in a rowboat heading out to sea, away from other people, away from lights, with a man she had never seen before.

20

As the rowboat was rocked by the wakes of fishing boats heading out to sea, Barbara huddled on the wooden seat, holding on as tightly as she could with both hands. Soon the oarsman turned away from the seagoing crafts until the little boat was far enough from them not to be affected, and the swells of the ocean lifted and lowered it. She continued to hold on even though being swamped didn't seem quite as imminent. Now she prayed she would not get seasick. When most of the lights were well behind them, the man at the oars began to turn the boat parallel to shore.

Dark hulks of boats loomed to her left, eclipsing shore lights, revealing them again as the little boat rode the dark water. Finally the rower began to slow his steady rowing, and he was turning again. Where the shore lights had been to her left, more and more they were straight ahead. He pulled in at the side of one of the big boats where pale lights revealed a ladder. On deck someone was standing, waiting.

"Go on up," her oarsman said, holding the boat steady.

She climbed the ladder. A hand reached out to her and she stepped onto the yacht.

"Welcome aboard, Barbara," Gabe Newhouse said. "Let's get you out of the light. This way." He led her to a narrow door, down several steps, and through a passage to a galley. "That's better," he said. "Have a seat. What can I get you? A drink, wine, water?"

"You can start by telling me what the hell is going on," she said as she sat down in a booth and drew in a long breath. "And if that's coffee I smell, that's what I'd like more than anything."

"At this hour? It's after four. I've been drinking it to stay awake, but you must be ready to get some sleep."

"It won't keep me awake. I won't sleep until I have a few answers."

He laughed. "Coffee it is. Have you had anything to eat all day?"

"No."

"Ah, then an omelette is in order. I'm pretty good with omelettes."

"Gabe, spare me the good host routine. I've had a rotten day. I want to know what's going on."

"Will you tell me about your day?" he said, pouring coffee into a mug. He brought it and the carafe to the booth. "Sugar, cream?"

"No. I suggest an exchange of information. I tell you nothing unless you talk, too."

"Ah, quid pro quo. Finally the lawyer in you rears its head," he said. "Fair enough. Who starts?" He was taking things from a built-in refrigerator as he spoke.

"You do," she said. The coffee was heavenly. "How did David know where we were? Who sent him to get us? Who are you both working for or with? I'm in a game I don't know, don't know the rules, don't know who the other players are, or even how many teams there are."

He nodded. "Right. But one suggestion. Let's establish some ground rules. We limit it to this one day for the time being. There will be time to talk tomorrow, actually later today, but for now we speak only of the day just past. Agreed?"

"Agreed."

He came back to the booth and handed her an ice bag wrapped in a towel. "Keeps the swelling down a bit," he said. "Who did it? Santos?"

She nodded. The ice bag felt good on her cheek that was still hot and throbbing. He returned to the counter and began to break eggs into a bowl.

"Yesterday," he said, "around noon, Miles Ronstadt drove out to the finca to nurse his orchids, but he was turned back. Someone told him he couldn't tend them, an important meeting was taking place. It worried him. Some plants would wilt and drop the flowers if they weren't watered, or something like that. He turned around and drove to the little cluster of workers' houses down the road. He was friendly with some of the women there who went to the finca every afternoon to prepare the evening meal. He thought to have one of them water the orchids in his place." He began to grate cheese.

There was an alarming throb of engines and the yacht made a shuddering movement. "We're sailing? Where are you taking me now?"

"We're sailing. I've been saying for a week that I'm ready to take off, that any minute now we'll depart Belize. That minute just came."

"Where to?"

He turned to smile at her. "Cancún. But that's beyond our agreement."

Barbara finished her coffee and poured more.

"It seems," Gabe said, returning to the cheese grater, "that Robert and Anaia are both very popular among the people of the forest. Ronstadt's friend was concerned because the kitchen workers had also been told not to come today, and one of the field-workers told her husband that Santos had seized Robert and he was being held at the finca. They all know what's going on, of course, and they're afraid of Julius Santos and his hired guns. They didn't know what to do with the information they had. Since no one can trust anyone these days, they didn't dare go to the police. So she told Ronstadt. And he, poor man, was in the same quandary. Who to tell? What to do? I imagine his first inclination was to do nothing, put it out of mind. His informant said he should tell Papa Pat. See what I mean? They know things. They know Papa Pat and Robert are close, and they both are close to Anaia. Papa Pat would know what to do, was the implication."

He was watching his omelette now, and the aroma of food was overwhelming. Barbara suddenly felt faint with hunger and could hear her stomach complaining loudly.

"Well, Ronstadt told the woman he didn't know how to get in touch with Papa Pat. She told him the priest had registered births earlier and had mentioned to several different people that today was his day to exchange books in Belize City. Ronstadt might find him at the used bookstore if he hurried."

He added cheese to the omelette and carefully folded it.

"To make a long story short," he said, "that's what Ronstadt did." He turned to give Barbara an appraising look. "I think you put a little starch in his spine, Barbara. With your pep talk, your suggestion that he should write a book. Anyway, he drove back to Belize City and found Papa Pat coming out of a copy shop on the same street as the bookstore. And minutes later Papa Pat told me."

Barbara closed her eyes. Papa Pat was working with Gabe and David? One of them?

Gabe brought the omelette to the booth, went back for a plate with a thick piece of bread and a butter dish. He sat opposite her. "Eat," he said, "and I'll wrap up my part of the bargain.

"About an hour later," Gabe said, "Papa Pat called again to tell me that he had sent a courier to you with some important documents, and that you were not there to receive them. The courier waited a while, but of course you did not return. Papa Pat found that quite disturbing, as I did, since he said you were expecting the documents and you had agreed to wait for the delivery. It wasn't hard to find out that you had left with the boy, Philip. Nor was it hard to figure out where you had been taken. End of story."

She took another bite, then opened her purse to get her notebook. She handed it to him. "My side of the bargain," she said. "You can read it while I eat. The omelette is wonderful. Thank you."

Neither spoke again while she finished eating everything he had provided and finished drinking her coffee.

"A long day," Gabe said, handing back her notebook. "I wonder if they would have thought of that and taken it from you."

"I wondered the same thing," she said, and took out the Eliot volume. "It's in here, too. Santos had looked through it earlier, and I hoped no one would give it a glance again." She fanned open the pages to show him the many annotations.

He laughed softly. "Good thinking."

"How did David get sent out there?" she asked then.

"And why did you get in the Jeep with Philip?" he countered.

"He had taken me to meet Robert before and I thought he had been sent this time," she said without hesitation.

"David and I met on the terrace as we'd been doing almost every day, usually in the company of the broncos. But now and then we managed to talk alone. We worked out the plan. It had to wait until very late, very dark. He couldn't take on all the king's men by himself."

"He didn't have to," she said angrily. "How many resources do you actually have? The men who picked up Robert, the crew on this yacht, the man who rowed me out here, probably others, as well. You sat by and let that boy get killed, let Robert get tortured. Did it even matter to you and your allies?"

He regarded her soberly for a long moment, then nodded. "It mattered, but there are bigger issues involved. I think few here have any idea of what you call my resources, and it has to be that way for the time being. Robert would have suffered unimaginable agonies before he told them where to find Anaia, and he would have given them some false leads first, but eventually they probably would have broken him. It was imperative that he not reach that point, and it did not take an army of men to achieve that goal."

Barbara felt a deep chill with his words. If it had proved too inconvenient to attempt her rescue, she would have been left behind.

As if reading her mind, Gabe said, "And surprisingly, Barbara, all at once it had become equally imperative to get you out of there, although now I wonder how much help you really needed." In a much lighter tone, he asked, "Had you actually gone into the forest, made your getaway, before David came upon you?"

She nodded. "He jumped me in the dark and scared the hell out of me."

"Did you have a plan for if they came after you, looked for you on the road?"

"At the first glimmer of light I would have dived into the jungle."

"Ah. Barbara, I truly believe that you would have made your way into Belmopan." He stood and held out his hand to her. "It's five o'clock in the morning. In an hour the sun will be up and it's hard to fall asleep after that, but quite easy to stay asleep. Let's call it a day. You're out on your feet, even if you don't know it."

When she stood, she did know it. She reeled and held on to the tabletop for a moment. "More questions and answers tomorrow?" she asked.

"As much as possible," he said, leading her from the galley. "Your stateroom is down this passage."

Barbara stood at the open door to the deck and took in long breaths of air. It tasted good, smelled good, and felt good on her skin. As far as she could see there was nothing but ocean, deep blue and deeper blue. She was dressed in blue jeans, T-shirt, and sneakers, and she was clean and not sweating, even if her hair was still wet, but now it was wet from a long shower. Although the bottoms of her feet hurt, two toes had Band-Aids, and she had a swollen face, she felt good physically. And she was alive. She smiled wryly at how little surprised she had been to find her suitcase in her stateroom, her jacket on a hanger in a small closet. Nothing could surprise her any longer, she thought, savoring the ocean air. She took the next step onto the deck.

"Over here, Barbara," Gabe called from a table under an awning.

As she approached, he closed a book and rose, to hold out a chair for her. "Good day," he said. "Ten minutes ago I might have said good morning. Did you sleep well?"

"Very well," she said, sitting down. "Rocked to sleep, in fact."

He peered at her cheek. "I don't think it will bruise much at all. A little discoloration for a day or two at the most. Good. Now, for something to tide you over until lunch, which will be at or around one thirty. Our cook, Franklin, doesn't like deadlines or schedules. I humor him when I can. Coffee, juice, some pastries. Or would you prefer something more substantial?"

He poured coffee from a carafe and juice from a pitcher. She lifted a napkin from a basket that held several sweet rolls.

"This looks fine," she said, helping herself to a Danish. "Did you sleep at all?" The napkin, like the towels and washcloth in her bathroom, had the neat little iconic graphic of a house, such as a child might draw. A box with a triangle for a roof. Newhouse, his trademark that preceded all his films, much as the MGM lion did.

"I slept a bit before you arrived, in fact," he said, "and out like the proverbial light as soon as your door closed. I always sleep well when we're at sea. Some people don't and I pity them. They're the ones who tend to get seasick. You seem to be a natural for life on the water."

She shook her head. "I like to look out and see trees and mountains, little things like that. A river is nice, too." She waved her hand generally at the ocean. "Doesn't that get monotonous after a time?"

"I've been sailing for about five years now, and it hasn't yet. If and when it does I'll do something else, I expect." He was gazing out to sea as he said, "I had a rather serious heart attack six years ago and during my convalescence I realized it was time to get off the merry-go-round I was on, racing faster and faster day by day. I opted to go sailing, and it seems to have suited me. Maybe I should have been a sailor from the start, instead of a frivolous director."

She knew he was referring to what Ronstadt had said or implied, and that it amused him. "Frivolous" was not the word to apply to him quite obviously. She changed the subject. "You said we were going to Cancún. Why?"

"It seemed a good idea to get you out of the country, and that's where I was heading," he said with a smile. "I wonder what Santos thinks. Did you escape first and rescue Robert? Did he make a miraculous recovery and take you out with him? Did his friends of the forest come to his aid, and yours, of course? Did his own people spring both prisoners? Are they scouring the nearby forests searching for you?"

"Not that," Barbara said. "Someone was following us in black car. They know we left by car."

"That's too bad," he said ruefully. "I like to think of them all out beating the bushes, searching."

"When will we get to Cancún?" she asked.

"Sometime tonight. I'll ask Fitz for an estimated time of arrival if you like."

"How can I enter the country without a visa or something?"

"It's been taken care of, but let's not talk about that right now. Have you eaten all you want?"

"Yes. And I want to talk about it now. I can't stay in Cancún. I have to go back to Belize."

"You know you can't do that," he said.

"I have to. I have unfinished business there. I don't intend to go home empty-handed. I came to do something and I have to do it."

"I see," he said. His easy relaxed air had changed subtly as he watched her and listened. He stood and said, "We'll talk about it later. First, there's something I want to show you." There was a note of finality in his voice.

She rose and carefully put down her napkin. "Gabe, no more games. Okay? I understand that you're on your own mission, and I don't give a damn what it is or what's involved. I don't want to play spy with you. I fully understand that I'm as much a prisoner on this boat as I was locked in that room at the finca. But unless you have me locked up in a real prison, or throw me overboard, I tell you here and now that I won't remain in Cancún any longer than it takes to make arrangements to return to Belize. If you send me all the way home, I'll make the same arrangements there. I have my own job to do and I fully intend to do it. I have to go back to Belize."

21

Come with me, Barbara," Gabe said. "Around this way." He led her along the deck to another door and inside to a spacious lounge with two pale green sofas, rattan chairs with colorful flowered print cushions, a large television, and a rolled screen. Tables and lamps were by all the chairs and sofas. If there hadn't been a constant rhythmic undulation of the boat itself, the room could have been in any well-furnished home.

Gabe walked through the room to the far side and indicated an L-shaped desk with a computer and printer set up on one extension. On the desk was a large bulging white envelope.

"That's for you," Gabe said, pointing to the envelope. "You'll find paper, notebooks, pens, the usual assortment of office supplies in various drawers. Feel free to help yourself to whatever you require. The computer is also at your disposal. As I said, lunch will be at around one thirty, but I'd guess closer to two. I'll be on deck if you want anything." He turned, then paused to add, "I asked Franklin to make certain there was coffee for you, and I see he did so. On the sideboard there. See you later, Barbara."

She sat at the desk without opening the envelope until he was gone, then slowly she undid the clasp and emptied the contents on the desk. Photocopies. Anaia's promised papers, photographs, copies of what appeared to be everything they had talked about and possibly more than that.

Barbara drew in her breath sharply as she moved the papers to uncover those still hidden and revealed a photograph of Anaia and another girl, her sister, Binnie's mother, or possibly her aunt. She gazed at it a long time. So similar, and so like Binnie, both of them. They were beautiful, laughing or close to laughter, with big dark eyes full of sparkle, dark blond hair that fell in waves to their shoulders where it was curlier. On the back on the photograph they had signed their names and the date, 1959. A note beneath the names read: ON SHALA'S FIRST DAY OUT OF THE SISTERS OF MERCY SCHOOL.

Barbara touched Shala's face gently, unable to stop the surge of mixed sadness and rage at what that lovely girl had suffered before death freed her. She put that photograph aside and picked up the next one.

It was of Lavinia Santos, their mother, when she had been about the same age as Anaia and Shala in their picture, and, as Anaia had said, Binnie resembled her grandmother even more than her mother and her aunt.

Barbara spread out everything and began to sort through it. The birth certificate appeared to be perfect, she thought after a rapid scan. Quickly she looked through the rest of the documents: Anaia's marriage certificate, her signature and that of Lawrence Thurston. His passport number. Augustus Santos's will. Anaia's account of the destructive hurricane, the cholera epidemic, why she sent her child away with Shala, only to receive news that they both had died at sea with the attack of pirates. Then, years later, the joyful discovery of her daughter's survival.

Absently Barbara opened the top desk drawer looking for paper clips. She began to clip papers together. A copy of the handwritten will went with the marriage license. There was a newspaper article about Augustus Santos's murder that included some details about the estate he had left to his daughter, Anaia Santos Thurston: the Santos Shipping Company, a sugar mill in Belmopan, the finca acreage, hacienda, other holdings. She clipped his will to that. Good—one anecdotal, one the real will. Barbara had not thought of the newspaper article, and appreciated that Anaia had included it. It could be helpful.

When she had things a bit organized, she started to examine more closely the various documents. Soon she got up and crossed to the sideboard for coffee, then sipped it as she read Anaia's will. Anaia had stipulated that her attorney transfer immediately 10 percent ownership of the shipping company to Binnie, and then continue to process everything else in accordance with the discussions they'd had previously to establish a nonprofit corporation. . . .

Her personal items, including but not limited to her jewelry, she bequeathed to her daughter, Lavinia Santos Owens. She had remembered to add Barbara's address as a contact for Binnie.

The will would take another careful reading or two, but Barbara felt satisfied that it did what it had to do, establish Anaia's claim of Binnie as her daughter, and to ensure that Binnie was not seen as penniless. She next read Augustus Santos's will and found it had included all children Anaia had or might have in the future. She leaned back in her chair, thinking how to present the material, how to arrange it to make a compelling narrative, wondering just how much she would have to reveal. If her birthright was not questioned or disproved, Binnie would be next in line to inherit the estate in the event of Anaia's death, if she died intestate.

If both Anaia and Binnie died, then Julius, as the only surviving member of the family, would get it.

After a few minutes, she opened desk drawers until she found a legal-sized notebook, and she began to make notes, now and then going back to the documents, now and then staring at nothing, now and then walking back and forth in the lounge, writing again.

"Barbara, lunch is ready." Gabe's voice startled her. He was standing in the open doorway to the deck. "You can leave all that," he said. "It's perfectly safe where it is."

She glanced at her watch. It was fifteen minutes after two and she was hungry, although she had not thought of time or food since opening the big envelope. She stood, and walked around the desk.

"You've read it all, I assume," she said, joining him.

"Yes. As I've said, we'll talk today, at lunch, after, whatever you decide. And, Barbara, I don't consider you to be my prisoner, but rather my very honored guest. I hope you like blue crabs. That's on the menu, or so Franklin tells me."

They returned to the table under the awning. It had grown appreciably warmer, but a cooling and constant breeze had also increased, making the heat welcome rather than a problem.

"Why didn't you tell me you had that material last night, or even this morning?" she asked as she took the same chair she had used before.

"Last night was out of the question," he said. "You wouldn't have slept at all, I'm afraid. As for this morning, my inclination is to get to the important things first, and that meant food, revelations later. Sore?"

"No. Relieved. I was afraid Papa Pat had returned it to Anaia. It didn't occur to me that he would have given it to you." She became silent as a man approached with a tray.

"Barbara, this is Franklin, our man of all trades. And our cook. Franklin, meet our guest, Barbara Holloway."

He looked to be in his forties and was built like a wrestler was her first impression. Bulging biceps, thick neck, blond hair in a ponytail. And a smile like an angel, was her second thought as Franklin grinned at her and put down the tray. She held out her hand to shake with him and his grin became even wider.

"If you don't like crabs, just say the word. I'll make you whatever you do like," he said in a voice that sounded like a rumbling truck.

"I love crab," she said, and pulled back her hand that he was still holding.

Gabe was laughing quietly. "Knock it off, Franklin. If you propose to her, I'll heave you overboard."

Franklin held his hand in the air. "I'll never wash that hand again," he said, and proceeded to serve them small dishes of avocado halves filled with something.

Barbara tasted hers. "My God, what is it?" The avocado was hot, the filling creamy smooth and delicious.

"Heavy cream, Stilton cheese melted together, something else he won't reveal," Gabe said as Franklin walked away, whistling.

"It isn't fair," Barbara said. "Killer food is always irresistible."

They talked very little as they ate crabs and salad. After the table was cleared and coffee had been poured, Gabe said, "Barbara, will you answer a few questions for me?"

She nodded. "But first, let me speculate a little. This operation you're involved in started some years ago, long enough ago for you to establish yourself as a familiar figure in Belize, an idle American who has the means to come and go as he chooses, and long enough ago to get to know various people, and to make reliable contacts. David allowed the broncos to hire him long enough ago to make it clear he worked for them. You, your people, have known about the Santos marijuana for a number of years, and possibly helped to ensure that those fields were never sprayed. To all appearances there are a significant number of people involved in the whole operation, enough that if you, your people, had wanted to take down Julius Santos you could have done it one way or another. You didn't want to do that even though it put Anaia at risk with the possibility that Julius could gain control of the estate, which you also don't want to happen. Pure speculation, of course, but it seems quite obvious to me that you want Julius to lose, but in such a way that he becomes useful to you. He is bait for something bigger."

She had kept her gaze out on the ocean as she talked. Now she looked at Gabe, who was watching her intently. "One more thing," she said. "You have kept this operation so secretive and well coordinated that Santos doesn't have a clue that it's ongoing. However, by rescuing Robert and me, there is also the possibility that he now suspects something is in the air, and he may change whatever his strategy was and do something totally unexpected."

"Barbara, you are one scary woman," Gabe said softly when she lifted her coffee cup and fell silent. "You would be a most formidable opponent in court, one I would not like to go up against." He poured more coffee for himself. "All the above is close enough," he said. "If there were a little more time for Santos to react, your last point would be a main concern, but there isn't. Yes, he's bait, and we believe he'll cooperate with us, starting quite soon. At midnight tonight, Anaia will become mistress of the Santos estate, and tomorrow he will be notified by the court of that, and he will be ordered off the property. And we think that at that time, he will become a marked man. Not by us, but by a much more dangerous enemy. Our operation has been going on for a number of years, as you surmised, but so has another one. And that one is by a very big drug cartel who saw the perfect setup in the Santos estate. Fields adjacent to a river, in a small country butting up against both Mexico and Guatemala, and very, very close to Colombia. And one with a hundred or more inlets, coves, waterways to hide fairly large ships, as pirates discovered and used centuries ago. Moreover, with an estate that includes a legitimate shipping business already well established and apparently with a political fix in place. Santos was to seize that estate and it would have become a major shipping center for cocaine and marijuana. Although he's just a pawn in the game, he knows the principals, and where and how to find them. He knows names. He believes he's one of the big shots, but he isn't. When he fails to gain possession of the estate, he will no longer be useful, and he will be quite dangerous for them."

"What if he simply runs and hides?"

"He knows he can't hide from them," Gabe said flatly. "We will be his only chance to stay alive."

"There's major corruption in Belize, of course," Barbara said, "but it has to extend to other countries as well." She was thinking of Nicholson, who had Drug Enforcement Agency identification.

"Several other countries," Gabe said.

"Of course. The question isn't whether there's corruption in . . . other countries, but rather how high up it goes."

Gabe had been speaking softly, and his voice was even lower when he said, "Leave it alone, Barbara."

"To make things clear," she said, "I have a client, and my only concern is for her welfare, her particular problem."

He nodded. "You have the broad outline, the details are irrelevant for now. It's your turn to tell me things I don't know. For instance, how did you get involved? We thought things were going more or less as expected, and out of the blue here came a wild card, in the form of a lovely young attorney from that mysterious state of Oregon, a wild card that no one could account for."

Barbara smiled. "I like 'that mysterious state of Oregon.' I stumbled into it." She told him about Martin and Binnie, and Shala's enslavement without mentioning the letter Shala had left in the sealed tube. "There were too many things that didn't make sense," she said. "Why hadn't that pirate Domonic Guteriez pressed his kidnap charge against Martin? Apparently he simply let it drop and that's hard to believe. A rich, well-known sports figure such as Martin Owens would be an irresistible target for a large settlement. I think now he must have been silenced by people he was afraid of. I thought for a time that those responsible for his silence were people who did not want the risk of an investigation if the name Santos came up in connection with the country of Belize. After talking with Anaia I wonder if that's right. It could have been Augustus himself that silenced Guteriez. Shala had made her bed and she and the child had to lie in it as punishment, so he made no attempt to save them. On the other hand, when Binnie escaped, he did not try to harm her and he could have done so. He let her go to her own fate, whatever it was to be. A month ago Augustus was killed, and soon afterward Binnie was singled out for deportation. It would not have been hard to find Martin Owens. I think when Julius seized the finca, he must have found something that told him for the first time that a child, a direct heir, was alive and he immediately took steps to eliminate her. None of that was apparent at the beginning."

She paused, waiting for a comment from Gabe. When he remained silent she continued. "Then, hours after Martin and Binnie's first visit, another caller came. He showed me ID from the DEA and said his name was Nicholson." After describing that visit, she added, "If it hadn't made sense in the beginning, it was making even less as I thought about it. How had he known about them, their visit, and so on? I brought in a detective, who found a listening device in the restaurant, and I knew something bigger than a simple deportation was in the works. I put Mr. and Mrs. Owens in a place that would be safe for them until I knew more. Nicholson returned to learn where they were or how to reach them. My own investigation revealed the date of the piracy and I went on from there. No response from Augustus Santos when I tried to call, and Binnie didn't know Lawrence Thurston's name. I couldn't call Anaia. I came instead, and you gave me her name on the day we met."

Gabe laughed. "I tossed out several possibilities. The broncos. One of the rich daddies might have sent you to keep tabs on them, rein them in if necessary. The local official with too many women.

One of that bunch could have brought in a savvy attorney. Or the Shakespearean drama. You played it cool. As far as I could tell you didn't bite on any of my hooks. But you went to the finca, which made me wonder if you were part of the Santos plan. Then you gave the broncos some good advice, and I had to think maybe that was it, that you were a designated babysitter. But David said you saw something at the Santos finca that startled you, spooked you. You see, every time we thought we had you placed on the board, you moved somewhere else. And you even vanished for one whole day, Saturday. What spooked you at the finca?"

"I saw Nicholson, the man who said he was from the DEA."

"At the finca?" His eyes narrowed and he leaned forward almost imperceptibly, but she had seen that reaction in court when a witness was confounded by an unexpected bit of evidence. Nicholson must represent a second wild card, she thought.

"Yes, I saw him, and he saw me. That's why Santos had me grabbed and taken out there." She paused a moment thinking, then said, "More, Gabe. When Nicholson came to my house a second time, he was driving a car that belongs to a man named Emerson, who is a partner in a shop in Eugene. Marcos Import. Marcos is suspected of being a drug supplier, or so I've been told."

Gabe regarded her for a long moment, then rose and walked to the rail of the deck, where he stood with his back to her. She helped herself to more coffee.

When Gabe returned to take his seat again, he asked, "You think Nicholson was the one who tipped off the immigration people?" At her nod, he said, "How did he learn about her is the question, isn't it? After so many years, how did they know about her?"

"Early on, that pirate, Domonic Guteriez, made Shala write to her father, pleading for ransom money. Someone went to Haiti, but he denounced Shala as an imposter and left." Barbara hesitated, then said, "Anaia thinks Shala saved Binnie by claiming her as her own child, threatening suicide if the child was harmed or killed. I don't know why Shala didn't speak up when the emissary arrived, and Binnie knows only as much as Shala told her. She escaped believing Shala was her mother, and she still thinks that. I went to Belize believing that. But, as I said previously, Santos knew his daughter was being held captive in Haiti, and if he thought she'd had an illegitimate child, Anaia said he would have abandoned her to preserve his honor. I also don't know about that."

"The revision sounds most likely," Gabe said, then added, "This is a puzzle with many missing pieces, Barbara. It may never make a complete picture."

"Incomplete for both of us," she said. They both became silent for an extended time until Barbara said in low voice, "Gabe, one of the unexpected things that Santos might try is to redouble his efforts to find Anaia in the coming days, before she has a chance to deliver her will to her attorney. He could stake out her attorney's office, his home, approaches to Belize City, who knows what else, and have Anaia shot on sight by one of his men. If her handwritten will is destroyed, he'll inherit everything, according to Anaia's account of her father's will, which would again become relevant."

"But you have a copy of Anaia's will," he said.

"It's not a legal document. The original could have been amended many times after a copy was made."

"And Binnie Owens? Wouldn't the parent-child relationship determine who inherits?"

"It would be contested, and Binnie's name appears nowhere in any official document signed by Augustus Santos. If Anaia is dead, no longer there to defend and verify her identification of Binnie as her lost daughter, that would come under dispute. Besides," she said slowly, "Binnie is as much at risk as Anaia is. Even without Anaia's will, once her identity is established, she is next in line to inherit under Augustus Santos's will. Anaia's will, the birth certificate, and marriage license will go a long way to make verification justifiable, of course, but they don't have the same force as a mother's testimony. But if both Anaia and Binnie are dead, the whole matter is moot. No lengthy court battles. Julius would simply be declared the heir."

"I was thinking that the daughter might provide some insurance for Anaia," Gabe said after a moment. "No point in killing the mother since her child would then come forward to claim the estate. Barbara, you've brought us a new can of worms, I'm afraid. And we never even heard of Binnie Owens before. Or you, either." He stood. "I have a few things to attend to. Please feel free to explore the boat, walk about, look inside wherever you'd like. Some doors will be locked, but for the most part it isn't."

"One last thing," Barbara said, rising. "You said we're going to Cancún. What am I to do there? I have to get home as quickly as possible. I don't know if I was granted an extension of time for Binnie's appearance, or if she is now considered to be a fugitive. And I have to make certain that she is safe, and remains safe."

"Cancún," he said. "Ah, yes. We'll arrive late tonight, and you will be driven to an airplane that eventually will fly to New Orleans. A reservation at the airport Hilton is in your name, and there will be a message for you, an envelope containing a ticket for your flight to Portland, Oregon, on Wednesday. You should be back in your state tomorrow night."

"Thank you," she said.

He regarded her soberly, then said, "You realize, of course, that not only is your client at grave risk, but so are you. Santos probably doesn't know what all you accomplished here, but he won't want your identification of the man you call Nicholson to interfere with other plans."

"I know," she said. "Anaia plans to tell him about Binnie as soon as she is legally heir to the estate. He'll know then what I have."

"Shit!" Gabe said. "I'll try to get a message to her to hold off on that for a time, at least until he's turned."

Barbara suspected that he doubted his ability to get a message to Anaia speedily, especially now that Robert had been injured and was no longer available, and Papa Pat was probably in that remote jungle village once more. How many others would be likely to know where to find Anaia? She suspected the answer was none.

She also suspected that Julius Santos would not be "turned" as long as he thought he had the slightest chance of getting Anaia and Binnie out of the picture before his drug lords took their own measures against him.

22

Fluffy mountainous clouds ringed the boat where sea met sky, while overhead, it looked as if she could see forever. As the yacht cut through the water, the cloud ring kept pace, kept the same distance, all of a piece. She paused her walking at the prow of the boat, pretending . . . pretending what? Explorer? First one to glimpse an undiscovered shore? Pirate searching for prey? Masthead, forever looking forward? Voyager eager to return home? Pretending she knew what faced her at home, what she had to do? Nothing, she told herself sharply. Pretending nothing. She continued to walk.

The ocean was too big, too incomprehensible, untamable. She couldn't put it in human terms that made sense to her. It seemed that one direction was as good as any other, since all directions were the same. It would be easy to sail endlessly in a great circle.

She frowned as it occurred to her that it was only her own thoughts that circled endlessly, a loop that had no exit, no entrance, only the loop. "In the end is my beginning," she thought. Exactly so. She had joined the loop the day Binnie and Martin appeared on her doorstep and she had taken their problem as her own because she had seen Binnie's hand reach for his as if reflexively. Because they were so very much in love, and she had lost her lover.

Since she had said yes to them, she had been like chaff on the wind, blown here, there, onward irresistibly, and she was still being taken here, there, onward, not by her choice, but the choice of others, nameless, faceless others. Another pawn in a game she had not chosen to play, a deadly game into which she had been drawn by an irrational act of her own, taking on a case for which she had not been qualified.

She walked the length of the boat again, rounded the corner, and saw Gabe descending the steps from the upper deck.

"Barbara, come sit down," he said. "You've been walking for over an hour. You'll exhaust yourself." He indicated the upper deck. "It's a pleasant place to sit and watch a spectacular sunset while sipping a glass of wine."

She nodded. Her bruised feet hurt, she was tired, and no amount of thinking seemed to lead anywhere. She didn't know what awaited her in Eugene, what the next play must be, or who the players would be.

Gabe stepped aside to allow her to precede him up the stairs, where he or someone had placed lounge chairs with thick cushions on the west side of the boat. A table between the chairs held a tray with wine in a bucket, a bottle of red wine, glasses, and a plate of snacks. It was like being in the Beast's castle with invisible hands tending to the needs of those inside. She had no idea how many crew members there were, or where they kept themselves. The only one she had seen had been Franklin. But it was good to sit down, she admitted as she lowered herself into one of the chairs, which proved to be as comfortable as a mother's lap.

"My inertia button jams," she said. "There are times when whatever I'm doing, I tend to keep doing until someone says stop."

Gabe nodded as if in understanding. "This is a dry Lambec

from Chile," he said, holding up the red wine. "Or do you prefer the white we had at lunch?"

"The red, please." He poured and handed a glass to her, and she found it as fantastic as she had expected it to be. "Wonderful," she murmured. "Just what I needed."

"I like it," he said. "Now this," he said, pointing to the plate, "is ham from Holland. You know that ham? Big slices, as big as dinner plates, almost as thin as paper, and delicious. Franklin likes to roll various things in it and cut it into bite-sized pieces. I think the pink toothpicks indicate a sharp cheese, yellow a mild Edam, and only God and Franklin know what the miscellaneous ones are."

"You seem to have a way with waiters," she commented, and took a pink toothpick-secured piece.

"I guess," he said. "Working people, like me. I had my first job when I was fourteen, paperboy. Up at four thirty, picked up my bundle of newspapers, rolled them, biked my route, tossing them on people's porches, quick breakfast, and on to school by eight thirty. I think I've worked ever since, until my heart attack."

"You quit cold turkey, but you then went back to work. Couldn't you stand the life of ease?"

He was silent long enough for her to assume that she had stepped into his do-not-enter zone. She picked up one of the miscellaneous ham tidbits and found it to be filled with a sharp, savory mushroom filling.

"I imagine you're had to deal with some addicts as a defense attorney," Gabe said at length.

"I have."

"My Bettina was a beautiful young woman when we met," he said. "Not a novelty in Hollywood, of course. Beauty is the standard, but Bettina was different. She could also act. One of the best in the business. I was an addict, addicted to work, and she discovered heroin and became an addict. Our fifth picture, *Roller Coaster,* was a nightmare from start to finish. It was our last together. Her last, period. When I began casting *Tripoli* I used Sandi O'Brian, and Bettina said I did it on purpose, to cheat her of the Oscar she had coming. Two nominations under her belt, she was due an Oscar, and that picture might have given it to her, but she was an addict. It isn't pretty watching that happen, that slide into the abyss by someone you've loved. La dolce vita, for a while, then Dante's *Inferno*."

When he paused, Barbara said, "That movie won you an Oscar for director, didn't it?"

"Yes. It made matters worse somehow. I'll never know if I could have helped her if I had tried harder."

"You couldn't," Barbara said. "No one outside can help. It has to come from the inside."

"Funny thing is, I know that intellectually, but I'll never really know it. Anyway, there was the blowup and divorce, and a few months later, heart attack. I went to a place up in Big Sur to recuperate, took a bunch of scripts with me and thought I'd get a lot of reading done but, instead, I sat and looked at the ocean, forever rolling in and out. And I knew I was done, finished, tired of it all. I wanted a boat. I told my attorney to sell everything, told my manager to start notifying people to look for other work—gardeners, house staff, secretary, personal assistant. My God, I was keeping a dozen people employed full-time!"

He gave her an appraising look and said, "I guess you don't follow celebrity news, read the tabloids, keep up with the antics of the rich and famous."

"Good guess," she said.

"Right. So there were rumors. Bettina had broken my heart. I had incurable cancer or something like that. I'd had a disabling stroke and couldn't cut it anymore. I was shacked up with a new sweetie half my age. Actually, I went shopping for a boat as soon as I could move without doubling over because it hurt." He laughed. "And I found one, this one. *My Bettina*. One of the best days of my life, having a crew who could run her and teach me how. We took her out on her maiden voyage, and afterward we fixed a few things, made a few changes, and went out again. It was grand, exhilarating, liberating. Then, back onshore I had a visitor. David came calling."

He stopped there, and Barbara thought he was finished. He poured wine for both of them, ate a little ham roll, and sipped his wine before he spoke again. "I'd known David, correction, I had thought I knew him. He'd done some still work for me three or four years earlier and we had a number of good conversations. He can be misleading because he's fairly quiet, but there's a lot to him that doesn't meet the eye, as I was about to find out. I invited him to a cruise, and he went out with us the next week." He laughed a low rumble of amusement. "I should say rather that he permitted me to invite him for a cruise. We were sitting here, where we are now, when I began to really know him. I had a seagoing yacht, I was unattached, I was of a political persuasion that was acceptable, and so on. Did I want to help a good cause? Not quite that raw, but that was the gist of our conversation that night sitting here. It took more than one conversation, of course, but in the end, I said yes. And here I am, with a new crew, some new equipment on board, and now and then a new assignment."

He finished the wine in his glass in one long drink and refilled it. He said with an intensity she had not heard before, "Barbara, if there is any way on earth that I can help smash a drug cartel, I'm in all the way. I'm being used, of course, and I completely accept that. Aren't we all to some extent? I know if there's a vacuum created in the drug business, there will be others to step in to fill it, but meanwhile I'll do what I can with the ones at hand."

He had found purpose for his life, Barbara thought when he became silent. He had a need to avenge the loss of his loved one, a need to assuage the guilt he suffered for not saving her. That mission, others like it, would never free him from those dual needs that would spur him relentlessly onward, forever on his own loop without an exit.

While Gabe was talking, the sun had slid behind the clouds in the west, turning them into ghostly white glowing mountains in the sky. Abruptly an eruption of brilliant scarlet flared, followed by green and gold bands that shot sideways, and the sky mountains came alive with dazzling colors. Barbara caught her breath as the eruption of brilliance ballooned and grew even brighter with new colors. Pink and coral, gold and green, aquamarine, violet . . .

Neither spoke until the clouds faded, leaving bands of dark blue and purple that gradually merged into darkness, and the sky overhead turned into a blue-black velvet studded with diamonds.

"Once a scientist started to talk about prismatic effects, refractions and such," Gabe said softly. "I excused myself and left him talking to the air. There are some things I really don't want to know."

"Good for you," Barbara said. "Thank you for bringing me up here, Gabe."

"You're welcome. I wanted you to see that." A pale boat light had come on with sunset and now was the only light. "I'm afraid we won't be able to tell one toothpick from another any longer," Gabe said. "Running lights, required at sea, or you might get rammed by something bigger than you are. We take our chances with the snacks." He picked up another tidbit, then said, "Good draw. I like the mushroom ones best. Barbara, do you think you could take a nap, rest a little? You're in for a long night, I'm afraid."

"I'm fine," she said. "And no, I couldn't nap now. I was thinking while I took my walk. Thinking about the man who called himself Nicholson, not likely his real name, but it will do. If what you say about Santos is right, it seems that he doesn't have the organization or the power to have people in the States working for him. Perhaps he thinks Nicholson is his man, but he isn't, is he?"

"As I said before, Barbara, you are a scary woman. No. Nicholson is most likely working for the same people Santos is primed to join, regardless of what they've let him think."

She sipped her wine. That meant that even if Gabe's outfit took Santos down, others might well remain in place, including Nicholson. Mentally she rounded another curve in the loop.

"One more thing," she said. "If Nicholson is their man, chances are good that Emerson and Marcos are also. They are the import shop partners. Their Eugene connection. Who needs the French connection?" she added bitterly.

"Barbara, you can tie Nicholson to Santos, and it appears that you also can tie him to a possible link in the chain, completing the triangle."

"Let me guess how good a position that puts me in," she said, and drained her glass.

Neither spoke again for a time until Gabe said, "Barbara, please excuse me for a few minutes. I won't be long." He rose from his chair.

"And I hadn't even mentioned light refraction," she murmured.

He laughed. "You're a rare woman, Barbara. You have no need to fill every moment of silence with mindless chatter. That's an admirable quality. Back soon." He walked away.

All right, she told herself, first order of business: Find out if the extension was granted, and if so until when. They could have ordered Binnie to report in on Wednesday, nine sharp, and she, Barbara, might be in New Orleans, or forty thousand feet up, flying north. Or somewhere else. Nothing she could do about that. Next order of business: Meet with Binnie and Martin and fill them in on events. Hey, Binnie, you have a new mother, and you're something of an heiress. Oh, incidentally, you're also on the hit list of a drug cartel.

First, second, third, ad infinitum, she told herself: Keep out of the gun sights of Nicholson, and any other goons who might also have guns.

Next: Make a plan to get Binnie to and from a meeting with immigration, in spite of what seemed to be true, that Nicholson was aware of what was going on in immigration. She was back to the place in the loop where she wondered if Santos had real information concerning Binnie's appearance, if it had been scheduled and Barbara had missed being there, throwing Binnie to the wolves. He had been wrong about knowing where Anaia was hiding, he could have been just as wrong about Binnie's scheduled appearance. But if that turned out to be true, it probably was over already.

If he had been lying, the date changed to one she and Binnie could make, there could be a hit man at the entrance to the federal building, ready to spray everyone in sight with lead, but especially Binnie and her attorney, and escape in the ensuing panic and confusion.

So, don't take Binnie to a meeting. Demand to represent her alone. She shook her head in derision. Reason with immigration officials when they believed they had netted one they considered to be an illegal immigrant? Deprive them of a deportation that would be high-profile, involving a rich and powerful man? She was aware of the fact that if an immigrant failed to show up for a hearing, they would instantly declare her a fugitive. In that event, they were likely to seize her and ship her, incommunicado, to an unknown holding facility to wait for a flight. Then, in due time, let an attorney plead her case.

Overriding all other orders of business: Keep Martin from using the gun she was certain he possessed.

She closed her eyes and tried to find a different starting place, or a different set of priorities altogether.

Sokolosky, she thought then, apparently in charge of immigration statewide, superior to the Eugene official Dennis Linfield, and either of them might have been given the tip by Nicholson. Or someone further down the chain of command, she added tiredly. Or Sokolosky and Linfield might both be in on it. Two feathers, two caps. Unknown players, all of them. But, damn it, Nicholson had given the tip about Binnie to someone in immigration, that much alone she felt certain about. And it was the only thing she felt she knew.

She sat up straighter and poured herself more wine, sick and tired of treading the same water over and over and over. Getting nowhere. And she was getting chilled.

She took a sip of wine, then put the glass on the table. She no longer wanted wine. She wanted a cup of hot coffee and she wanted to walk and think. Wearily she shook her head. No more walking in circles on a goddamn boat.

She had risen and was starting back to the stairs to the lower deck when Gabe returned. "I was getting cold," she said. "Time to go inside, or get a sweater."

"Good. I was going to suggest the lounge. The air does cool off fast after dark."

"Is a cup of coffee possible?"

"Of course it is. In the lounge."

There was more light on the lower deck as they made their way to the lounge where she had pored over papers all afternoon. It was comfortably warm inside.

"Barbara, before you settle down, I have a request. May we have your notebook with the account of your miserable day?"

"Why?"

"While you're getting it, I'll tell Franklin we want coffee, and then I'll explain. Okay?"

She shrugged. "Sure. But not the Eliot."

"No. Just the notebook." He walked to her stateroom door with her, then left to speak to Franklin.

She had everything packed and ready to go, her sweater and

jacket on top of her suitcase, her purse on the bed. She retrieved the notebook and flipped through it to see if she had jotted down something or other toward the back. It was clean except for her crude map of the finca house and driveway, the start of the gravel road into the jungle, and her account of her kidnapping. She left both pages intact.

Then, in the lounge, seated in the rattan chairs, as they waited for coffee Gabe said, "Later, perhaps after dinner, you'd like to watch a movie. Something frothy and comic. Marx Brothers?"

"You really don't have to entertain me," she said.

"I know, but there it is. I can't seem to help myself. Good, here's the coffee."

Franklin entered with a tray and put it on the table by Gabe, looking and smiling broadly at Barbara as he did so. "Do you like lamb? A rack of lamb?"

"Very much," she said. "I've had so much seafood gills are starting to develop."

"Lamb it is," he said. "Or will be at about nine. You want it earlier, or later?"

Gabe said, "That's enough, Franklin. Beat it."

Franklin backed up to the door, grinning at Barbara all the way before he turned and left.

"He's mad about you," Gabe said drily.

"I rather suspect he's mad about all your female passengers."

"Only those he thinks worthy of his attention. Well, maybe most of my female guests under a certain age. Above that age he treats them all like his mother. But he makes a decent cup of coffee." He poured it and handed her a cup.

"Barbara," he said then, "I've said you're a scary woman, and you are. A wild card in our midst, and you are that, also. But more, you're a catalyst. Because of you some plans have been rearranged, changed a bit drastically, in fact. Tomorrow morning, Santos will be served notice to vacate the finca. That remains in place. But he will also be arrested and charged with kidnapping, assault, conspiracy to commit murder, and as an accessory to murder. The grounds will be searched for the body of Philip Carnero, and he will be found, I'm sure. Probably buried hastily not far from the hacienda. Santos will be held in custody while the kidnap charge is under investigation, and he will be told that you will be brought back to testify against him and against the man who killed Philip. You witnessed that murder, Barbara. That blow to the head was his only injury, according to David."

She shook her head violently. "You can't make me do that," she said.

"No, we know that. And we won't ask you to, but he won't know that. He will be shown a copy of your account, with your signature and date, and he won't be allowed to make any phone calls for at least twenty-four hours. He will be told that no bail for such serious charges will be permitted, and he will await trial in prison. He knows that prison for him would be a death sentence. He would be a sitting duck there. I think within twenty-four hours, he'll know it's over, and that's when we'll approach him."

She thought about it, then slowly nodded. Twenty-four hours, long enough for the others to learn enough to know he was no longer a player in their scheme? Long enough for them to order his death?

"We, of course, will offer a safe house, offer to fly him out under our protection, and continue to protect him." Gabe had not taken coffee for himself. Now he did. "I think I'll recommend a safe house in North Dakota, one without air-conditioning. Have you ever been to North Dakota, summer or winter?"

She shook her head. "Might I suggest that in his new identity he is a South American writer, who needs his own hundred years of solitude to write his opus. He would need a secretary, of course, one who is very big, blond, and blue-eyed, maybe a little overweight, from the Deep South. Alabama, Mississippi, someplace like that.

One who has not lost his accent. He should enjoy things like ⟍
country music, chicken-fried steak, french fries, quiz shows and
cartoons—" She stopped. Gabe was laughing, not his usual soft
laughter, but explosive deep laughter.

"You are also more diabolical than even I am," he said when he
subsided.

Barbara handed him her notebook.

"Now for the rest of it," Gabe said. "Our resources are not as
vast as you assumed earlier. This entire operation has been organized with the accent on secrecy. Not a hint can emerge until the
time is right, and that means it was limited in personnel as much
as possible. All available people are already deployed, here, there,
in various places. But what that means is that we don't have anyone
in Eugene, and we don't have anyone to send there at present. Until you arrived, no one even considered Eugene, your client, Mr.
Marcos, Nicholson, any of that whole new chapter of the ongoing
drama. I'm very much afraid, Barbara, that we will be counting
on your ingenuity and skill to keep you and your client safe for
the next week or so."

23

Throughout the excellent dinner Franklin flirted outrageously with Barbara whenever he was in the lounge, where he had set up a dining table for two. She assumed there was a real dining room, but no doubt the invisible crew was having dinner there. She asked no questions. Gabe talked charmingly about mishaps on various sets during filming, about Hollywood foibles, many things, but not about the situation at hand. After coffee had been poured, dinner remnants cleared, he asked if she would like a brandy.

"No, thanks," she said. "It's wasted on me, I'm afraid. Not a fan."

"The first flaw in you that I've discovered," he said. "I hereby remove your halo."

She laughed. "Gabe, you've said several times that it will be a long night. How about a few more details than that."

"Right. At eleven thirty or so, a motor launch will rendezvous with us. I'll hold a brief conversation with someone, and then you will be escorted ashore to a waiting car that will take you to an airplane. It's an army plane with few amenities, I'm afraid. I can't tell how long the plane will be on the ground waiting for other passengers, but it will take off and fly to New Orleans. There, another driver will escort you to your hotel, where your tickets will be waiting for the rest of your flight, or flights. You may or may not have time to rest in your room, also already reserved in your name. And from then on, you're just another passenger trying to get to your home base. Enough?"

She nodded. "So, if ever I'm asked which countries I've visited, I can say Belize, but don't ask me about the ruins or the waterfall or anything else. And my experience in Cancún will be a passing acquaintance. Okay."

"I've held a number of conversations with others today," Gabe said, swirling brandy in the snifter he held. "I was told to reveal nothing to you, and I explained that there was little danger of that, since you already had pieced it pretty much together yourself. I was also instructed to explain to you the necessity of maintaining silence about this operation. I doubt I have to do that, either. I mentioned that you have been very cooperative and helpful, even if they declared you a pain in the ass." He looked from his glass to her and said, "Thanks."

"Gabe, what choice have I had? You could have taken my notebook at any time, and unless I jumped overboard and swam to the nearest shore, I was a captive on your lovely yacht."

"There is that," he said ruefully. "Another time I would like nothing better than to invite you as my guest for a cruise to a destination of your choosing. I'm afraid, however, that our paths are not likely to cross again, and I want you to know, Barbara, that I think you are a remarkable woman. Your client is very fortunate that you came to her rescue." He stood. "And now, I insist on a movie or two. Buster Keaton, my favorite after a trying day."

She did not protest, although a movie was at the bottom of the list of items on her mind. Rising, she said, "Gabe, may I ask a favor?"

"Absolutely. What?"

"I imagine that there are times when you provision your boat in the States. Someday when you do that, would you mind buying some hot dogs for Papa Pat?"

He looked blank for a moment. "Hot dogs? Wieners?"

"Yes. Good-quality hot dogs, if there is such a thing. He misses them."

Gabe pulled a notebook from his pocket and jotted it down. "I wonder if he has relish, mustard, catsup, or even buns." He made another note. Closing the notebook, he said, "I lived in New York City for a number of years when I was young."

"Sauerkraut?" she asked.

"Good God, I forgot sauerkraut." He opened the notebook and added it. "Consider it done, Barbara. He will include you in his prayers, I have no doubt."

And she, she had already decided, would ship a box of northwest McIntosh apples to Papa Pat.

It was a little after eleven thirty when a motor launch pulled up to the yacht. Gabe and another man talked for a few minutes, and he gave the man a metal box and what looked like a diplomatic pouch. Franklin handed her suitcase and jacket to someone else still in the launch. Then Barbara was motioned forward.

"Take care, Barbara," Gabe said at the ladder. "Be very careful." He kissed her forehead and she descended the ladder.

From where they were the lights from Cancún looked distant and nebulous. No one spoke in the launch or in the car that awaited them. Not until she boarded an airplane did anyone speak to her, and then a sergeant asked if she would like to stretch out on the bench that was on one side of the plane. She didn't. Eight double seats were on the other side. It was a long wait on the plane before two more men boarded, one in camouflage, the other an army lieutenant who looked exhausted. The door was closed, the captain said to fasten seat belts, and they took off.

At seven in the morning, Barbara checked in at the hotel in New Orleans, picked up the envelope at the desk, and went to her room, where she sank down on the bed, more tired than she could remember ever being. She had not slept on the plane except in brief snatches, and she had been cold throughout the flight.

She took her tickets from the envelope and groaned. Her departure was for nine thirty, just enough time to call Bailey, have breakfast, then out again. She ordered breakfast, and immediately afterward made her call.

She left a message on his machine, her flight numbers, and time of arrival in Portland. She would drive to Eugene and be home by seven thirty. He was to call Frank's office, ask Patsy if her letter had arrived, go get it, and be at her house by eight. It was five in the morning in Eugene, she thought sourly. He would be snug in bed, sound asleep.

When she walked from the ramp into the Portland terminal, she was surprised and alarmed to see Bailey waiting for her. She hurried. "Bailey, what's wrong? Is Dad okay?"

"Your old man? Sure, far's I know. Who slugged you?"

She touched her cheek. "Later. Why are you here?"

"Let's get out of this mob first," he said, taking her carry-on. "You look like hell warmed over, by the way."

"Thanks. Let's get all the way out of here."

"Not a good idea. Rush-hour traffic, stop and stop and stop and maybe get to go. Let's have something to eat and wait it out. Better in here than in the car."

The restaurant he steered her to was almost as crowded as the rest of the terminal, and it was noisy. After they ordered, Bailey said, "You know what they say, you can't go home again. There's something to that. You've got a stakeout at your place. Martin's restaurant, and their house have them, too. Now, about that cheek."

It was too noisy to talk. Instead, she took the Eliot volume from her purse, opened it to the right place, and handed it to him. "Did you get a letter for me?"

"Jeez, Barbara, you want me to read poetry?" He reached into his pocket and brought out a crumpled envelope, gave it to her.

"Read the footnotes," she said crossly, opening the letter.

Their appointment was for Friday morning at nine. This was Wednesday night. Not enough time, she thought despairingly. One day! God, not enough time.

She watched Bailey read her account. When done, he snapped the book shut and said, "Jeez, you put your foot down on a hornet's nest and all you got was a slap across the jowls. Miracles do happen, after all. How'd you get out of the dungeon?"

"Walked," she said.

"You just got up and walked away. Right."

A couple at the table next to theirs left, the busboy cleared it rapidly, and another couple, this time with a toddler, was seated. The child began to yell as soon as he was placed in a high chair.

"Tell you all about it later," Barbara said. No real talk was possible. Their steaks were served, making Barbara wish she had ordered something she did not have to cut or deal with in any way except to lift food to her mouth.

When they were ready to leave, Bailey said, "You parked over in long term?"

She nodded.

"Give me the keys and I'll get your car. Have another cup of coffee or something. It'll take half an hour and I'll meet you at the United exit."

She found her keys and handed them to him. "Third row from the gate, left side."

"Okeydokey. And, Barbara, I'll drive us down, take you to a motel, not your place."

"What about your car? I'm perfectly capable of driving. Don't be an idiot."

"Alan and another guy can pick it up in the morning, or even later tonight. See, if you drive, sooner or later I'd have to scrape you off a tree. Worse, I'd have to try to explain to your old man, and he would hand me my head. Half an hour."

He left and she had to admit that she was grateful not to have to drive, not to have to do anything except sleep.

Not until they were on the interstate heading south, heading home, did she tell him the whole story. Frank had always said Bailey had to know it all in order to do his job, and she knew that telling him was like telling a rock. Classified secret be damned, she thought.

He did not interrupt her. When she finished, with her head resting against the side window, her eyelids so heavy she had to concentrate to keep them open, Bailey said, "Jeez, Barbara, you're messing with big-time trouble. You know that?"

"I suspected as much."

"Yeah. You think Binnie and Martin will buy it?"

"What choice do they have?"

"Right. So our local hotshot, Marcos, is part of it. Any idea what to do about him and the goons on stakeouts?"

"No idea about them or anything else. No ideas, period."

"Right. Let's think."

"You think," she said wearily. "Bailey, I've been kidnapped, threatened with death at dawn, assaulted, alone in a pitch-black jungle in the middle of the night, a jungle complete with jaguars, alligators, poisonous snakes and spiders, part of an insane car race on a highway where a guy was gunned down a few weeks ago, a prisoner on a luxury yacht, flown in a boxcar overnight, sleep-deprived two nights in a row, and my brain has shriveled up and died. Maybe permanently."

"Gotcha," he said. "You want pictures of the stakeout goons?"

Her answer was a groan as she closed her eyes.

"You ought to use a sleep mask and earplugs on airplanes, let's you get some shut-eye."

She wanted to kill him.

"We're here." She heard his voice as if from a cave, and tried to shrug off the hand on her arm shaking her.

"Come on, Barbara, wake up. You've got a bed just a few feet away."

She pulled herself away from the window, stiffer and sorer than she had been before. Blinking, she saw a motel entrance, and knew they had arrived.

"I'll go in with you, see you get to your room, then take off," Bailey said. "I won't let you fall asleep on the way, promise."

She didn't even bother to tell him to just shut up. They went inside, she registered, he took her key and found her room for her, put her suitcase inside.

"There's a restaurant next door," he said. "I'll be there waiting for Sleeping Beauty in the morning. See you."

As soon as the door closed, she began to pull off her clothes, and minutes later fell into the bed and a dream-laden sleep in which she was chased through a black jungle alternately by Santos with a machine gun and alligators with mouths big enough to swallow buses.

24

Barbara was happy to see her own car parked outside her room when she left it, and happier to see Bailey's outside the restaurant next door. Inside the restaurant she spotted Bailey reading a newspaper in a rear booth.

"Hi, ya," he said, putting the newspaper on the seat beside him. "I was down to the classifieds. Obits were next."

"Keep a book on hand at all times," she said, and helped herself to coffee. A waitress came to the booth and she ordered scrambled eggs and juice, then waited for the woman to leave. "Bailey, I haven't had thinking time yet, but there are a couple of things for now."

"Okay. Shoot."

"About the only thing going for us is the fact that no one here knows I'm aware of the bigger picture. I want to keep it that way. You said something about pictures of the stakeouts. Have any of them spotted you?"

"Barbara, come on. But they might have a clue since you walked away from their locked room, don't you think?"

"I don't know, but chances are they believe Robert's jungle pals got us both out."

He looked skeptical. "So, what about pictures?"

"They might come in handy sooner or later, but not at the risk of being spotted. Can do?"

"Already got two of them. Barbara, some really big-time effort is at work here. And real big-time bucks are at stake. At least six guys are working shifts keeping three places covered. Could be more, but I know of six. I'll get Alan to get more pics, and maybe another guy if we need him. Then what?"

"A couple of prints of the Binnie pictures." She opened the bulging envelope and brought out the picture of Anaia and Shala. "I'd want Binnie's image to be about that size." She passed the picture to Bailey, and he whistled softly.

"She could be their sister," he said, handing it back.

"I know. And she's even more like her grandmother." She returned the picture to the envelope. "I also want prints of the stake-outs. I don't know if I'll use them, but I'd like to have them on hand, just in case.

"If what I was told goes as planned, Santos was arrested yesterday, charged with some serious felonies, and he was to be held incommunicado for at least twenty-four hours, to give him time to repent his sins. That means his bosses won't know what's going on until later today, or maybe not for several days. And that means that whatever the plan was for Binnie and me probably won't be altered or dropped right away. We'll have to base everything on the assumption that those goons intend to shoot on sight. I doubt anything less than murder is on their minds at this point. Earlier you said you thought they were not locals. Do you think they're imports from Colombia, Mexico, somewhere like that?"

"Best guess," he said. "That's all, a guess. Could be L.A. imports, or from Texas or somewhere else."

She nodded. "My guess is Central America. Again working on assumptions, if they're immigrants, illegal aliens, or even homegrown with unlicensed weapons, they're at risk if they're fingered. I'm going to keep that in mind."

She became silent as the waitress approached with her breakfast. Another assumption, she thought, was that Anaia had survived, and would continue to survive for the next few days, until Santos was under control and his drug lords realized that the estate had moved beyond their reach.

As soon as they were alone again, she said, "I watched the weather report this morning. Rain moving in tonight, heavy rain tomorrow."

Bailey grunted. His usual gloomy expression became even gloomier. "Your fault," he said. "Not a drop of rain while you were gone, and now days of it in store."

She ignored that. "This morning I have some things to do, shop for a briefcase and stuff to put in it. And a hooded raincoat for Binnie. I'd bet she doesn't have one with her, and I want her hidden as much as possible tomorrow."

"Something else," Bailey said. "You shouldn't be tooling around in your own car today. There's heavy-duty stuff going on, and they might have been alerted to watch for your car. Eugene's not like L.A., where you could ride around on an elephant for a month before anyone noticed. Nicholson had plenty of time to get a take on your car at your place. I'll drive you to a rental agency when we're done here. Something dark, cheap, tourist-type car."

Slowly she nodded. She hadn't thought of that, but he was right. Heavy-duty stuff going on, money being spent, six or more guys sent in to do a job. God alone knew where Nicholson was or when or where he might pop up, or anything else about him. And she had some driving around to do.

"Okay," she said. "After I shop I'll go out to talk to Binnie and Martin. I hope to God I can think of a game plan for in the morning while I'm driving out there. Come over to the motel at about four." She began to eat her eggs.

"Okeydokey," Bailey said. "If you're not back yet, I'll wait in here." He was eyeing her toast.

She pushed it closer to him. "Help yourself to one. One," she repeated, and nudged the little jar of jelly his way.

Driving usually was a distant second to walking to turn on her thought processes, but it was not working that morning as she drove out to Turner's Point. She couldn't even stop at the small general store in Turner's Point and walk the rest of the way. Someone might recognize her and word would get back to Frank. She had not been willing to involve him at first for her own personal reasons. She had not wanted his rational argument to try to make her see how foolish it was to take on this case. Now she knew she didn't dare let him get involved in any way, put him at risk.

Stop that, she told herself. Stop veering off into irrelevancy like that. He was not involved and would not become involved. But she needed more time, that refrain kept intruding. "You don't have more time," she muttered. "Get on with it."

It hadn't helped to give herself orders. When she pulled into the driveway of the big house at Nell's property she still didn't know how she would manage the following morning. She parked, took out her briefcase and a shopping bag along with her purse, and went to ring the bell.

Martin met her at the door and took both of her hands. "Did you find anything for us?"

At his side Binnie's eyes were very wide with apprehension. She reached out and put her hand on Barbara's arm.

"I have a load of stuff," Barbara said. "Anyone else at home?"

Martin shook his head. "Tawna's teaching and has a meeting, and James is making house calls, or barn calls all day."

"Good. Let's sit at the dining-room table where I can spread out some stuff."

She shrugged off her jacket and they went to the dining room. Before she opened her new briefcase, she said, "First, I want to tell you what's been going on in Belize. You need a little background to prepare you for the rest. I found Anaia Santos Thurston. That's the name of the man she married, Lawrence Thurston. Her father, Augustus Santos, was murdered a month ago, and his brother, Julius Santos, is the prime suspect. That's your grandfather and your great-uncle, Binnie." She sketched in the rest of it, without a mention of a drug cartel.

"Apparently Julius has nursed a grudge, resentment, even hatred for his brother all his life, and he saw a chance to grab the whole estate, but only if Anaia died before the thirty days ended. No one knew about you, Binnie, except him. And he was the one who tried to get you deported and out of the way, because you would otherwise be in line to inherit it all."

Binnie was holding Martin's hand with a white-knuckled grip but she made no sign, and Martin did not say a word. Barbara was aware that his gaze had lingered on the bruise on her face, although it was fading and no longer so obvious.

She brought out the pictures of Anaia, Shala, and their mother, Lavinia. Spreading them on the table in front of Binnie and Martin, she said, "It can't be denied that Binnie belongs in that family."

Binnie caught her breath, released Martin's hand, and picked up the picture of Anaia and Shala reverently. Tears filled her eyes, and she turned to Martin and signed.

"That's how she remembers her mother," he said huskily.

He picked up the other picture. "Binnie's grandmother," he said in a low voice. "Lavinia, Binnie's name. She's almost exactly like Binnie."

Barbara nodded. "When I was taken out to talk to Anaia, she told me a story that took me by surprise. I won't try to paraphrase it, but let you read her own words for yourselves." She found

Anaia's statement about the birth of her daughter and sending her away from Belize with Shala. She handed it to Binnie.

She and Martin read it together. Binnie began to shake her head violently and her hands flew as she signed to Martin.

"She doesn't believe it," he said. Binnie continued to sign until he put his hand on hers. "Shh," he said. "Let me. She knows Shala was her mother. What about the letter she left her? The one rolled up in that sealed tube for years? Why would she lie about it? She never lied."

Barbara held up her hands. "I know this is a shock, but let me tell you what Anaia said to me. She and her father were estranged after she married Lawrence Thurston. She believed he had completely disowned her and they hadn't spoken since the wedding, not until they were notified that Shala had died at sea. At a memorial service he told Anaia that he was glad Shala had died because she had brought dishonor to him. For the next eighteen years they did not speak to each other, and he never learned about her child. She believes Shala lied to Domonic to save you, Binnie. A mother will do anything, including commit suicide to save her child, and she thinks Shala saw it as the only way to protect you, to lie to him and say you were her daughter. If he harmed you she would kill herself. Why she didn't tell the emissary when he arrived, no one knows, unless she was afraid Domonic would have exacted a terrible revenge. Remember, no one knew Anaia had a daughter. Would the emissary have believed it if Shala had told him? Anaia doesn't think so. And, Anaia said, if the emissary had reported back to Augustus Santos that his younger daughter, Shala, had an illegitimate child, he would have abandoned her to preserve his honor. She thinks he knew you existed and he believed you were Shala's child, and we know that Julius Santos must have found out about you."

Binnie was watching her as if hypnotized. Gently Barbara said, "It's a dark and filthy story of the misplaced pride of one arrogant man and the filthy overwhelming greed of another. And neither one has anything to do with you or with Anaia."

Binnie was shaking her head again. Her hand had found Martin's once more.

Barbara brought out the birth certificate next and handed it to Binnie. "That's what immigration demanded, and I can produce it for them. I also have Anaia's marriage license, and the number on Lawrence Thurston's passport. Your mother and your father, Binnie." She put the marriage license on the table.

Barbara tapped the birth certificate. "Binnie, listen to me. That document means no one can deport you to anywhere. Period. It means that you are a citizen of the United States of America."

She watched a range of emotions sweep over Binnie's face: more shock, bewilderment, disbelief redoubled . . . Martin's hand must have tightened on hers, and she winced and turned to him, but his gaze was locked on Barbara, his jaw was clenched so hard a ridge had formed that looked as solid as rock.

"Barbara, is that the law? Is that a fact?" he whispered, as if his voice had failed.

"It is the law. She has an American father and that confers citizenship on her."

Abruptly Martin rose. "I'm going to make some coffee," he said. "Binnie, want to come with me?"

She jumped up and they walked out together. Barbara leaned back and closed her eyes. They needed private time, time for one of their silent discussions. Time to comprehend what she had just told them.

She had told Binnie that the woman she knew in her soul was her mother was instead her mother's sister. Binnie would never believe it, could not believe it. But could she accept having others believe it? Would she see it as renouncing her own mother, denying her? How heavy a burden of guilt was she, Barbara, laying on that young woman?

She was quite suddenly plunged into her own guilt-ridden past. When her mother died of cancer, she had denied, rejected her death, had abandoned her father to his grief and had fled, unable to accept the guilt she had felt over doing nothing for her mother. She could have been, should have been with her more, been more of a comfort to her, more of a companion, more loving, more . . . just more, she thought wearily. And she had failed. It didn't help at all to know there had been nothing anyone could do, the cancer was master, not to be defeated. She could have, should have tried.

When she opened her eyes, she brought out the other papers she had, the newspaper account of the piracy and the death of all those aboard the freighter, the account of the will Augustus Santos had left, and the handwritten will Anaia had included.

The minutes stretched out without a sound from anywhere else in the house. Barbara got up and went to the window to gaze at the back of the property, thinking of the peacefulness of the walnut grove, yearning to be out there under the trees, remembering Frank's words in his house over by the river. He had told her for the first time about his sleepless nights after that death that changed them both for all time. He had come out to the river, he had said that night, and the susurrous whisper of wind in the fir trees had done what sleeping pills had failed to do. He had been able to sleep again. He, like her, had been able to find peace under the trees.

She was still at the window when she heard them coming back, Martin carrying a tray with the coffee and cups.

"There's a little more," she said, returning to the table. "A few more things for you to read, if you will." She motioned toward the copies and accepted coffee gratefully when Martin handed her a filled cup.

When they looked at her again after reading everything, Martin said in a wondering voice, "She's an American citizen and an heiress?"

"Well, she'll get something now. You should understand that when the shipping business stops dealing in marijuana, profits probably will plummet. So there may be little return there in the near future, but eventually, yes, Binnie will be an heiress. But not soon. Anaia is a very strong, very vibrant woman who, I suspect, will live many, many years. Let me tell you more about her and what she's been doing all these years."

She had to make Binnie accept it now, here, not have that look of confusion and denial in the morning at the immigration office. She told them about Anaia's years teaching in remote jungle villages, her plans for the estate with schools for adults and for children, the foundation she planned to establish, the multitude of friends she had and the love and protection they had given her.

When she paused, Martin said, "Barbara, there's more, isn't there? Something you've not told us yet."

She passed her cup across the table for a refill. "There's a little more. Until it's established that Binnie is Anaia's daughter, in the event of Anaia's death Julius will still get the whole estate. Remember, no one knows about Binnie, and he might fight having her recognized."

"How can you prevent that?" Martin demanded. "He's there, apparently with enough money to send someone here to try to get Binnie deported and to plant a bug in the restaurant."

"I gave the authorities a written statement accusing him of kidnapping me, assault, conspiracy to have me killed," she said slowly. "He will be investigated, arrested, and sentenced to a long time in jail." Binnie's hand had flown to her mouth as Barbara said this and the look of terror had returned to her face.

Martin's gaze had fixed on her cheek as she spoke and she nodded. "You obviously escaped," he said. "How?"

"Anaia's compatriot, Robert, and Anaia both have many friends there. They rescued me."

Martin's close scrutiny was still focused on her face and she shook her head slightly. Whatever he had been about to say went unspoken. Binnie turned to Martin with a questioning look. He took her hand. "So until all that happens," he said, "we will all have to be careful. Is that the message? If Santos killed his own brother and was trying to kill Anaia Thurston, Binnie is still in his way. And so are you. Be careful seems to say a little less than what it means."

"You've got it," Barbara said. "Santos apparently has others in the area who will be watching for you, Binnie. Establishing that you are Anaia's child may take a little time or may happen almost immediately, but we'll have to be careful. We can't know when word will get back to Santos and he'll be forced to accept it and the threat will end. This afternoon, after I leave here, Bailey and I will put our heads together and figure out the best plan to get you both to a hearing tomorrow morning. That's the time they granted, one week. We're due there at nine in the morning. I want Bailey to pick you up and he'll have instructions for you about how to go on from there. We should allow at least an hour and a half to get to town, but he may want more time in the morning. Will that be a problem?"

Binnie looked terrified again and Barbara said to her, "I don't expect any trouble with the immigration people. It's just that the wheels of bureaucracy turn very slowly. I have more than enough to satisfy them, but they may have to confirm it before they give their stamp of approval. We'll have a good plan in place later to-day. I just got home last night and there hasn't been enough time to do it sooner. I wish there had been."

"The time in the morning isn't a problem," Martin said. "Whatever Bailey tells us to do, we'll be ready."

Barbara opened the shopping bag and brought out the rain-coat. "Binnie, I want you to wear this, with the hood up. It's a little too big, but that's good. Will you do that?"

She nodded. She still looked stunned, disbelieving.

Barbara reached across the table to take her hand. "Binnie, Anaia is a lovely, caring woman who has devoted her life to others. She is one of the bravest people I've ever met, and she is overjoyed to have found her daughter. She and Shala were extremely close, and she feels that close to you already. She plans to come to you as soon as she is free of the legalities of her situation, Julius is dealt with, and she is actually mistress of the Santos plantation without fear. She will need to apply for a passport, of course, and it all may take time. She is eager for you to go to Belize, see where she and Shala lived, share memories with you, tell you about growing up with Shala, how close they were, tell you about your grandmother. They used to go into the jungle, the three of them, and find orchids. Both girls adored her, and Anaia said that her father did, too, that something in him died when she died. Anaia thought she had lost everyone she ever loved, her mother, her sister, her child. She wept when I told her about you. She wept for you and for Shala, and now she will do everything in her power to make sure you are safe, that you share the Santos fortune, the estate, and the joy she finds in it. She loves you, Binnie. She loves you very much."

She paused, then said, "Binnie, you will never stop loving Shala as your mother. That's a given. She was your mother in all ways and would have died to protect you. Anaia understands that and would do nothing to try to take her place. She just wants another place in your heart. She wants to be a mother to you exactly the way Shala was if you can let her do that."

Tears filled Binnie's eyes, and this time she could not contain them. With tears rolling down her cheeks, she mouthed the words "Thank you."

Barbara began to gather up all the papers on the table. "I have to make copies of everything, but after this is over, the photographs, all of it will be yours." She turned to Martin. "Anything else?"

He shook his head. As she pulled on her jacket, he said, "I'll walk out with you. Be right back, honey," he said to Binnie.

At her car door, he touched her cheek gently, "There's a lot more. I know that. Binnie will be all right. Like you said, it's a shock, but she'll be fine. You've given her a mother. It's as if you've restored Shala to her. Barbara, I hope someday you'll tell me the rest of it."

"Take care of her, Martin. Let her talk as much as she needs to. Bailey will be in touch later."

He embraced her, then kissed her cheek. "You saved the lives of two people today. We'll never forget that. You take care, Barbara. Take care."

As she pulled onto the highway after leaving, Barbara heard in her head once more the phrase "Heaven is high . . ." But now the emperor was not far away, she thought then. The emperor was in Eugene, waiting for her.

25

Driving back to Eugene, Barbara began a list of must-do items for the next hour and a half. It was two thirty already, she thought with a groan as her list expanded. Kinko's to make copies. Buy manila envelopes and folders. Something to eat. Some decent coffee to take to the motel, and a bottle of wine, she added with emphasis. Sort and arrange the documents into separate folders and envelopes. Plan for the morning.

She groaned again. Mist was forming in the forests, daffodils were fading, forsythia was finished and tulips appearing, spring had advanced, and she could already smell rain that was due later. She wanted to be in the woods with water still dripping from the dense upper story long after the rain ended. She wanted to go for a walk in the woods, her own clean, quiet woods. She shook her head impatiently, and kids want Santa Claus right now.

An umbrella, she decided. She had good enough clothes in the motel for the federal building and its fifties-style offices, but she shouldn't show up dripping, and her poncho and raincoat were at home, out of reach.

She kept seeing the image of Binnie's small hand in Martin's huge one, how he had held an umbrella over her the first time they had shown up at her house. Binnie was so small and next to him she appeared even smaller. The first nebulous outline of an idea came with the image of them leaving her house that first day.

By the time she finished her chores, it was a quarter past four and Bailey was in the rear booth of the restaurant looking sour. A booth filled with laughing teens was in the one closest to his.

She drew near and said, "Let's go to my room and talk. I'll go on over and see you there." She paused, then said, "Will you order a sandwich for me and bring it? Ham and cheese or something."

Back at the motel she unloaded her things and, before she took off her jacket, she found the coffee she had picked up and started a pot. It made only two or three cups at a time, but it had to do, no matter how many times she had to fill it again.

Minutes later Bailey knocked on her door. He had his duffel bag over his shoulder and was carrying a small bag that he handed to her. After looking with disfavor at the bed where she had strewn her own things, he edged around the small table to take a chair and put his duffel bag on the floor by it.

"Some beer in there," she said, pointing to the groceries on the bed. She unwrapped the sandwich. "Coffee coming along in a minute." She took a bite from the sandwich and went back to the coffeemaker to will it to finish.

Bailey got a beer from the six-pack. "I have pictures of five of the stakeouts. And my photo lab guy is getting tired of rush orders. He's got other work to do, he wants me to tell you. Also, another print of Binnie." He put an envelope on the table. "How'd she take the idea of a new mama?"

She scowled at him. "She's in shock. She'll be okay. I've been thinking of tomorrow morning. I bet those guys don't have a picture of her, just a general description, and God only knows how good that is, or how they got even that much. She told me no one had ever taken her picture, no one but Martin, until I did. But those guys will know what Martin looks like and he's unmistakable. They can't miss him. I don't want Martin and Binnie seen together tomorrow at the federal building." She poured coffee, finished the sandwich, and sat in the chair opposite him at the table.

"I took her a raincoat, but I also bought an umbrella for her, and one for me. Let's think about doing it this way. Have Martin go in through the main entrance and stand just inside the door as if he's waiting for her to show up. Check his watch from time to time, act anxious."

Bailey snorted. "Won't have to put on much of an act. Go on."

"Let her go in by way of the courthouse, escorted by Alan." Alan McCagno was his favorite and best operative, and Alan looked like a perennial college freshman. "They should use the parking lot across from the courthouse, go in through the tunnel, up to the second floor and courtroom two. You tag along and keep an eye out. The Sutherland embezzlement trial is happening and there are a lot of witnesses. No one will pay any attention to how long they stay in the back as interested observers, until you tell them the coast is clear. Then use the sky bridge to come across to the federal building."

"And you?"

"I'll get to the federal building early, a little after eight, and hang out in the Social Security outer office. If anyone asks me why, I'll say I'm waiting for my aunt to help her fill out forms."

"I don't like it," Bailey said. "Too loose, too many unknowns. There's a bunch of guys prowling around and, Barbara, I don't aim to get involved in a shoot-out in the fed's own building, not with all those U.S. marshals around. Not a good idea."

She rose to go to the bed and find her yellow pad in the briefcase. She sat down again and made a sketch of the building lobby. "The Social Security office has a glass front," she said, roughing it in. "Over here, IRS and immigration offices. From here," she said, putting her pen on the Social Security office, "I'll be able to keep an eye out. You've got pictures of the goons, all but one anyway. I know what Nicholson looks like if he shows up, and I can watch for two suits entering the immigration office. I won't budge until I see them, and not at all if I see a guy who looks like any of those pictures. One of them will be kept busy watching Martin. Maybe they'll even send a second one to help keep an eye on Martin, in the belief that he's waiting for Binnie. Meanwhile, you can nose around and spot the others if they're there. I think a tip to the marshals that a suspicious guy who looks like he's carrying might interrupt their game plan."

He reached across the short distance to the bed and got another beer. "They're getting warm," he said.

She pointed to the small refrigerator. He shrugged and opened the beer.

"I don't think I'll be their primary target," she said. "I think they'll want Binnie first. Remember, they don't know what all I know, or that we're on to them, and they don't know what I can produce regarding her. If she's out of the way, Nicholson can crawl back under his rock, never to be seen in these parts again. Even if I can prove she's Anaia's child, if she's dead Julius Santos is still next in line for the estate. At least until he's under lock and key, plus wearing an anklet for the next few decades."

Bailey began pointing out other problems with her plan. He suggested alternates and did not object when she shot them down. He was morose when they returned to the only one they both agreed had a chance of working, and for the next hour they smoothed out details.

She had made a second pot of coffee and he had emptied three bottles of beer when she stood and said, "I told Martin you'd call and tell them when to be ready to go in the morning. And remember to give the umbrella to Alan. See you in the feds' own building tomorrow."

244

"Yeah," he said. "You've done a lot of running around today. Maybe you should knock it off and order in a pizza or something later, and stay out of sight. I'd hate to have you a no-show in the morning."

"I'd hate it even more," she said with a nod. "I made copies of everything I have," she said then. "Wait a second while I untangle things and put copies in an envelope." She did not look at him as she added, "I want you to keep the extra copies. You know, insurance or something. If necessary give it all to Dad."

She made sure she had it all divided, and put one of each in a big envelope. When she handed it to him, he looked as grim as she felt, but neither one commented.

She glanced at the messy bed. "That's it. I still have some work to do, and I would like to catch up on sleep. See you in the morning."

He edged around the table and went to the door, where he paused a moment, then saluted and left without another word.

What else was there to say? she thought as she went to the bed to spread out documents, articles, and photographs.

It was always a mild degree of chaos at that time of morning Barbara well knew, seven thirty to eight thirty, with arriving jurors, clerks, secretaries, other staff members, trial junkies, all vying for the limited parking spaces in the lot across Seventh Avenue from the courthouse. That morning, with a hard rain and gusting wind, the chaos was worse than usual as the drivers all tried to get as close as possible to the tunnel under the busy street. She sat in her car for a minute or two, waiting for the inevitable car pool to disgorge several people together. When she spotted a van pulling into a parking space one lane over, she got out and hurried to join the four people who had emerged and were already rushing toward the tunnel. Joining them, she held her umbrella over herself and a woman without one. The woman smiled and said thanks and they hurried on.

Inside the courthouse there were clumps of people heading for the cafeteria, others hurrying to various offices on the main floor, many heading for the stairs to the upper floors with the courtrooms and the sky bridge to the federal building across the street. Again she dawdled, waiting for several people to start across the sky bridge in a group, and she fell in with them. Along with several of them, she turned toward the lobby on the other side, but crowds of people there caught her by surprise. Tables had been set up, and people were lining up in front of them, more crowding in through the main doors.

"What's going on?" she asked a woman walking at her side.

"AARP, helping folks with their taxes," the woman said. "It's going to be like this right up to April fifteenth." She kept going toward the far side of the lobby, and Barbara turned right to go to the Social Security office.

Inside the glass-fronted outer office she looked out at the lobby and said, "Shit," under her breath. All she could see were the backs of the tax advisers and dozens of people in lines beyond them, with others milling about at racks of tax forms, or streaming around them all to get to other offices. It was fifteen minutes past eight. "The best-laid plans," she muttered under her breath, and stepped to one side where she could still see the lobby and not be in the way of those entering or leaving the Social Security office.

People entered, took a number, and waited patiently to be called when other people emerged from the back room. Some went to a wall of racks holding pamphlets and leaflets: "How to Figure Your Benefits"; "Espousal Benefits"; "A Guide to Medicare" . . .

The outer office was getting steamy and smelled of wet clothes, wet shoes, wet hair. . . . In the lobby, even more crowded than before, it was getting harder to single out any one individual in the constantly shifting crowd seeking income tax help. Barbara had located the upper part of the door leading to the immigration office, but could not see past the bodies between her and it. She kept her eye on the top of the door. It opened at twenty minutes before nine, but she got no more than a glimpse of the back of a woman going in. A receptionist or secretary, she decided. It opened two more times in the next ten minutes, but one time she could not see anyone entering, and the last time, a glimpse again, the back of a tall man in a black raincoat.

A man nudged her arm. "I think you were here before me," he said, holding a number.

"Thanks, but you go on. I'm waiting for my aunt."

He nodded. "It's a bad morning. Hope she isn't too late." He walked toward the door to the back.

She moved to the information rack and picked up a sheet with instructions about applying for disability benefits for a dependent adult. Bailey walked in and straight to the rack and began searching for something.

"Okay in the courtroom," he said in a low voice. "Martin in place, one guy nearby, and a marshal. Marshal near the immigration door. Another guy by the sky bridge this side, and two in parked cars on the streets."

She nodded and glanced at her watch. "Can't see a thing out there. At two minutes before nine, I'll head over."

In a near whisper, Bailey said, "Marshal at immigration, sandy hair, five nine, tan coat, black pants." Then in a carrying voice, he asked, "Where are the tax forms? Schedule C?"

"Wrong office, buddy," someone behind Barbara said. He sounded impatient, irritated. "Out there where all the people are."

Bailey turned back toward the door. "Thanks, pal."

"Some damn fools can't read a sign to save their lives," the man said in disgust when the door closed behind Bailey.

Barbara replaced the paper she had been holding and moved closer to the door. She tried to see past many people, tried to find the marshal in a tan coat, and failed. What were they up to? The imported goons on the job along with marshals didn't make a lot of sense. A backup plan if Binnie made it past the guns? Have a marshal grab her and squirrel her away somewhere? Send her on her way to a holding center for deportees? It would be neater that way and the end result would be the same. Avoiding the inevitable investigation of a shooting might be more desirable than any other option.

She checked her watch. One more minute, then out. When she left the Social Security office, she did not hesitate but walked quickly around the people at the tables, others at the information booklet rack, ignored Bailey, who was scanning tax forms. She had reached the door to the immigration office when she heard Bailey's voice.

"Hey, what's with you? Can't wait like the rest of us? Stop pushing."

She glanced back to see him blocking the way of a man in a tan coat. She opened the door, entered the office. The marshal was right behind her. Without a word to the woman behind a desk, Barbara kept walking fast to a frosted glass door and pulled it open. The marshal was within reach when she entered the office and came to a dead stop. The marshal bumped into her as he rushed in also.

"Why, Mr. Nicholson," Barbara said. "This is a surprise. I didn't expect to see you here this morning."

He was seated behind a desk with a neat little Lucite name holder that said Dennis Linfield.

26

The marshal had come in at her heels. He touched Barbara's arm and said, "Ms. Holloway, please come with me."

"Don't be ridiculous," she said. "I don't even know who you are. Also, I'm here on official business by invitation of both Mr. Linfield and Mr. Sokolosky."

The woman from the outer office had edged in as she spoke. "Mr. Linfield," she said, flustered, "I'm sorry. She just walked right in before I could stop her."

Barbara took another step away from the door. "Don't touch me again," she said to the marshal. "Or I'll bring charges against you for assault." She looked at a tall, thin man who had been standing near a window at the right of the desk. For a moment it appeared that he had an abnormally large head, but as he moved away from the window it became clear that he simply had a great deal of hair. "Mr. Linfield?"

"I'm Sokolosky. Who are you and what do you want here?"

"Barbara Holloway," she said. "I was expecting Mr. Dennis Linfield and you." She looked at the marshal, who appeared to be confused. "Did you have orders, perhaps, to restrain me when I arrived?"

He looked at Nicholson and made no response.

"What is the meaning of all this?" Sokolosky demanded.

"Mr. Sokolosky, if I might make a suggestion, it seems a bit crowded in here at the moment. Perhaps this gentleman and lady could leave us to conduct our business. But before they leave, I'd really like an answer to my question. Was he ordered to restrain me when I appeared?"

Sokolosky looked at the marshal. "Were you?"

"Yes, sir," he said.

"Whose order?" Sokolosky demanded.

"Mr. Linfield's."

"Get out. Both of you."

The woman scurried out and the marshal followed.

"Now," Sokolosky said to Barbara, "you tell me what the hell is going on here? Who is Nicholson?"

"He is," she said, pointing to him. "At least, that's what he said his name was when he came to my house. He showed me photo identification from the Drug Enforcement Agency with that name on it." She glanced at Nicholson, who was staring at her, his face livid. "I didn't realize the government appointed anyone for dual positions, especially under two different names."

Nicholson snapped, "This woman is a raving maniac. I never saw her before in my life." His grating voice was even higher-pitched than it had been before, almost hysterical sounding.

"Mr. Nicholson, come now," Barbara said. "Actually this is the fourth time you've seen me. Twice at my house, if you'll recall." She turned again to Sokolosky. "The last time I saw Mr. Nicholson was at the Santos plantation in Belize last Saturday."

"I've never been to Belize," Nicholson said. "I told you she's a lunatic, and she's obstructing the deportation of an illegal alien immigrant. She aided her escape, has hidden her away, and the woman is a fugitive."

"When you came to my house, as I recall," Barbara said thoughtfully, "it was raining heavily. I hear it hasn't rained since then. I wonder if that identification is still in your raincoat pocket."

His gaze flickered to a coatrack where his wet raincoat was hanging. He said furiously, standing, leaning forward with both hands on his desk. "I demand that you leave this office immediately or I'll have the marshal place you under arrest." His voice was a near screech, the words nearly incoherent.

"But you already told him to do that, didn't you?" she said. "On sight, it seems, without waiting for me to obstruct in any way. Mr. Sokolosky, I prefer to say no more in the presence of Mr. Nicholson since I'll bring charges against him of intimidation, false representation of a federal officer of the Drug Enforcement Agency, extortion, and of attempting the illegal deportation of my client Mrs. Lavinia Owens, as well as a few other felonies and misdemeanors which I'm confident will surface in the next few days as I have more time to consider the recent past."

Sokolosky was shifting his gaze back and forth between her and Nicholson. Abruptly he turned to approach the coatrack. "This raincoat? Is this yours, Dennis?"

Nicholson sat down again without replying.

Sokolosky reached into one of the pockets and came out empty-handed. He reached into the other one and this time brought out the same ID that Nicholson had shown Barbara. Nicholson was picking up his telephone.

"Put it down," Sokolosky said. He showed the ID tag to Barbara. "Is this what he produced when you met him?"

"It is."

"Can you explain yourself?" Sokolosky asked Nicholson.

"I'm calling my attorney," Nicholson said with his hand still on the telephone.

"I wouldn't let him call anyone until after you hear the full story," Barbara said quickly.

Sokolosky walked past her to the door and jerked it open. "You, what's your name?" he said.

"James Warrenton," the marshal said.

"Get in here," Sokolosky said. He stepped aside as the marshal entered, then he closed the door. "Stay with Mr. Linfield and don't let him use the telephone or let him leave. Come with me, Ms. Holloway."

In the outer office he said to the secretary, "Ms. Womack, don't switch any calls to Mr. Linfield and don't interrupt us." She looked pinched and frightened as she nodded.

He strode past her desk to a door on the far side of the office. "In here," he said to Barbara. It was a small conference room, with a round table that could seat no more than six people. He pulled out a chair, indicated another one for her, and sat down. She sat across the table from him.

"Now just tell me what the hell is going on," he said.

She nodded and opened her briefcase. "Mr. and Mrs. Owens came to me for advice," she said, and she briefly described the situation to him. "She didn't know the name of the man Anaia Santos had married and since time was so short, I decided to go to Belize to find out, and to get proper identification for her. I found her mother, and found that the situation there was dire. There is a vast estate with extensive acres of marijuana being grown on it. Maybe thousands of acres. There is already a well-established shipping company owned by the Santos family. Julius Santos illegally seized the property after the murder of his brother and it appears that he and the man I know as Nicholson have conspired to prevent Mrs. Owens from being next in line to inherit the estate. I saw Nicholson there when I went to talk with Julius Santos."

She handed him the birth certificate and Anaia's marriage license.

He put them both down after a careful examination. "Ms. Holloway, why has this surfaced now, at this particular time? Why didn't the mother and daughter make any attempt to locate each other? Why didn't Mrs. Owens come forward to establish her status before? This is highly irregular, and it doesn't alter the basic situation of illegal entry without any documentation."

"I have Mrs. Thurston's written statement explaining herself," she said, taking it from her briefcase. "As for my client, Mrs. Owens, she grew up unaware of her true birthright. She believed Shala Santos was her mother. Remember, she was an infant when the woman she considered to be her mother was kidnapped, enslaved, and forced into prostitution. She knew only what Ms. Santos told her." She gave him the statement Anaia had written, and watched his face as he read it.

He was such a bony man, she thought distantly, watching him struggle with the story. Bony cheeks and chin, bony wrists and fingers. Strange for such a skeletal man to have such abundant thick hair. His hair was gray, but it would easily have been enough for two heads. He read the statement, then read it again. At last he put it down and said heavily, "What a goddamn mess. Has Mrs. Owens fled? Why didn't you bring her in with you?"

"I feared for her life," Barbara said.

At that moment the door opened and Ms. Womack stepped in, closely followed by the marshal Warrenton. He was holding a bloody handkerchief to his head.

"Jesus Christ!" Sokolosky said. "What happened?"

"He said he was getting heart medicine from a drawer, and he fell over, out of his chair. I went around to render assistance and he slugged me," Warrenton said. He was leaning against the doorjamb and he was pale, his hand holding the handkerchief shaking.

"He left," Ms. Womack said tremulously. "He just walked out."

"When? How long ago?"

"Ten minutes," she said. She was shaking more than Warrenton.

Sokolosky looked at the marshal. "Are you all right? Do you need immediate medical attention?"

"No, sir."

"Then get on the phone and call your superior. I want some marshals, at least three, as fast as they can get here." He looked at Barbara. "You stick around. We'll finish later."

"I have a private investigator in the building," she said. "He can provide information for the marshals."

"Get him in here," Sokolosky said.

She picked up the papers on the table and returned them to her briefcase and withdrew the envelope with the pictures of the five stakeout men, then went to the other office and the door to the lobby. She didn't have to go out. Bailey was standing near the rack of tax information. She motioned to him and he ambled over.

"What's up?" he said when he saw the marshal using the phone on Ms. Womack's desk.

"Plenty," Barbara said. "Nicholson was here and he slugged him and got away." Sokolosky had come to her side and she introduced Bailey. "Did you get the license plate numbers on the cars you saw earlier? And do you still have Nicholson's license plate number?" She hoped he got her meaning. Just supply the number and let the feds make the drug connection. "You might explain the photographs while you're at it." She handed the envelope to him.

"Sure," he said with a slight nod.

"In there," Sokolosky said, pointing to the conference room. "When the marshals come, send them in," he ordered Ms. Womack. "And when you're through you come in, too," he added to the marshal.

"What the fuck are you up to?" Sokolosky yelled at Barbara as soon as they were in the conference room with the door closed.

"And no more dribs and drabs. Why did you say you were afraid for the safety of your client? What photographs? What license plate numbers? Tell the whole goddamn story this time."

Calmly she said, "I told you I was suspicious of Nicholson when he asked me to relay the message to Martin Owens, asking him to be an informer for the DEA. It wasn't clear how he had known they had come to me for advice, unless he had been spying on them. Bailey found a bug, a voice-activated listening device, in the restaurant, and I instantly told the Owens to go into hiding, which they did. Nicholson returned to my house asking how he could get in touch with Martin Owens directly to make his appeal in person." She stopped when the door opened and Warrenton staggered into the room.

Sokolosky took him by the arm and seated him at the table. The marshal looked dazed and was pale down to his lips. "Just sit still. I'm sending you to the hospital as soon as your people get here," Sokolosky said.

"Handgun," the marshal mumbled. "No medicine. Handgun."

He cradled his head in both hands for a second, then put one arm on the table and rested his head on it.

Sokolosky stood by his chair helplessly. "Go on," he said to Barbara.

"Yes. Bailey saw the car Nicholson was driving when he came back to my house and he made a note of the license plate number. I left for Belize," she said, turning her gaze away from the marshal, who looked as if he had passed out. She hoped he wouldn't tumble from the chair. "In Belize I found the situation I already told you about. On my return, Bailey informed me that there were stakeouts at the restaurant, the Owens's house and my house, six men in all. Today he spotted four of those men, two here in the building, two others in cars parked nearby. Those pictures are of five of those men. He has the license plate number for Nicholson's car, and numbers for the two parked cars in the area. And that's all I know about it."

"I bet," Sokolosky said bitterly.

There was a tap on the door, followed without a pause by its opening and three men entering. One was in a gray suit, two in casual clothes, jeans and sweater for one of them, khakis for the other, and a windbreaker over his arm. The suited man handed Sokolosky his ID and nodded to Barbara and Bailey.

"One of your men should get this man to the hospital," Sokolosky said after identifying himself. "The man known as Dennis Linfield assaulted him with a handgun, and he's on the loose, as of about fifteen or twenty minutes ago. Armed and dangerous. The secretary can give you a description. This is Bailey Novell, and he'll explain the pictures. Two of those men are in the building, two others in nearby cars. Round them all up and for God's sake keep it quiet. There's a mob in the lobby and we don't want to start a panic. And no press."

"Those four guys are probably armed," Bailey said.

The man in the suit gave him a cold look of disdain. "We've dealt with armed men before," he snapped.

"Let's go to the other office," Sokolosky said to Barbara. "They can get on with it."

She looked at Bailey and said, "When you're finished in here, I want a word with you."

He nodded. "Yeah, me too."

When Barbara and Sokolosky passed Ms. Womack again, she looked even more frightened than she had before, and her eyes appeared to have grown larger. Think of it as something to tell hubby and friends all about, Barbara thought at her and preceded Sokolosky into the other office.

Sokolosky went to stand by the window where he had been when she first entered the office. She sat down in a chair near the desk and waited for him to start. He had his back turned, and again she was struck by how big his head appeared on top of his thin frame.

Finally he turned to her. "Now, exactly what did you mean by saying you feared for her safety? What do you think Linfield and those others were planning?"

She shrugged. "You know as much as I do about their intentions. But I was to be detained, we both know that much. And I had the documentation your office required. If she had shown up, doubtful in my opinion, she would have been helpless. But I don't think she would have been allowed to get as far as this office. Either a marshal would have seized her, sequestered her, and sent her to a processing center for instant deportation, or as instantly as possible. Or, possibly even more likely, those hired guns would have seized her, or shot her on sight. Take your choice. Mr. Sokolosky, I have no idea how much a thousand acres of prime marijuana is worth, but I suspect the answer is very, very high. They call it Belize Breeze, some of the finest marijuana to be had, premium pot, premium price. Julius Santos was, is, determined to control it and both Mrs. Thurston and Mrs. Owens were in his way."

"You think that somehow he got to Dennis Linfield, enlisted his help," Sokolosky said after a moment.

She made a rude snorting sound and no other response.

"Mrs. Owens has to appear," he said after a moment. "There is a routine to be followed, as you must know."

She shook her head. "No, Mr. Sokolosky. My client will not appear. There are at least six armed men, plus one you call Linfield and I know as Nicholson, also armed, who would not allow her to leave this building alive unless it's in custody for deportation to Haiti, where she would face the same hellish situation she saw Shala Santos endure. I will not produce her."

"Then you're breaking the law as much as she is," he said harshly.

"So be it," she said, in an equally harsh voice. "Mr. Sokolosky,

I don't know how far Nicholson's corruption extends, who else might be involved who are fully aware of the situation I've described, and with as much vested interest in seeing to it that Santos has his way."

He took a step closer to her and said, "My God, what are you implying?"

"I imply nothing," she said coldly. "I stated a fact."

He glared at her, then turned back to the window when there was a tap on the door.

Ms. Womack opened the door a little and said, "Ms. Holloway, that man, Mr. Novell said you wanted to speak to him before he left. He's out here."

"Thanks," Barbara said, rising. She took her briefcase with her as she went to the door. "I won't be more than a minute," she said to Sokolosky. Walking around Ms. Womack on her way out, she realized how tired she was getting of the rabbity woman and her tremulous voice, her big eyes. Bailey was at the door to the lobby.

"Out there," she said, and they went out together.

"They're waiting for the FBI," he said in disgust, jerking his finger toward the conference room.

"Let them," she said. "I want Alan to get Binnie back to Turner's Point as fast as he can manage. Is he good enough to make sure no one follows?"

Bailey gave her the same kind of disgusted look he had used for the marshals. "Yeah," he said. "What about Martin?"

"After you know she's on her way, and after they pick up the goon watching him, which I hope to hell they manage to do, tell him to go somewhere, I don't care where, and that we'll join him later and get him back out to the Gresham house. And tell them both it's fixed for Binnie, nothing to worry about and nothing they need to do from now on."

"You fixed it?"

"About to," she said. "Hang out where I can spot you after you play messenger boy, and be sure you know where Martin's going."

"Okeydokey," he said. "Maybe I'll get in line and see what deductions I've been missing all these years. See ya." He saluted and ambled off, and she returned to the office to start fixing things.

27

When Barbara entered the inner office again Sokolosky was seated behind the desk. He was taking charge, the authority now. She had a vivid memory of a time when as a girl, sixteen, maybe just fifteen, she had been in Frank's spacious office with its rich paneling, many glass-fronted shelves of books, a leather-covered sofa, and easy chairs grouped at a large coffee table. There were two comfortable chairs in front of Frank's desk, and his own big chair behind it.

"Why so many chairs?" she had asked.

"Psychology," he had said. "When I'm over here with my clients or prospective witnesses, it's informal, information-gathering, getting-acquainted time, something like that. But when I'm behind that desk, it's all business and I establish who's boss, who's in charge."

She had gone behind the desk and had seated herself in his chair, and from across the room Frank had regarded her for a long time, then had said, "Bobby, that's where you belong. You look good behind that desk."

The memory faded as fast as it had formed, and she took the

chair opposite Sokolosky and waited for him to assert his authority, establish who was boss.

She didn't have to wait long. "Ms. Holloway," he said, in a brisk, businesslike way, "I fully understand your reluctance to produce Mrs. Owens at this time under these circumstances. We will postpone her appearance for a month, or even six weeks, if you prefer, during which time there will be a complete investigation of Mr. Linfield's activities, and criminal charges will be brought against him for assault of a federal marshal. I'll have Ms. Womack set up an appointment for you and your client for, let's say, six weeks from today."

She smiled at him. "No, Mr. Sokolosky. Don't bother. Although I was prepared earlier to do so, I no longer have any intention of producing my client today, a month from now, or any other future date you could mention. We both know she's an American citizen and you have no authority to order her to do diddly."

He stiffened and drew himself up straighter. His voice was icy when he said, "Ms. Holloway, she is in our files, and her file must be closed officially under the rules and regulations of this agency. You, as an attorney, are under the obligation to assist a federal officer in fulfilling his duties when asked to do so."

She made a dismissive wave of her hand, brushing aside his rules and regulations with one motion. "I suppose you've been with your agency long enough to know those rules and regulations by heart," she said. "But, Mr. Sokolosky, I don't work for your agency, or any other government agency. I work for my client. It's my duty to assist in the event that my aid is sought in a legal endeavor. Having a file for Mrs. Owens is not legal and assisting in the closing of an illegal file is not in my job description. I suggest you tell Womack to bring her file in here, the complete file. I am curious to see if the deportation of Mrs. Owens has already been ordered and processed. Do you know just how illegal it is to attempt to deport an

American citizen? I confess that I don't at the moment, however, I will find out. I can assure you that I will find out. Depending on what I learn, I might be forced to sue your agency, Mr. Sokolosky."

"It is against our policy to share our confidential files with any unauthorized person," he said flatly. "I reject your suggestion."

"Very well. I'll subpoena that file, which is within my rights as attorney for Mrs. Owens."

He glared at her and she returned his gaze pleasantly. "Your move," she said after a moment.

He picked up the phone and snapped, "Ms. Womack, bring in the Owens file, the complete file."

"I imagine she's filed under the name Binnie Owens," Barbara commented. "I doubt that Linfield-Nicholson even knew that Binnie is her nickname."

His lips were tight and his jaw clenched as they waited for Ms. Womack. She was as timorous as before when she brought in the file, and she hurried out again as soon as she handed it to Sokolosky.

Barbara watched as he opened the file and got no further than the first document he saw. Although from across the desk she could not read anything on the paper that held his attention, she could see that it was an official government form, with blanks to be filled in, and that the blanks had been filled in. He kept his gaze on it for a long time, as if committing it to memory. She picked up her briefcase and began to search through various file folders and envelopes. After finding what she was after, she regarded him with something close to pity.

No doubt, she thought, he had devoted his adult life to this agency, that he thought of his job as an honorable mission and his dedication worthy. Probably he was not more than three or four years from retirement, and now he saw scandal, investigations, his career put in jeopardy, a cloud that he might or might not have deserved, but one that would shadow the rest of his years.

Finally he closed the file and folded his hands on top of it, as if to protect it from her. "What are you doing?" he asked in a deflated voice as she began to place photographs on the desk.

"Pictures. Binnie's grandmother, her mother and aunt, and one of Binnie herself. Have a look. You'll see them again, of course, in newspapers, on television, probably on national television since two different federal agencies will be involved. It will be a big story, a lovely young, voiceless woman being terrorized by the immigration service of her own country. The life of slavery, prostitution, and humiliation she witnessed being endured by the woman she loved as her mother. The knowledge that immigration officials were condemning her to the same sort of life. I imagine that the attempt to keep the Belize Breeze blowing will become a fairly large part of the story. A drug connection always sensationalizes any story, doesn't it?"

"What do you want?" Sokolosky demanded.

"A copy of her file, and that order clearly stamped closed or resolved, or whatever term you use, signed and dated by you. I want her file placed in a dead file, or resolved, or closed, whatever procedure you use. When she applies for a driver's license, a passport, or a Social Security card, I don't want any vestige of that file to interfere with her right to do so. If you tell me you can't do that, then I want that file to be destroyed altogether."

He made an involuntary motion with both hands, as if to pull the file to his chest, to safeguard it. "You know I can't destroy a government file!"

"I can," she said. "Those are the only two options, Mr. Sokolosky. My client has lived in absolute terror these past weeks, and it is not over for her, as you also know. The same men who were staking out her house were here in your own building this morning, and the man who was determined to send her to her death was behind that chair you're now in. They are all still at large. It isn't over for her, but this particular chapter is finished. Done.

Choose one of the two options, or as soon as I leave I'll have a press conference, and I'll share those pictures with the media and let the circus begin today."

"That file is confidential," he said. "It's illegal to give an unauthorized person confidential files. You want too much. I can mark it case closed, and I will do that, but I can't let you have copies."

"You don't get it, do you?" she said coldly. "Was Linfield-Nicholson alone in his scheme? Are others involved? Is someone in the DEA involved? How many in this agency, how high up? Perhaps Womack is in on it. I want that file. I'll put it in a safe-deposit box where it will remain unless someone else steps in to finish the job Linfield-Nicholson started. If you don't want Womack to know anything about it, tell her to take a walk and I'll make the copies on the Xerox machine in the outer office. Or you can make them yourself. The two options haven't changed."

"You're threatening me," he said in a harsh whisper. "This is extortion!"

"So have me arrested, and we'll both testify under oath, as will Warrenton and Womack."

He lowered his gaze to the pictures again.

"She'll testify also," Barbara said. "She's adept at ASL and through an interpreter she will tell the story of Shala Santos, and what she would have faced if deportation had succeeded."

"What assurance do I have that you won't go public even if I agree?" he said after a moment.

He did not look at her. She suspected that he was looking inward, trying to assess which was worse, involving his agency in a scandal that would assume national notoriety and force his early retirement, or breaking a rule, committing what he perceived to be an illegal act in giving an unauthorized person confidential files.

"You have no more than my word," she said. "I told you I work for my client, and with that file stamped closed and signed by you, I am done with this agency. How you conduct your internal investigation will be none of my business. Mr. and Mrs. Owens want nothing more than to return to the quiet life they led before this started, and once those gunmen are rounded up and put away, that's what they will do. I told you that file will be in a safe-deposit box as long as there's no threat to Binnie Owens regarding her status as a citizen. That's all the assurance I can give you. Whatever we say and do in this room I consider absolutely confidential, exactly the same way that any conversation I have with any client is confidential."

She picked up the photographs, replaced them in the envelope, and put it back in the briefcase. When she looked at Sokolosky again, he was regarding her with a bleak expression.

With a heavy sigh he rose. "I'll tell Ms. Womack to go to lunch now," he said. He walked stiffly to the door, leaving the file folder on the desk. At the open door, he said, "Ms. Womack, it's past lunchtime. It's been a hectic morning and the office will close for the rest of the day. I'll lock up in a few minutes. Tomorrow come in as usual and do whatever routine work you can manage. I'll have a temporary replacement for Mr. Linfield as soon as possible since he won't be coming back. I'll take the Owens file with me to the Salem office and handle it from there."

When Barbara and Sokolosky left the inner office a few minutes later, there was no sign of Ms. Womack, but a young man in a business suit was seated near the outer door. He jumped to his feet and said, "FBI, Special Agent Dwight Zimmer. Ms. Holloway, we would like a statement from you early next week. Please call this number to arrange a time that's convenient." He handed her a card, then said to Sokolosky, "Will you be available at your office next week, sir?"

"Yes, of course."

"Someone will call you there to get a statement from you also, sir."

Barbara put the card in her purse. The agent nodded to her and Sokolosky and left. Silently Sokolosky went to the Xerox machine and made copies of the file he had stamped CLOSED, signed, and dated. Just as silently Barbara put her copy in her briefcase, nodded to him, and walked out into the near-mob scene still in the lobby.

"Done," she said to Bailey when he drifted over. "Is the coast clear?"

"Dunno," he said. "No one out front, far's I can tell. And the guy at the sky bridge entrance is gone. Let's go that way." It was so noisy in the lobby she could barely hear him.

"I'm parked in the lot across Seventh," she said. "Where's Martin?"

"I'll drive," Bailey said. "I'll get Alan to pick up your heap later and take it to the motel."

The noise level decreased as they left most of the people worrying about taxes and headed for the sky bridge. "Did he take Binnie out to the Gresham house?" she asked.

"Yeah, and he'll hang out with her until we get there." He was talking to her, but he was scanning faces, keeping watch on everyone around them, and his slouching walk was covering the ground fast without giving an appearance of hurrying. She didn't know how he did that.

They crossed the sky bridge, went down the stairs to the lower floor of the courthouse, and toward the tunnel. He steered her around to the front of the building.

"Wait inside," he said. "I'll get my car and bring it around."

Rain was still pouring steadily, and she was happy not to have to go out in it any longer than necessary. She realized that she had left her umbrella someplace, the way she always did, the reason she always had to buy a new one when she felt she needed one.

A few minutes later, in the passenger seat of his car, she said, "I have to go by my bank. First National."

"Jeez, Barbara, now?"

"Now. It won't take long. I have to put something in my safe-deposit box. Don't bother parking, just drive around the block."

He gave her a look. "Oh. You robbed him? Swiped his watch while he wasn't looking? Stole a whole box of paper clips?"

"Something like that," she said.

It was a surprise to feel so relieved, she thought when she finished at the bank and watched again for Bailey to drive up. She had not wanted that file in her possession over the weekend, or any other time. She had wanted it in a safe place and now it was. Bailey double-parked in front of the bank and she dashed out.

"Now for Martin," she said. "Did you give the feds everything they wanted?"

"Sure. Three license plate numbers, and they asked me for the key to the restaurant. They'll get that bug. They wanted to know if I handled it," he said with disgust. "Rondell's in for a shock when they get around to asking why Nicholson was driving his car."

"Who's Rondell?"

"Rondell Emerson of Emerson Property Management, partner in the Marcos Import business. Good old Ronny, happy to lend his car to a DEA officer."

"Good," she said softly. "Let them make the drug connection. So far not a word about anything bigger than the Santos marijuana scam. They might make that other connection as well eventually, but not because of us."

"The two parked cars were gone," he said. "Don't know when they took off, but they're gone. Maybe the feds rounded them up, maybe not. I saw them grab the guy keeping an eye on Martin. Slick as a whistle. One FBI, one marshal, one for each arm. Just walked up, said something or other, and next thing three guys walked down the steps in the rain. I think the guy in the middle might have had a hurt finger."

"One out of six or seven isn't enough," she said. "They didn't want to cause a panic. Kept it quiet. Okay, so that's what we've got to work with. The immigration trouble is over, now all we have to worry about is staying out of the firing range."

28

Bailey drove to a steak house in Springfield. "He's in there," he said. "You want a burger? I'll get takeout. We can eat in the car."

"God, yes! And coffee." The restaurant had not yet opened that morning when she left the motel, and the piece of cold pizza left from the night before had proved to be inedible. She was ravenous.

Minutes later, with Martin in the backseat, Bailey began the long drive to Turner's Point. After reassuring Martin that Binnie had already been taken there, Barbara ate her hamburger before she got into the morning's events.

She twisted around enough to see Martin and Bailey both, and said, "Nicholson and Linfield are one and the same man. In the immigration office he's known as Linfield, but he still had that fake Nicholson ID, and it was still in his pocket. Sokolosky and I went to a conference room, leaving a marshal to watch Nicholson. He faked a heart attack and got a gun from a drawer in his desk and used it to slug the marshal. So he's on the loose. We don't know how many of the others the FBI or the marshals managed to grab. Meanwhile, Sokolosky and I came to a deal and the file for Binnie has been closed. That's over."

"We don't have to go back?" Martin asked, almost disbelieving.

"Never. You have nothing to do with immigration and they have nothing to do with you. Done. Over. Finished."

"How—? But—"

"She's a citizen, Martin. That's all there is to it. Both Bailey and I will poke around to try to find out if those other guys have been caught, or if Nicholson has been. But while there's still any uncertainty about that, it's best if Binnie doesn't surface yet. Can you both live with that for the time being?"

"Yes. Sure. But, Barbara, if they can't deport her, what else do you think they might try? Are you saying they might kill her? Or try to? Why would they if Santos can't get the farm? What's in it for them?"

He was leaning forward with both hands gripping the back of her seat as if he might rip it out from under her.

"Easy, Martin," she said. "The problem is that we don't know yet if Santos has been booted out, if their orders have been rescinded. They could still be operating as if it's all still on, but we just don't know. I'll call someone I met in Belize to try to find out about Santos, but he might not know much yet, either." Who that someone would be eluded her. No number for Gabe, and he was off-limits anyway. Not David. Not Anaia. No telling where she was. She could be in the jungle somewhere, in Belmopan, even at the finca. Not Papa Pat. No number for him, not even sure he had a telephone. She hadn't seen one. She let it go until later.

"Binnie's safe where she is," she said, "that's what matters now. A question is how much do you want to tell her? That all but one of those goons might still be running around? Or that it's safe to get back to a normal life?"

"I can't say that, can I?"

"I don't think you can. I couldn't make that statement."

"Yeah. We'll stay put for now. Tawna and James have been terrific and I know they won't object. And Binnie has to be told the truth. I don't lie to her." He settled back in his seat. "You know what's funny? She was more afraid of being deported than of hired gunmen."

Funny, Barbara thought, was hardly the word for it. She said, "For what it's worth, I don't think this will last very long. Those guys will be caught, or they'll pack their bags and take off fairly soon, I'm sure. As you said, what's in it for them to hang around if the game's over?"

Ronstadt, she thought then. She could call Ronstadt. He would know if his beloved orchids were in safe hands, in Anaia's hands.

When they arrived at the big house, Alan opened the door, saw who it was, and called over his shoulder, "It's okay. You can come out." He grinned at Barbara, looked at Martin with a bit of awe, as if he wanted to ask for an autograph, and nodded to Bailey. In jeans, an oversized U of O sweatshirt, and sneakers, he looked as if he belonged in a classroom. "No problems," he said. "She's been teaching me ASL."

Binnie had emerged from a back room. When she saw Martin she raced to him and was swept up in his arms.

Barbara knew that brief separation of several hours was not the first time they had been apart since Binnie found him in Miami, but they acted as if it were.

"We won't stay very long," she said to Binnie when her feet were on the floor again, her hand in his. "Martin can fill in the details, but I want to tell you that officially you no longer have anything to fear from the immigration people. That part is completely over and done with. In a few weeks you should apply for a Social Security card and a driver's license. You'll need to take your birth certificate with you. And when that's done, get a passport. You never know when you might want a passport on hand, a sudden yen to go traveling to Paris or something like that."

Binnie's smile was radiant, her eyes luminous. She looked hesitant, but then seemed unable to restrain herself and almost threw herself at Barbara to hug her fiercely and kiss her cheek.

When she drew away she began to sign furiously to Martin and, laughing, he said, "Barbara, she wants to know what she can give you, do for you. Work for you, do anything. Keep your house clean, cut your grass . . ." He was laughing too much to continue and he took Binnie's flying hands in his and held them. "She gets the point," he said to her.

Bailey made a grunting noise, cleared his throat, and said, "Barbara, your car keys for Alan. Remember? Do you know the license plate number?" She shook her head. He gave her a disapproving look and said to Alan, "It's a black Honda Civic, late model, rental car." He looked at her again. "Do you know about where it's parked?"

"Almost dead center of the lot," she said. "How many black rentals do you think might be in the lot?"

He scowled at her and drew Alan aside to give him further directions, after which Alan waved to them all and left with his jacket over his head.

Binnie signed to Martin. He nodded and said to Bailey, "She said he's sweet, and thank you for sending him to help out."

Bailey had an expression of incredulity at the word "sweet" applied to his best operative, one he claimed was the best shot on the West Coast and as mean as a snake. "I'll tell him," he said.

"We'll take off, too," Barbara said. "You both have some plans to make about the future, I imagine. I'll be in touch just as soon as I find out anything at all, but it may not be until Monday. Weekends can be a problem. Even the crooks seem to prefer fishing or hiking or something instead of attending to business."

In the car a little later, Bailey muttered, "Sweet! Jeez."

"When this is really all over," Barbara said, "if she tells me that you were sweet to help out, do you want me to pass it on to you?"

He floored the accelerator and the car shot forward. She laughed. "I get the point," she said. "What are the chances of finding out anything from the feds?"

"Low," he said, easing up on the gas. "I know a guy or two who might know something, might not. Depends on how much they want to keep everything quiet."

"That's what I'm afraid of," she said. "There's going to be pressure to keep things under the table for a long time. Two federal agencies involved means a hell of a lot of pressure. On the other hand, I have to know when it's safe to stick our heads aboveground again."

It had occurred to her that even if Ronstadt knew what was happening in Belize, word might not get to the Eugene connection very fast. She frowned at the rain-obscured windshield. "You need new wipers."

"Tell me about it," he snapped.

When they were nearing Franklin Boulevard and her motel, she said, "As soon as Alan brings my car around, I think I'll check out and go to the coast. I'll go bonkers if I have to stay in that motel another night, a whole weekend. I'll leave my phone number on your answering machine when I get a room. Give me a call if and when you hear anything worth reporting."

"You realize what the weather's like out there this weekend?" he asked.

She was looking at the rain running crazily down the windshield and she laughed. "I know exactly what it's like."

On Sunday night Barbara sat wrapped in a blanket watching lights up and down the coast go out one by one. No boats had been at sea that stormy weekend, no lights out there, but luminous waves rose and crashed, rose and crashed high on the shore. She was tired, a good kind of tired, the kind that left her relaxed and at ease. That evening, coming down from a hike behind the campground at Strawberry Lookout, she had met two couples standing under a cover at the beginning of the trailhead. One of the young women had looked at her curiously and asked, "Did you go up there alone? Aren't you afraid alone like that?"

"There's nothing to be afraid of," she had said. Wrong, of course. A fall, a predatory human being, a once-in-a-lifetime chance of coming across a bear, but no, she had not been afraid. It hadn't even been a real hike, since she had no boots or proper gear for a real hike with her on this trip. Her one concession to an impromptu coast trip had been to buy a rainproof hooded poncho that reached her ankles. She had walked miles on the beach, and twice up into the woods. Today's walk had been just a walk in the woods, her kind of woods, without snakes or jaguars, and certainly without alligators. She smiled to herself realizing that young woman had been the mirror image of how she had regarded the jungle in Belize. Yet Lavinia Santos had taken her two young daughters out there looking for orchids, and they called it a forest, not a jungle. That was their kind of forest, one in which they felt comfortable, a forest they loved.

If Binnie went down there to meet Anaia, would she be taken out into the forest to look for orchids? Feel the same kind of trepidation Barbara had felt?

She yawned. It was ten thirty and she was more than ready for bed. She pulled the drapes closed, remade the bed, replacing the blanket she had pulled off, and lay down, listening to the wind and rain, listening to the crashing waves. All the sounds became fainter and faded away within minutes.

She was already half awake when her phone rang the next morning at eight o'clock. She groped around for it, and muttered, "Hello."

"You awake?" Bailey asked.

"Enough. What's going on?"

"All hell's broken loose. Double shooting overnight. Emerson and Linfield both got it in the head."

"Jesus," she muttered. "I'm leaving as soon as I can get my stuff together. Meet me at our favorite restaurant. I'll give you a call when I get into town. And bring everything you've got about the shootings, anything you can find out about it."

Half an hour later she turned from the coast road inland to start the drive over the Coast Range and to Eugene. The rain had stopped overnight, leaving pockets of fog that had not yet burned off. The Siuslaw River was high with spring runoff, and there were stretches of roadway covered with water, making driving slow and treacherous. Logging trucks were already out. She cursed under her breath. Her sneakers had not dried out overnight and her feet were cold. The car heater seemed reluctant to release anything except cold air. She searched the radio dial for a signal and got static, or a Florence station, nothing from Eugene.

It was a slow drive all the way until she was close enough to town to call Bailey and leave a message that she would be there in another half hour or so. Linfield-Nicholson and Emerson, she kept thinking. Both of them just tools to be used, and when no longer needed, discarded? Finally she had a local station on her radio, but there was not a word about the killings. Disco music, fast-talking morning talk show hosts mouthing nonsense, national news . . .

She drove straight to the restaurant where they had met before, and as before Bailey was already in a rear booth with the remains of breakfast and a carafe of coffee still in place.

"Took you long enough," he said in way of greeting.

"Tell all," she said, and waved the waitress over.

"It was on TV this morning, and on the radio. Nothing in the newspaper yet. They were both in Marcos's house, shot in the

277

back of the head, both of them sometime last night. Not a word about Marcos, if he was there, taken by the cops, nothing. And that's just about all I have."

"Executions," she said in a low voice.

He nodded. The waitress came and Barbara ordered coffee and toast.

"Anything about the rest of that gang?"

"Nada. Not a peep. They're playing it as close as I've ever seen. FBI case, up to now. But this was local, so our own boys in blue will be on the job and I might be able to get a scrap later on today."

They became silent as the waitress appeared with Barbara's toast and coffee. Barbara found the card the FBI agent had given her. As soon as the waitress had asked the mandatory question, if everything was all right, and left almost before she was reassured that it was, Barbara said, "I have to make an appointment with the FBI. With any luck I can get in today and maybe they'll tell me something." Bailey snorted and took a piece of her toast. She stood and went to a phone near the restroom doors, and placed the call.

"Today at two," she said when she returned to the booth. "Good. I doubt that Martin and Binnie have heard a thing about all this yet. They don't seem the type to be listening to early morning radio, and TV out there is lousy. No newspaper until late in the day if then, unless Tawna or James picks up one. Let's leave it like that, not a word until we have something real to tell them."

"What are you going to tell the FBI is more to the point, don't you think?" Bailey said.

"Whatever they want to know about Nicholson and my client. Nope, never heard of Emerson or Marcos, except what my private investigator told me on my return to Eugene this morning. And that was what he heard on the newscast. Period."

Bailey glanced around, then said, "You know if the feds catch you in what they decide could be a lie, they like to nail you."

"Tell me about it," she said drily. She moved the rest of her toast out of his reach and spread jelly on a piece. "It looks like Marcos was the big cheese in these parts, that is, unless his body turns up with a bullet in his brain. Anyway, if he's running back to his base, it might really be over as far as this area is concerned. That's what I want to know. Is he flying south, driving south, holing up locally, or what? Keep it in mind."

He nodded gloomily. "Right. I'll ask my paperboy first time I see him. For what it's worth, no more stakeouts. My bet is that those that got away are piled up in a van or SUV or something like that and driving as fast as the rig will go toward the border. And," he added, "unless they have a private crossing point, they'll be nabbed when they get to the border. Just my guess."

"I'd bet that there's a ranch in southern Texas, Arizona, or California that stretches right to the border where they'd be more than welcome and can cross at their leisure."

Bailey's expression became gloomier and he nodded again. "I wouldn't bet against that."

29

Barbara walked into the FBI office in the federal building that afternoon promptly at two o'clock. A plump, pleasant-faced woman seated at a computer smiled at her. "May I help you?"

"Barbara Holloway. I have an appointment."

"Oh, of course, Ms. Holloway. One moment, please." She picked up her phone, pushed a button, and announced her. "Very good, sir. Just go on in," she said to Barbara, hanging up. "They're expecting you." She pointed to a closed door and went back to her keyboard.

Barbara opened the door and entered the other office, where three men had already gathered. She recognized Lieutenant Hogarth of homicide. With his fading red hair receding fast, a very pink scalp, sharp blue eyes, and florid complexion, he was a memorable detective.

"Good afternoon, Lieutenant," she said.

He nodded without speaking. A tall, handsome man came forward with a smile. "Eric Heilbrunner, FBI," he said, extending his hand. He was as elegantly dressed as any 007, and as good-looking. Mid-years probably, but it was hard to tell because he was so sleek and well built. His handshake was firm without that little bit of excessive pressure many men felt it necessary to exert.

"And Roger Dorman," Heilbrunner said, indicating the third man, who did not offer to shake her hand. "Roger will take notes, if you have no objection."

"Not at all," she said, taking off her jacket.

Heilbrunner took it from her and went to the door, where he said, "Will you please hang this up for Ms. Holloway?" He handed the jacket to the receptionist and closed the door again.

The office was sparsely furnished with several straight chairs, a large desk with one file folder and a telephone on it, and a smaller desk with a computer. Dorman had already taken the chair at the computer desk. Heilbrunner motioned toward the straight chairs. Barbara suspected that this was not Heilbrunner's real office, but rather one he had borrowed for the occasion or possibly for the duration of his stay in Eugene. She did not think he was one of the local FBI agents. She would have seen him at one time or another, and women remembered such handsome, elegant men every bit as much as men remembered beautiful women.

"Please, Ms. Holloway, be seated," he said. "Both the lieutenant and I have a few questions, but I don't want to take up a great deal of your time."

The more charm he exuded, the warier she was becoming, she realized as she sat down. She placed her briefcase on the floor, returned Heilbrunner's smile with one of her own, and waited to see who would play good cop, who bad cop. He went to the big desk and perched on the corner of it with one leg swinging slightly.

"Ms. Holloway," Hogarth said, standing in front of her, "how well did you know Dennis Linfield?"

"If you mean as Dennis Linfield, I met him one time along with Mr. Sokolosky and was in his presence less than five minutes in his office. I wouldn't say I knew him at all from that brief encounter."

"You know what I mean," he said. "Under any name."

She stood, and he frowned at her. "I find it awkward to have to crane my neck to see the person I'm talking to," she said. "If you mean under the pseudonym he used, Jeffrey Nicholson, only slightly better. About five to eight minutes in my house, less than one minute at my front door, and a glimpse of him in Belize and, again, I wouldn't say that means that I knew him in the usual sense of the word."

"Sit down," Hogarth snapped. "Why was he in your house for any length of time?"

"I'll sit down if you will," she said. "You go first."

He yanked one of the other chairs around and straddled it. She promptly sat down again. "Lieutenant, this will all go a lot faster if I just tell you from the beginning how I met him and why."

His face had become noticeably pinker, his eyes narrower as she spoke. "From the beginning," he said. "All of it."

"Of course," she said agreeably. She started with the arrival of Martin and Binnie that rainy day. "They had a problem with our immigration service that I agreed to help with. I thought the matter little more than a misunderstanding," she said, "until Jeffrey Nicholson came to my door, representing himself as an officer of the Drug Enforcement Agency. He was in my house for no more than eight minutes, probably more like five minutes, just long enough to give me a message to pass on to Martin Owens. He wanted him to become an informer for the DEA. I agreed to do so and he left."

Before he had a chance to demand more, she said, "The next time I saw him was a day or two later, on the next Monday. I had advised Mr. and Mrs. Owens to go to a safe place out of sight, and they had done that. Nicholson came to my door to ask where they were, and I did not admit him that time. I told him they would get in touch when they had decided about his proposal. He left." She held up her hand when Hogarth drew back and seemed poised to bark another question. "The third time was when I went to the Santos finca in Belize. Finca means farm, as you know. I caught just a glimpse of him that day. We did not exchange a greeting. And I already told you about my encounter with him when he was using the other name, Dennis Linfield. So I insist, none of those meetings constitutes what any reasonable person would interpret as my knowing him." She smiled at him and spread her hands. "That's it, Lieutenant. All of it."

"How well did you know Rondell Emerson?" he asked in the same barking manner he had used before.

"Never met him, never saw him that I'm aware of."

"What does that mean, that you're aware of?"

"Well, you know Eugene is not a huge metropolis and we do pass people in the street, or in a restaurant, a mall. I can't swear our paths never crossed in such a way, but if they did, I'm not aware of it. I wouldn't know him if he walked in here. But, of course, he couldn't do that, could he, since it appears that he's been executed?"

Hogarth's face darkened even more and he all but snarled, "What do you know about his murder?"

"What Bailey told me he heard on the news," she said. "For heaven's sake, Lieutenant, Nicholson said there's a big drug operation here in Eugene, there are hundreds, up to a thousand acres of marijuana being grown on that plantation in Belize. Nicholson represented himself as a DEA agent looking for a stool pigeon, and in his role as an immigration official he was trying his damnedest to get a legal heir to that plantation deported to Haiti. He failed to accomplish that, and he and another man ended up with bullets in the backs of their heads. Sounds like a gangland killing, an execution to me. How and why that other man got involved is something I don't know a thing about. That's your job to connect the dots, not mine."

"How well do you know Herman Marcos?" Hogarth demanded in an abrupt change of subject.

"Never heard of him," she said.

Hogarth looked disgusted. "Have you been to his import shop?"

"Marcos Imports? Yes, once or twice. If he was there, I wasn't aware of it. I wouldn't know him if I saw him."

"Ms. Holloway," Heilbrunner said before Hogarth could continue, "please tell us why you became suspicious of the man you met as Nicholson. And why you went to Belize, and what you know about the finca and Julius Santos."

"Nicholson came within hours of the Owens' visit, and it was too soon, unless he had been spying on them. My investigator found the listening device in the restaurant, confirming my suspicions. I went to Belize because I didn't know the name of the man Anaia Santos had married, and I could not reach Augustus Santos by telephone. I had to get the proper documentation for my client and time was too short for anything other than having someone go there to find the family and get the birth certificate that was required. There, I learned that Augustus Santos had been murdered, his brother, Julius Santos, had been occupying the property, that Anaia Santos Thurston was in hiding in fear for her life, and that the plantation and the shipping company were involved in growing and shipping marijuana. And I learned that the man I had met as a DEA agent, Nicholson, was somehow involved with Julius Santos."

A flickering smile crossed Heilbrunner's face and he nodded. He left the corner of the desk to go behind it and sit in the chair. He made it seem more a matter of comfort than asserting his authority. His easy manner did not change when he said, "Thank you for such a succinct summary. It gives us a few talking points, doesn't it? I understand that the misunderstanding with the immigration service has been straightened out, and there's no reason to go into it again. Instead, I'd like to focus on Nicholson or Linfield as the case may be. Why exactly were you suspicious of him?"

Hogarth had continued to straddle the chair he had pulled closer to Barbara. Abruptly he jerked out of it and swung the chair around to where it had been, some five or six feet away. He sat down again, with his legs stretched out.

Barbara was thinking furiously. Apparently Heilbrunner was telling her that he had already talked to Sokolosky. And he was taking command of this interview, probably explaining Hogarth's evident frustration, since he wanted to talk about two murders, his department, and the FBI agent was more interested in the drug connection and organized crime.

She explained her reasoning for distrusting Nicholson, and Heilbrunner went on to the next point. It was all easygoing, no bluster or disgusted expressions, just a gentleman asking a lady a few questions very politely.

How had she managed to get out to the finca on such short notice? She told him about the broncos and their photographer. Why hadn't she brought up the subject of Mrs. Owens if that had been her reason for going out there? She had not liked or trusted Santos once she met him. On and on over each and every point she had made.

"I never saw any marijuana," she said, answering one of his questions. "That was hearsay. I heard about it and Mrs. Thurston confirmed it."

"Will you speculate just a little," he said with a smile. "How do you suppose a man like Julius Santos from Central America found Dennis Linfield in a city like Eugene?"

She shrugged. "No idea. Anaia Thurston said Julius returned to Belize about three years ago after years of absence. What he was doing in those years is anyone's guess. He might have spotted Linfield walking around with a dollar sign on his back for all I know."

"You're sure he was there in Belize?"

"Absolutely."

"More speculation. Do you assume that he was working for Julius Santos?"

"I believe he was doing a job that Santos wanted done, at least attempting to do it."

Finally Heilbrunner had no more questions and before Hogarth could begin again, Barbara said, "I would like to be able to reassure my client that she is no longer at risk, that she and her husband can return to a normal life. I can't do that unless I know if those men who acted as stakeouts, and later were in the building here or in parked cars nearby, if they have left the scene or have been apprehended." It was not a question, but it was directed at Eric Heilbrunner.

"I quite understand your concern," he said. "In any homicide investigation there are always a number of leaks, no matter how much the investigators try to prevent them. There are neighbors who see things and talk about them, and within every department at every level there are always a few people who can't resist mentioning things to friends, relatives, sometimes even to reporters. I trust your discretion, Ms. Holloway. Two of those men were indeed apprehended. And there are multiple signs that a number of people have been coming and going in the Marcos house in the past few weeks, and signs of a hasty departure. Except for two dead men, the house was empty when a housekeeper arrived there early this morning."

Hogarth made a choking sound and jumped to his feet. "If we're through here," he said in grating voice, "I'm going back to my office. I've got work to do. Ms. Holloway, I'll get back to you in a day or two." He nodded to Heilbrunner and stalked out.

Heilbrunner rose and came around the desk. "Thank you, Ms. Holloway. This has been helpful. I appreciate your cooperation."

They shook hands. She retrieved her jacket in the outer office and walked through the lobby out into the fresh air. She had a very strong feeling that Heilbrunner knew that this whole affair was bigger than just the Eugene connection. How much more she couldn't guess, perhaps the whole story, perhaps not, but something. She also suspected that Hogarth had sensed the same thing, that both she and Heilbrunner knew things he was not to be told. As she walked to her car she thought that it was possible that she herself had been tested, and that she had passed. She was discreet enough to be told some of the truth.

Before going to her car she stopped at a pay phone to call her father, to tell him she was back in town before someone else did.

"Welcome home," he said. "If you're in the neighborhood, come on by. You have a package here that's driving Patsy crazy with curiosity. It's perishable."

"What on earth? Sure. I'm on my way. Five minutes."

It would have been little more than a five-minute walk to the office, but she drove. At that time of day, close to five, there should be easy parking right behind the office building. She was right about that and soon pulled into a slot, got out, and walked into the foyer.

In the outer office the receptionist had her purse out, ready to leave, and she simply waved Barbara on through. "Mr. Holloway said he's expecting you," she said.

Not only was Frank waiting, but Patsy was there also, pretending she wanted a letter signed or something. She had been with Frank for decades, ever since he had been able to afford a real secretary, and she was determined to remain there as long as he did, although she hinted broadly from time to time that perhaps he should give more thought to his own retirement. She was a tubular woman, an almost perfect cylinder. Her hair had always been jet-black and still was, with never a hint of white or gray root showing.

"Hi, Dad, Patsy," Barbara said as she entered his office. "You received something for me? That's odd. Where is it?"

"Overnight delivery, special delivery," Patsy said. She pointed to a box on the big round coffee table and both she and Frank went with Barbara to the table.

He was as curious as Patsy, Barbara knew, and more honest about it. He already had a pocketknife out, ready to cut open the cardboard box. It was long, a foot and a half, and about eight inches deep and that wide. He looked at Barbara inquiringly and she said, "Do it. I can't imagine what it is or why it came here."

Inside the cardboard box was another lighter, white one, fastened with Scotch tape. Frank cut through that, too, and stood back to let Barbara open it.

She lifted the top, moved cellophane paper aside, and caught her breath. There were two sprays of orchids, one with nearly transparent petals that had red streaks, the other with dark violet verging on purple. A heady perfume wafted from them.

"Oh, my goodness!" Patsy said. "My goodness, they are beautiful!"

Frank stared at them, then at Barbara, and back to the orchids without a word.

Barbara picked up an envelope and removed a card. It was a postcard with a facsimile of a playbill from around the turn of the century advertising the coming attraction of *All's Well That Ends Well*. In very neat lettering at the bottom of the card was the line: *Coming soon to Fargo*. A casual glance would accept it as part of the playbill. She turned the card over. There was no address, no return address, but centered on the bottom was a small drawing of a simple house, such as a child might draw.

"No name or anything?" Patsy asked. "A secret admirer? My goodness!"

Barbara smiled. "No name. Nothing else." She was aware of Frank's shrewd gaze and said, "A penny postcard. It could be a collector's item."

"You'd best keep it then," Frank said. "Want some dinner later on?"

"Rain check? Tomorrow night? I have one more appointment today, and I have to run. Thanks for keeping this for me," she said, putting the card in her purse. She replaced the top on the box.

"Tomorrow night," Frank said. "I'll give you a call."

"Thanks," she said, and kissed his cheek. Then she kissed Patsy's cheek and hurried out with the box.

"Goodness," Patsy said. "A secret admirer! How romantic!"

Frank nodded. Secret to them, but not to Barbara. She knew damn well who had sent them and why. And she most likely would never mention the orchids again, he added with some regret. And he'd be damned if he ever would, either.

Barbara had one more call to make and used the pay phone in the lobby to call Bailey. "Hi," she said when Bailey picked up. "It's over. Done with. All of it. Come by the house tomorrow and we can compare notes and clean up accounts or something. I'll tell all then."

"Over? Here and down there?"

"Both. I'm going out to tell Binnie and Martin. They shouldn't have to wait a minute longer."

"This time of day? You know what traffic's going to be like?"

"I'll sail right over the top of it," she said. "See you whenever you can make it tomorrow. At my house."

In her car Barbara smiled at the box on the passenger seat. One for her, one for Binnie. She would let Binnie have first choice. She started her car and was ready to sail over the rush-hour traffic.